BOYS OF SUMMER
An Erotic Anthology
Edited By
Mickey Erlach

Herndon, VA

Published in the United States by STARbooks Press, PO Box 711612, Herndon, VA 20171. Printed in the United States

Many thanks to graphic artist John Nail for the cover design. Mr. Nail may be reached at: tojonail@bellsouth.net.

Herndon, VA

STARbooks Press Titles
Edited by Mickey Erlach

Contents

SUMMER CAMP
By Rob Rosen

"You're going and that's final," said my mother, her back toward me as she slammed the pan down on the stove.

"But this is my last summer before college," I tried, for the umpteenth time that day.

She turned and glared at me. "Which means you'll be lounging around here for three months, expecting me to be at your beck and call, three square meals a day?"

I shrugged. "Sounds like a fun summer."

She shrugged. "For you." Then she turned and went back to making lunch. "You're going to summer camp. It'll be an adventure, a learning experience. Case closed."

I flipped her the bird, behind her back of course, and nodded. Then I replied, just beneath my breath, "We'll see about that."

"What did you say?" she spat, whipping around, lightning fast.

I jumped. "I, uh, I said, well how about that. Can't wait."

She paused, hands on her hips, and stared at me, causing my legs to quake. "Me either, Sean. Me either."

So that, as she said, was that. But I planned on having the last word. And who could've guessed that that word would've been *arrivederci*?

In any case, I was gone not two weeks later. She'd signed me up months before. Neglecting, of course, to tell me until the last minute, claiming she was just too busy. Thankfully, I was to be a counselor and not an actual camper. Then again, maybe thankfully was too strong a

1

word. Mainly because the kids I'd be taking care of were all between the ages of seven and eight, sugar-charged boys with more energy than a small hydrogen bomb. And just as lethal.

In other words, about all the learning I was experiencing was how to effectively hide. No easy feat, mind you, because these kids had authority-seeking-radar like there was no tomorrow. That is, when they weren't chucking water balloons at me or replacing my deodorant with itching powder. Meaning, amen for nap time.

Which is how and when I'd found the spot, actually. They were asleep, and I was out of ear-shot, taking a much needed break along a stretch of forest trail that hugged the lake. The day was hot and muggy, my shirt off and tucked inside the back of my shorts, sweat dripping down my chest as I followed the winding path around ancient oaks and towering pines. My sneakers were the only sound I heard, crunching twigs and leaves as I made my way, staring at the wide expanse of lake as it sparkled in the midday sun. For the first time in days, all was peaceful. And quiet.

Well, almost, anyway.

I stopped when I heard it, the faintest sound of music carried on the slight breeze. I squinted into the forest, but couldn't spot the source. Just trees, endless trees, and the occasional scampering squirrel. So I tilted my head up and followed the sound. Lo and behold, I came to the source a few minutes later, my head craning up to a well-concealed tree house high above the forest floor.

Up the rope ladder I climbed, soon poking my head through the door as sweat poured down my face. I gulped at the sight of him, prone on the floor, head bopping to the music, fists air-drumming above his head, balls dangling out of his shorts. He was shirtless, like me, and a counselor as well, not to mention handsome as all hell. Beyond that, I knew nothing about him.

"Uh, hello," I said, just slightly louder than his iPod and mini-speakers.

He jumped, shot up, and scampered to the rear of the tiny cabin, flicking off the music as he did so. "What the fuck, dude?" he coughed out, hand to chiseled chest, eyes wide, big and blue.

2

"Sorry," I said. "I, uh, heard the music and came up to investigate."

He caught his breath and grinned. "Fucking kids," he said, by way of an explanation. "Thank God for this place, though. Built by counselors years ago, I hear. Only way to get the fuck away from them." He laughed and waved me in. "Brats are like fucking flies, always buzzing around no matter how many times you swat them away."

I echoed his laugh and ducked inside. Place was just barely big enough for the two of us, him leaning against one wall, me on the opposite one, both of us dripping with sweat in the small enclosure. "Cool," I said, reaching my hand across the divide. "Sean," I told him.

"Tony," he replied, hand in hand, a spark running up my arm before exploding down my spine and spreading to my crotch like wildfire. "Hot as an oven in here, but at least no one can find me."

I nodded and reluctantly released his grip. "Except me, of course."

He shot me a lopsided grin, a splash of red running up the side of his neck. "Better than a swarm of flies, anyway."

I kicked his bare foot. "Thanks."

I got a kick in return, balls again bouncing into view. Dude had quite a pair on him, apparently. That combined with the heat probably made them hang something fierce. The thought, of course, made my shorts start to tent. I placed my hands in my lap to be on the safe side. No use tempting fate just yet, I figured.

"What age kids you got?" he asked.

"Seven to eight," I replied, with a grimace.

He chuckled. "Worse for me; I got the eleven to twelve year olds. All they can talk about is girls and sex. And they don't know anything about either one."

"So they come to the expert?" I couldn't help but ask.

His blush returned, face a deep red, dripping now in a stream of sweat. He chuckled. "Kind of like the blind leading the blind, though, on that one."

3

"Good looking guy like yourself?" It came out before I could think of how it sounded. And then the comment floated there, hanging all around us, my blush twice as crimson as his all of a sudden.

"No options where I live," he replied. "The sticks, dude. Middle of fucking nowhere. More remote than even this place." He pointed out the tiny window to his side. Then he laughed, nervously eyeing me. "Just me, my girlfriend, Palmela, and her five sisters." He beat the air with his fist. "If you know what I mean."

I gulped, because indeed I did. All too well, in fact. And my breath lodged in my throat as the image of him stroking away filled my addled brain, which was now swimming in teenage testosterone. "Desperate times," I managed.

"Desperate measures," he tacked on, repeating the chuckle and the air stroke.

And then I spotted it, sitting by the mini-speakers: a Kleenex pack. Suddenly, the small space around us shrunk even smaller. His eyes followed mine, the silence nearly deafening. Then he looked back up, sapphire blue eyes locking on to mine, vice-tight. "Desperate times?" I repeated, voice barely above a croaked out whisper.

He shrugged. "Only measure," he said, jokingly grabbing for his crotch, which now seemed fuller than when I last looked. "Can't do it back in the cabins, too many kids. Same for the showers and the crapper stalls, which stink way too much to even consider it." He laughed, but with an edge now. It was tinged with something, something that made my cock swell, my Adam's apple bob in my Sahara-dry throat. And still his eyes stayed locked on mine, not even a blink to break the contact.

I moved my hands from my lap, my tenting very much noticeable. "I see your point, dude."

His eyes went wide. "And I see yours."

My ears starting ringing, and my heart was beating hummingbird-fast all of a sudden. Then again, his chest, almost bare save for a smattering of curly black hair down the cleft between his tight pecs, was also madly rising and falling. Meaning, we were both in the same

4

boat, in the same rocky waters. So what could I do but throw him a life preserver?

"And are you pre-desperate or post?" I squeaked out.

He glanced down at the box of Kleenex again. "Uh, pre." And suddenly his shorts went from pup to circus tent. Matched, of course, only by my own.

And so I upped the ante. After all, it seemed like I was playing with a winning hand. "There enough tissues for two in there?"

He laughed and held it up for me. "Full pack, dude."

I grabbed at my straining prick. "Good thing."

He grabbed at his. "Amen."

"You first," I said, nodding down to his midsection.

"You," he said, also with a nod, that and a twitch just above his left eyebrow.

By then, we were both drenched, both breathing erratically. "Count of three," I offered.

His nod continued, his fingers grabbing for the elastic waistband, a smattering of black pubes coming enticingly into view. My fingers reached inside my shorts a second later. "One," he said, voice unsteady.

"Two," I added, eyes now glued to his crotch.

"Three," we both said, in unison, yanking down on our shorts, which we kicked off, the pair flying to the side, out the door, and to the forest floor far down below.

He laughed as his cock sprung out, thick and wet at the head, balls even bigger than I imagined. "Oops," he said, ogling my stiffy, which pointed up and rested like a steel bar against my belly.

"Should we go get them?" I asked, fairly drooling at his tool, which stood out like a fifth limb. Thing looked like it could pry open a safe.

He stood up, his cock swaying as he did so. "Probably best."

I stood, the two of us now a few inches apart, naked, hard, sweating profusely. His eyes found mine again, his breathing still labored. I pointed at his dick. "Big one," I commented, stating the obvious.

He glanced down, from his to mine. He shook his and replied, "But yours is thicker." Then he surprised me by grabbing mine, a rush of adrenalin racing through my veins as he slapped them both side to side. "Mine is longer, yours is thicker."

I stifled a moan. "But your balls hang lower."

He laughed, still holding on to our pricks, eyes again beaming at me. "It's the heat, dude."

Tell me about it, I thought. "Better, uh, better go get our shorts. Just in case," I said, voice fairly trembling.

"Agreed," he said.

He let go of our pricks, and we grabbed our stuff. Then I made my way to the door and started the climb down, with him close behind. Literally. Because when I looked up, his alabaster rump was right above my face, cheeks splayed, hair-rimmed asshole winking down at me, mammoth balls swaying to and fro, dick still rock-solid-thick and bobbing up and down. I stopped, as did he. "Not something I would've imagined seeing when I woke up this morning."

He chuckled and pushed his prick down my way. "Not on the camp's daily roster, huh?"

I reached up and grabbed it. It pulsed in my grip, a thick bead of sticky jizz dripping down from the tip. His legs bucked, but he held on to the ropes. "Don't fall," I said, stroking it with my free hand as I held on tight to the swaying ladder with my other one.

"Easy for you to say, dude," he fairly moaned. "You just shot off almost every nerve ending in my entire fucking body."

I leaned in and stared up, locking eyes with him again, a swarm of butterflies taking wing inside my gut. "Almost every?" I closed the gap between his dick and my face. "How about now?" And then I was on it, sucking the head as his body quivered and a stream of groans shot out

6

all around us. His precum hit the back of my throat like a bullet as I downed him as best I could, a gagging tear streaking down my cheek.

"Fuck," he rasped. "Every fucking nerve ending." His eyes fluttered as he said it. "But you better stop, dude; I'm slipping here."

I popped his prick out of my mouth, reluctantly, and made my way back to the ground. He joined me there a second later, both of us out of breath. I eyed him, nervously. "Was that, uh, was that okay?"

He grinned, blue peepers sparkling. He answered by leaning in, the kiss at first tentative but soon rough, eager, and wet. Sloppy if not downright awesome. "Very okay, dude," he said, pulling me in, our sweat-drenched bodies gliding together, hands roaming as the kiss was repeated and repeated again. Then he pulled away. "Suddenly, I realize how naked we are."

I looked around. It was just me and him and the trees, our clothes on the ground. Still, he had a point. "You brought the tissues," I said, pointing down at the pack.

He nodded and grinned. "Pays to come prepared."

I squatted and yanked him down with me. "Then get prepared to come, Tony."

He reached for my prick and I did the same with his, adrenaline once more coursing through me upon contact. Again our mouths pressed up tight together, his lips soft as down as we made out and jacked away. I pulled his nipple with my free hand; he aped the action on mine. Both of us moaned and groaned, the sound echoing all around us as a breeze whipped up and helped to dry up all that sweat. "Close," he soon said, exhaling down my throat.

I pulled my lips from his, our foreheads together now as we stared down, both of us eager to watch the show. His hand went into double-time, a blur around my cock. I matched his pace, watching, waiting, as those giant balls of his swayed. And then his legs started to bounce and mine started to quake, and we both spewed together, our cocks shooting off thick bands of cum, white streams that hit the ground and splashed up as we huffed and puffed and moaned, my entire body on fire as I came and came and came some more.

He laughed and fell backward onto his ass. "All of a sudden, I like camp, dude."

I joined him there and wrapped my arm around his shoulder. "Ditto."

He turned my way and the kiss was light as a feather, so perfect as to take your very breath away. "And I like you, too, dude."

I nodded and returned the kiss in kind. "Ditto."

Naturally, we did a lot of dittoing that summer, camp turning out way more fun than I could've ever imagined. Especially at nap time. Especially in that old tree house of ours. Kleenex pack after Kleenex pack. But summer quickly dwindled, as did our time there together.

Still, I did have the last word on good ole Mom, just as promised.

I came home, tan and happy and full, of course, of surprises. She hugged me and quickly said we needed to go clothes shopping for college. "Nope," I replied, nervously but with much-practiced resolve.

Naturally, she eyed me with well-founded suspicion. "Nope?"

I shrugged. "Well, not for college, anyway."

Her smile, at once, disappeared. "You have five seconds. Explain."

And so I did. "You know how you love an adventure and learning experiences?" I asked, tossing her own words back at her. She merely nodded. "Well, I'm about to get a whole lot of both." I paused and moved out of striking distance. "Because I'm going backpacking through Italy and not starting college in the fall."

She gritted her teeth. "No, you're not."

I backed up an additional two inches. "Afraid so. Already called the school and postponed everything a semester. And it can't be undone this late in the game." I stifled a grin. "Camp was just so busy. Guess I forgot to mention it. You know how that is."

"And just who are you going with and how do you plan on paying for it?" she asked, clearly thinking she had me on that one.

I held up my check from the summer. "This ought to do it," I told her. "Plus, Tony's been saving for over a year."

She sighed, resigned to her fate. "And who's Tony?" I gave her the abbreviated answer, minus the tree house and the Kleenex, of course. Her sigh repeated. "Anything else you want to tell me, Sean?" she asked, eyes now cast downward.

I turned and headed to my room, hollering over my shoulder, "Just *arrivederci, Ma! Arrivederci!*"

MOBY'S DICK
By R. W. Clinger

1. Banging Bly

No joke. Mike Moby really does have his face nuzzled against my ass while I stand on a ladder, searching out a copy of Robert Bly's *Iron John*. My fingers graze copies of a short story collection called *Raw Recruits* and Dave Benbow's *Summer Cruising*, finding the moment with Moby completely unbelievable.

What's he want with a guy like me, anyway? I'm just an average nineteen-year-old with spiked black hair, azure-colored eyes, a five-ten muscled frame, 190 pounds, clean-shaven cheeks and chin, broad shoulders, and muscular looking thighs. I'm dressed in a tight navy tee and jeans; nothing special, of course. Trust me, there's better looking in the world, and smarter, and sexier, and ...

In truth, I never believed the guy queer because he spends his summer working on cars down at his uncle's auto shop, taking the season off from college. The guy hangs with jocks like Luke Dane and Track Palmer, who just happen to be total straight assholes, exactly as they were when we all went to high school together. Plus, I never thought Moby really liked me. He is one of those clients at Broad-Shouldered Books that comes into the store and says pretty much nothing. He finds what he wants, pays for it, doesn't look at me, and leaves. There's never any flirting. Never any light conversation. Nothing.

Today is different, though. It's a totally naughty Moby that I've never been introduced to before. The six-plus guy with grease on his shoulders and white wife-beater asks for a copy of *Iron John*, which I know is hidden in the ALTERNATIVE LIFESTYLES section in the back of the bookstore, parallel to the CLASSICS. And, like a good part-time bookseller in the June-July-August evenings, making some extra cash for college, I want to help the blue-eyed 200-pound dream guy with a muscular build, five-eleven frame, and waves of blond hair. So I find the store's six-step ladder, scale a familiar shelf, and ...

"Moby, is your face in my ass?"

His nose nuzzles denim.

I see a copy of *The Straight Road to Kylie* by Medina. "Moby," I whisper, enjoying his breath against my hidden hole. "Tell me what's going on back there."

"Nothing," he mumbles, taking a strong whiff of my center, and maybe enjoying it.

I see a copy of *Iron John*, but accidentally grab a copy *Men on Men 2012*. I close my eyes and take in his nose-nuzzling for a minute, and let out a soft moan of satisfaction. The man-handled copy of *Men on Men 2012* falls out of my grip and plummets to the floor, missing his right shoulder by millimeters.

Tuesday nights are slow at the store, and we're alone. It's just the two of us. And honestly, the blond-haired beefcake can do whatever he wants to me, and get away with it. But why would here? The city has a lot of bookstores, and better looking college guys tending their counters. The cream of the crop for his gay ass-sniffing can be widespread outside Broad-Shouldered Bookstore's doors. The sky's the limit for his nose-nuzzling needs. What does the twenty-one-year-old want with me?

"Moby," I whisper his name on the ladder, feeling dizzy, ready to fall.

His hands reach around my sides, and palms run up and along my jeans. Moby's fingers find my belt buckle, single button, and zipper, all of which he masterfully undoes while positioned behind me. And, slowly he pulls the denim down to my knees, leaving my white briefs in position, keeping my ass covered.

With my right hand, I hang onto a shelf filled with Edmond White hardbacks. My left palm and fingers discover a shelf of Armistead paperbacks. I become lost above him as his lips cross over my cotton-covered balls. His warm breath blows against my guy-hole in fabric and stirs a boner to life at my middle. Two of his straying fingers rub the hole, and I begin to shiver on the ladder, swept away and ...

"Don't fall, Evan. Enjoy it, just like I'm enjoying it."

My tighty whities are pulled southward to my knees, and now both pieces of material are yanked down to my ankles by his thrifty hands. Now, I feel three of Moby's fingers against my tight hole, which gently rub its pink flesh. One finger begins to slip inside me, but just a little, and I let out a soft hmmpph sound, overwhelmed by the moment. The fingertip compressed inside my bottom does not further its adventure, though. Moby pulls the digit out and replaces it with the tip of his slender tongue. The slippery appendage presses inside me, pulls out, and presses in again. There is no ass-rimming like in the dirty movies I watch and masturbate to on Friday and Saturday nights. Moby gets right to the action with his face buried against my rump, enlightening my world by his tongue-escapade.

"I'm going to fall," I whisper, elated and on fire above him.

He pulls away from my ass for oxygen, breathes heavily, and replies, "I'll make sure to catch you."

His palms spread my legs apart, and his face buries itself into my bottom again. The traveling tongue dives between my cheeks, pulls away, and plunges inside yet another time.

I'm going to shoot a load over an arrangement of fiction novels, which are mostly hardbacks, if he doesn't stop his tongue-and-mouth game behind me. The feeling that sweeps throughout my body is pure energy, and causes elation to build in my eight-inch cock. Pre-bubbles of ooze drip out of my hose and fall to the floor.

Again, Moby surfaces for air. He instructs, "Hold it in. I'm not done with you yet."

What transpires next is unthinkable. Straight Moby continues to nuzzle his face and tongue against my rump. His right hand reaches around my body and finds the swollen shaft between my legs. Fingers immediately wrap around the tool and begin to stroke the beef up and down in a slow manner.

"Moby, stop or ... I'll shoot," I beg, vibrating with euphoria.

Laughter is muffled against my taut backside as he ignores me. One stroke causes my hips to jut forward, smacking against the ladder. Two strokes prompt an unidentifiable string of naughty words to exit my mouth, plus another jut of my hips against the ladder. Three strokes enables a hearty gasp and white sap to fly out of my hose, splattering against an assortment of gay novels, which include: *Latter Days*, *Jim the Boy*, *A Home at the End of the World*, and *The Snow Garden*.

Moby is not finished with me yet. After he drops his face away from my bottom, and his hand from my still-hard dog, he instructs, "Carefully turn around."

I listen. Why not? What's done is done, right? I've already blown my load and ...

I turn around and look down at him.

He chants, "You're so fucking hot ... You make me sting for sex with you."

My eyes roll into the back of my head, and I begin to waver on the ladder. Balance is eventually lost, and I fall off the ladder, head-first.

To my surprise, as Moby promised before, he catches me in his beefy arms. He kisses me next, burying his face against my face, and he gently places me down on the carpet, next to him. I say, "Thanks for all that," smiling from ear to ear, numb and confused.

The summer mechanic doesn't stick around, though. He bolts away from my side. And, before vanishing from the bookstore, he calls over his right shoulder, "What happens in the bookstore, stays in the bookstore, got it?"

"Yeah," is all I can reply with, watching the guy's exit, and feeling mystified, euphoric, and spent.

2. Fingering Truman Capote

Two days later I see Moby at his uncle's garage, bare-chested and working on a Cobalt's engine. The muscled grease monkey looks hot with a wrench in his hands. He makes eye contact with me, winks, and eventually goes back to work, until his shift ends.

I swear, if I had a car, I'd purposely rip something out of its engine just so Moby could work on it. A hose for a hose, perhaps? Or maybe I'd flatten one of my own tires just so I could watch him change it; this would be nice.

Following his shift at the garage, he comes in the store this evening and looks around. The guy is drop dead handsome in a clean pair of jeans, yellow T-shirt, and faux-Diesel loafers. He fingers Walt Whitman, Michael Cunningham, Herman Melville, Truman Capote, and a biography of Tennessee Williams.

I know his history because of research, stalking ... something. He attends Temple in the fall and spring, studying engineering; parents live on Ossner Street for the last forty years; two brothers, Shane and Alex; his Facebook page says that he enjoys photography, football, and cars; he's afraid of spiders; graduated from high school at the top of our class; enjoys camping and mysteries and horseshoes and painting and ...

I follow him as if he's a shoplifter, ready to pin him to one of the shelves and frisk his ass for a paperback copy of *David Copperfield* or *Hollywood Husbands* by Jackie Collins. His reaction is not unpleasant, of course. He confronts me in CLASSICS, presses my back against a Jack London shelf, and licks the side of my neck. The mechanic's body is flush against my own, and he whispers, "I've been thinking about you all day."

I'm bone-hard between my legs, feeling his taut nipples mix with my pecs. His denim-covered rod presses against my rod, which drives me mad.

"You're shivering," he says. "What's wrong?" one of his palms slides between our connected bodies, and he cups the firm package between my legs.

"What do you want with me?" I sound weak and helpless, under his spell, completely intoxicated by his brashness, but love every second of our encounter.

"A kiss. Just a little kiss, Evan," he replies, and caresses his lips with my own, dazzling me once again.

I melt against the shelf, lost under his touch. The kiss is extraordinarily sexy, and causes my stomach to go topsy-turvy with excitement. Dizzy. Lost. Confused.

Following his mind-blowing kiss, Moby pulls away from me, fingers the cotton fabric covering my chest, and explains, "Lose the shirt. I want to check out your chest." He pulls up the tee, exposing my cut abs, puckered navel, and line of black treasure trail. The shirt is pulled over my head and dropped to the bookstore's floor.

Before I can respond, uttering a plea of deep satisfaction, he drags fingertips over each pec and nipple, keeping them hard. Five of the fingertips travel down the center of my nervous chest, explore my navel, and head southward, over the black line of hair between pleasure and sin. He fingers my jeans, but doesn't open their buttons. Instead, he teases me with his fingertips, touring my chest again and again. Keeping me occupied, his tongue plunges into my mouth, melting us together.

His naughty behavior drives me wild. If he wasn't against me, I'd fall to the floor, overwhelmed by his impromptu visit. When the kiss ends, his mouth travels down and along my chin and neck. His tongue grazes the cords that line my muscled right shoulder, and his lips fall to my right pec. Moby gently strokes the nipple with a flick of his tongue, which causes me to moan. And, after three consecutive flicks, his mouth travels to my left pec and nipple, where he carries out the same motion.

"Moby," I moan in bliss, "you're straight. I've seen you kiss a number of girls."

His tongue-flicking ends, and he pulls off my skin for air. He huffs, "It's only a show. You're the one I want this summer. Truth is I can't get you out of my head."

Again, I cannot respond because he breaks my concentration. His tongue-dance continues down and along the center of my chest. Saliva moistens each ab, and he kisses my navel, groaning with pleasure.

On his knees, coming off my skin for oxygen, he stares up and along my muscle-crafted torso with a serious smile, and says, "This is our secret that no one needs to know. I'm not ready to admit I'm gay yet."

I nod my head in agreement. I understand. If our little bum-fucked country town found out that the all-star football player of the class of '09 was queer, all hell would break loose. If those dicks, Luke Dane and Track Palmer, learn this side of Moby, he'd have the shit kicked out of him. Why wouldn't I understand?

The buttons on my jeans are thumbed open. My extension of eight inches is pulled out and ...

He's hungry for his find, licking and lapping at my rod. He sucks the cap of my dog, and then my balls. He strokes the tool with his right hand while he sucks it off. His other hand massages my balls.

I cordially pump his face with my dong. Four inches of my dick slide into his hole with such ease and bliss ... five inches begin to gag him ... six inches cause his face to turn a rose madder hue, and the last two inches choke him. I crazily ride his throat, banging my pubic triangle against his face, burying his nose in the curls. I hold onto his head for balance, murmur his name again and again, and continue to thwap his face with my goods for five minutes ... eight minutes ... twelve minutes. It's as if he doesn't come off for air at all. It's as if he has this superhuman blowing technique that ...

What transpires next occurs in less than ten seconds, I'm quite sure: the mechanic pulls his mouth away from my shaft and I unexpectedly gush a thick load of jizm against his right cheek, glazing his neck with hot ooze. The three bells on the front door jingle, announcing a new customer, which catapults the two of us into a panic. Moby stands and runs for the bathroom, hiding. I pull up my jeans, covering my semen/spit-wet dong, button them with speed, snatch up my shirt from the floor, and slip it over my torso. I push the swollen beef away under my denim jeans, walk to the front of the store, and say, "Mrs. MaCombler, what a pleasant surprise this evening. I'm sure you've come for your copy of Nora Roberts's latest."

While I wait on the old bag, Moby slips out of the bathroom, past the sci-fi paperbacks, the book club reads, the mystery section, and escapes the store unnoticed – exactly the way he wants it to be, of course, until we meet again.

The next day I'm on Sutner Street, across from Moby's uncle's garage. I'm busy watching the sexy mechanic fix a Ranger truck; something to do with the driver's side wheel. I stare at Moby's greasy biceps in motion, sweat clinging to his forehead in the day's heat. I study his hands at work, his strength with the tools, his skill, and ...

He makes eye contact with me, decides to cross the street, and says to me, "Tonight ... wait for me at the bookstore. I'll be there when it closes."

"What for? What are you talking about?" I play his game, challenging him. In truth, I know exactly what he wants – me!

He quickly returns to the garage where he works, back to his greasy and hot job, a place where he works with his hands on cars, and back to his straight world where he is a stranger, hidden, underneath his life.

3. Humping Hemingway

At six minutes after nine o'clock this evening, Moby walks through the bookstore's front door. He locks the door behind him, finds me at the cash register, pulls me back to CLASSICS, and begins to undress himself, and then me.

Four-play is lost. Kissing is not on his personal agenda. What Moby has in mind is purely raunchy, lust-driven, and exactly what a needy summer boy wants to accomplish with another needy summer boy's succulent skin.

I'm spun around and pushed against Hemingway and Hardy by Moby's force. My left cheek meets Homer's *Odyssey* and my lips graze a vintage copy of Nathaniel Hawthorne's *The Scarlet Letter*. My cock slides against a soft leather copy of Henry James's *The Turn of the Screw*.

Behind me, Moby slips a condom down and over his pole and dribbles lube from packet down my crack. My legs are cocked apart by one of his hands. He licks the center of my back, up to my neck, curves right, and whispers into my ear, "Are you ready for me?"

If he only knew how honestly ready I really am. I reply, "Go for it. Don't be a shy boy, and bang me hard."

With his left palm positioned tightly on my left hip, one of his inches slides into my tight bottom. I let out a hearty humph sound, blown away by his swollen mass. The timber between his legs has to be at least two inches wide. I whisper, "Moby, you're huge," trying to catch my breath, pushing away the pain.

"Another secret," he chuckles. "I'm loaded with them."

The second and third inches of his firm mass slide into my bottom with just as much pain as the first inch. I loosen up on the fourth and fifth inches, breathe heavily, and hang onto the wooden bookshelves with all my strength. With one chaotic but desirable movement of his hips, he throttles my ass with the rest of his stick. Before I know it, ten inches of his protein starts to bang my bottom, pulls out, and bangs my tight opening again. His stomach and pubic triangle brush against my back. His palms clamp to my hips as he guides in and out of my core. Repeatedly, he plunges himself inside me, pressed against me. A copy of *The Sun Also Rises* tumbles from the shelf and falls to the floor. A battered paperback copy of *The Iliad* bounces off another shelf, landing by my right foot. My weight rocks against the wall of novels, shaking the shelved tomes to and fro with my body, and making a horrendous banging noise. Continuously his bolt bangs my insides, and pulls out. This motion continues for the next eight ... eleven ... sixteen minutes – I'm not really sure. His energy is non-stop though, a potion that drives both of us wild, into the reaches of ecstasy and connected harmony.

As his steady and rough romp inside my backside continues, my cock glides against the soft leather spine of *The Turn of the Screw*. Endlessly, it builds up a friction with the tome. Gasps of pleasure exit my pursed lips. I become breathless against the wall of books. Saliva drips out of the right corner of my mouth and falls against the spine of a misplaced copy of Greg Herren's *Murder in the Rue Dauphine*. Oxygen is lost. My chest bangs against the paperback and hardback novels. Pores covering my flesh perspire, under the summer boy's thrusting spell. His colliding breaks my rump, splitting me into two pieces of man-lust. I jolt forward, backward, forward again, and my stick rubs against a pair of spines. My breathing becomes intense, falls, and grows again. Fingers clamp onto wooden shelves, preventing me from tumbling to the bookstore's floor.

Moby is a monster behind me regarding his movement. He lashes into my collapsed rear, sliding in and out of its fiery-warm slit. Bang after bang ensues: heatedly, unstoppable, and with much rhythm. He uses me like a summer toy, bouncing on my upright frame, pleasuring the both of us. Quick, kiss-dabs are applied to the back of my neck, which sometimes turn into harmless bites. The man groans chaotically behind me, pinning me to the H-section of classical fiction within the bookstore, obeying his thirst for my masculine flesh. The mechanic pounds me with hyper motion that is continuous, building up his climax, enjoying his ass-ride, and finds my rump a perfect fit for his extension of pulsating rod.

I ... I ... I hallucinate against the fiction. My eyes semi-close and a glazed and comfortable black-and-white movie unfolds beneath my eyelids: Moby asking me to be his boyfriend; Moby taking me to Las Vegas for a weekend and spending thousands on me; Moby undressing me at every opportune moment and taking advantage of my body; Moby digesting my skin again and again; Moby unleashing his hunger for my summer flesh; Moby enjoying me like a carnival ride. The visions pass quickly between my temples, which are all absorbed into my consciousness. I become numb under his valid and exceptional work, bedazzled by his actions, and movie after movie unfolds within my mind, each becoming most naughty by his every thrust.

"Bang it, Moby," slips out of me, words that sound gruff and to the point, a demand regarding my own pleasure. "Make it hurt."

He listens. The mechanic pumps his weight into me, pulls away, and continues to pump me. His search for oxygen becomes frenzied as his chest rises and falls against his hips-thrusting action. Behind me, he informs, "Take it like a man."

"I plan to take all of it, for however long you intend to give it to me."

"You feel great on my cock, Evan. Just so you know."

I moan, share a grunt, and add in a painful sounding manner, "Trust me, I like having you inside me. Pound away, dude ... and don't stop."

Was this act of sex ever a consideration in the boy-man's summer repertoire? Did he ever – for a split second in his secretly queer life – think that he would be banging my bottom in Broad-Shouldered Books? I think not, which only causes this moment between us to feel even better, a drug of sorts that prompts me to become high and fully enlightened by our unexpected entanglement between college boys.

As I am being pulverized by his speedy shaft, faggot writers wash through my mind: Jonathan Asche, David Holly, Jack Stevens, John Patrick, John Butler, Denis-Martin Chabot, and Milton Stern. Each of these queer writers scrawls naughty gay-with-gay paragraphs of my connection to Moby. String after string of details fill my mind of the authors' works, cum-scenes followed by cum-scenes and ...

The Turn of the Screw is washed with my spew. My junk empties its creamy and sticky load as it rubs up and down the tome's leathery spine. Ejaculate pours out of my hose, damaging the book, ruining its leather for good and making it unreadable for future use. The feeling that surfaces within my core is nothing less than a throbbing vibration of pure joy. Ripples of delight careen throughout my torso, tease the nape of my back, and rise to the rear of my head. A light throbbing ensues, which soon turns into an emotional swabbing as my orgasm unfolds. More gasps exit my pursed lips. My fingers dig into the shelves, holding my weight up. I become absentminded in front of the mechanic, used and spent, exactly how he wants me to be.

Moby releases his tool from my hub and exclaims, "I want you to wear my shit, pal." Quickly, with brutal force that I find rather tantalizing, he grips my right shoulder with his right palm, spins me around, and faces me.

I imagine my face is bleached white with splotches of candid red. A smile forms on my mouth from my euphoric explosion. Never in my life have I ever popped a load between my legs without my crank being touched. Never have I ...

The summer boy cocks his feet apart, grasps his pole with both fists, aims the meaty extension at my torso, and begins to pump it up and down with some mighty force. What follows is a succession of thick grunts and constricted murmurs that escape the chiseled man. Noises fill the CLASSICS area with such ease. Moby's guttural voice echoes off the shelves, walls, and ceiling of the bookstore.

Fierce and brutal jacks occur to the guy's knob. His hips rush forward, backward, forward, backward ... and keep this action up for the next two ... three ... four minutes. Perspiration covers my friend's chest, dripping off his perky nipples. More sweat flies off his brow, splashing against my chest. His grunts and murmurs of deep satisfaction continue, spilling out of his mouth. "Shooting," also tumbles out the boy-man's mouth, finishing himself off with a last, pelvic-thrust, ready to spiral his churn against my torso.

Hot spew twirls against my shaft and balls, flying out of Moby's pick. String after string of the gooey stuff clings to my tool's uncut head and furry bag of balls. The liquidy burst is thick and sticky, goopy and pungent. It clings to my body and ...

Following his orgasm, Moby says, "Let me take care of that mess." He drops to his knees and begins to lick the sticky stuff up, sucking it down into his system. One lick turns into a dozen as he takes his good old time moaning and groaning and feeding himself his own spurt from my spew-splattered privates. The mechanic relishes the moment, enjoying his treat, making sure not a single drop is left over, cleaning up all of his mess, completely.

Chests clinging together, arms around naked bodies, spent from our upright sex-connection, Moby says, "That was the best fuck ever."

"You're not so bad yourself."

He leashes my head to his, and downs his tongue into my throat. When he finally pulls off and away, he says, "You liked Moby's dick then?"

I roll my eyes, chuckle, and say, "Nice play on words."

22

Again, he kisses me: tongue, saliva, and some light force. Following this second intoxicating kiss, he shares, "I have a request for you."

"A request?" I inquire with wide eyes. "What kind of request?"

Trusting me with his body and soul, he sweetly whispers, "I want you to thump my bottom before the end of the summer. I've always wanted to try that with a guy."

"And I'm the lucky guy?" I ask.

"The only one I like, Evan."

My stick bounces between us, thrilled with the idea, overjoyed with his company, and our connection. I reply in a mischievous tone, "No time is better than now," and lead him into the small office to our right, and eventually push him over a battered desk to fulfill his request, need, and what summer boyfriends usually carry out in private.

RAINBOW CRUSH
By Joshua Skye

My hometown of Warren, Pennsylvania, drew an interesting assortment of visitors during the summer months. It always had. The Mafioso families once vacationed here. The homes they built were every inch as opulent and beautiful as the ones commissioned by the oil and timber barons that founded the area. The wealth was vast, the excess was sickeningly apparent. Even now, after all the old money has dried up and the extremely wealthy have abandoned Warren, the specters of the past lavishness linger on. The massive skeletons of those ancient homes remain ... but they are mere shadows of their once former glory. Most of them have been converted to apartment buildings or commercial sites with ailing businesses residing therein. Warren is a sad place ... not just because of the visual melancholy inherent in perhaps every similar small northeastern town but because there seems to be a genuine and palpable unhappiness that enshrouds the residents.

I am not immune to this. My legs are heavy, and my arms are a chore to move. I find that looking at the ground is quite preferable to the road ahead and the eyes of the strangers that may perhaps walk by. The recent winter was rather harsh, even by northern standards. The deep freeze had killed many of the trees about town and the leisurely spring was grated by the sound of chainsaws as the dead things were removed. I sat on one of the DeFrees Park benches and watched with disinterest as all the trees were cut to the ground ... even the old chestnuts that wreathed the Cornplanter Council building. Someone would miss them. Perhaps.

Summer emerged from the rains of spring to unusually high temperatures. It was quite uncomfortable to be indoors where few had the luxury of cool air conditioning. Outside didn't bode much better ... the winds were hot and the sun felt scorching. As Warren rests at the convergent of the Allegheny River and Conewango Creek the humidity was suffocating at times. I found myself abandoning my shirt and walking around with loose shorts on and nothing else. Underwear was too confining and way too hot to even remotely consider wearing. I preferred bare feet to wearing shoes. With an interesting lineage of Caucasian and Seneca bloodlines, I would turn an embarrassing shade of red but tan just days after. I had blond hair that grew nearly white in the sun and ice blue eyes that popped intensely juxtaposed to my skin tone. The white man part of me was Irish and my features reflected this only in the thin run of my nose. The native in me gave me high cheekbones, a strong jaw-line and deep-set eyes.

At nineteen-years-old, I had only just graduated from Warren High and like most of the people I was associated with I had no clue what I wanted to do with my life. I didn't want to work at the oil refinery. I didn't want to work for Blair Corporation. And I sure as hell didn't want to work for Wal-Mart. There was little else in town. I needed to get out ... but I didn't really want to think about it. I didn't really want to think about anything. I just wanted to be. Why was that so hard for people to understand? My parents sure as hell didn't get it. They didn't get quite a bit, to be honest ... especially when it came to me. I don't think they ever really tried to get me. They understood my brother just fine ... the little football player with all the friends. And they seemed quite enamored about my sister ... the swim-champ princess down at the local Y.

I watched them all that day ... that hot day in late June ... as they frolicked together on the grassy stretch near Kinzua Beach. It used to be the premier beach of the area, but neglect had allowed outdated septic systems to rupture, and business quickly went elsewhere ... specifically to Chapman State Park and Onoville Marina. Once the forestry service agreed to a partnership with local leaders the beach was restored and reopened as a free service to the community. It was indeed a beautiful and picturesque area during the summer ... indeed it is lush, green and gorgeous. There were some other families there ... some swam in the cool water, others played or hiked. To be honest, I was rather bored. I sat on an oversized cotton towel surrounded by my family's belongings and wished I'd been smart enough to have brought a book. I was a fan of Anne Rice, Stephen King and Clive Barker ... perhaps the three greatest imaginations of my, or any, generation. I adored them and their work.

I decided to stare at people as they meandered about ... watching them as they moved ... the way their bodies gestured ... the way they articulated ... how animated their eyes were. Did their expressions say something quite opposed to what they conveyed with their bodies? Was there sinister or carnal intent behind their eyes? The game was fun, and I found that I imagined that every single person I gazed upon had a deep, dark ulterior motive that only I could fathom. Their loved ones wouldn't know what hit them when they discovered the secrets behind the Norman Rockwell facades. The paintings were false ... gruesomely deliberate guises designed to conceal the darkness they coveted in themselves.

There was an outsider, perhaps my own age, strolling leisurely along the beach with what was perhaps his mother. He had on a raggedy pair of cut-off jeans. His skin was pale, but his muscle tone was that of a disciplined swimmer. I could practically count his abdominals from here. His short auburn hair was tussled ... tufts of it swayed in the breeze. Even from my coy distance I could see that his eyes were a brilliant emerald crowned by thick eyebrows. His smile begat adorable dimples speckled with freckles. His mother wore a demure outfit ... a long and flowing sundress in a pastel floral print that, as odd as it seemed, perfectly complimented her extremely long crimson hair. I imagined her as an aging hippy that smoked pot and listened to Janis Joplin in darkened rooms as she reminisced about the past. How many times had she told her son, in whispers and coughs, all about the 'good old days?' And did he laugh? Did he get in a few harsh and bitter tokes as well?

My gaze drifted over him ... smooth shaven, mysterious and alluring even in the bright light of day. The mound of his package left little to the imagination. He was quite well hung, and I could just make out his religion. I felt a flutter in my tummy ... a tightening in my shorts that made me immediately uncomfortable, but still I could not take my eyes off of him ... until ...

"Are you hungry?"

My mother's jovial voice yanked me almost violently from my personal reverie. I was more uncomfortable than before and guiltily covered myself with both hands in an inadvertent gesture. My eyes were pulled away from the red-headed beauty to the friendly, kind features of my mom. She was smiling broadly down at me. I forced a smile and nodded. She said, "Let's set up for lunch."

As I sheepishly helped her unpack the basket, I tried desperately to conceal my erection from her and everyone else as the rest of my family still frolicked. My eyes drifted about in search of the pale stranger. It wasn't long before I found him ... sitting with his mother not far away at all. They were eating as well ... with a particularly large group of people, and I had to chuckle. I was right ...she was a hippy ... they were with the unjustly maligned Rainbow Family, a hippy-trippy organization that camped out in the forest every so often. Local conservative prudes couldn't stand them, but I found them to be utterly fascinating ... and their message of love and peace was much more preferable to the message of hate and discrimination that conservatives preached. Suddenly, his eyes met mine, and the fluttering in my tummy became an abrupt swarm of butterflies. I automatically looked away ... down to the paper plates my mother was spreading out on the towel ... one plastic fork on each. And as she folded matching paper towels, I chanced another glimpse up at the crimson stranger. He was staring ... smiling ... eating an apple that glimmered in the sun. Oh, the fluttering!

Instantly my eyes turned down, but I could not help but grin with awkward curiosity and longing. The butterflies refused to settle, and as my mother dished out potato salad, I found that my stomach turned. The very sight of food made me slightly ill at ease. I was not hungry. I kept my gaze down and helped her divvy the food. I found that much to my dismay I could not bring myself to look back up. I forced myself to eat right along with my family but kept my eyes firmly focused on my plate. By the end of the meal, the fluttering in my tummy was gone, but my mind ran wild with embarrassing scenarios I'd imagined. What if he was watching me, and I missed my mouth completely with a fork loaded with brisket and the barbequed meat tumbled pathetically down my chest and settled with a deep red splash right in my crotch? What if I suddenly developed a hole in my bottom lip as I sipped my lemonade and poured it down my chest where it, too, would splatter down over my crotch making it appear as if I'd pissed myself? What if my father, in one of his infinitely dorky-assed moves, slapped me playfully across the back of my head as I was chewing, and I revoltingly spit my food out? Or worse, choked on it? None of those awful things happened. Thank God!

When I finally mustered the nerve to look back in the direction of the Rainbow Family ... they were all gone. As my family darted toward the water, in direct violation of the well-known warning to never swim right after eating, I searched the beach for the red-haired stranger. I did not find him. Disappointment welled up inside of me, and I found that a different kind of fluttering began in my stomach. It was a bitter and intense sensation of regret. Even as I told myself there had been little that I could possibly have done I found myself condemning myself for not having the balls to have somehow manipulated a situation in which we would have spoken to each other. No matter what scenario I envisioned, the potential endearment of actually having talked to him was completely overshadowed by the potential humiliation that was surely inevitable. The absolute worst case scenario was that he wasn't even remotely ... well, like me ... and my clumsy advances would be his ultimate amusement. I pictured him laughing at me ... right in my face ... his hippy kin-folks finding it utterly hysterical as well.

Used to my brooding ways, my family didn't even bother trying to coax me into the water. They noticed that I dusted myself off and began a casual walk toward the woods, but they didn't say a word. Why would they? I couldn't help but wonder if they stopped trying not because I never responded enthusiastically with what they were doing but because secretly they really just didn't care if I joined in their reindeer games anymore. I suddenly wanted them at least to have asked and felt thoroughly dejected that they hadn't. I loved to hike in the woods, and I stared longingly at the trees as I strolled leisurely toward them. Everything was a brilliant shade of emerald crowned by a cerulean sky pillowed in pallid cottony clouds. The earthy smell thickened the closer I got, and I found that my gloom melted away to a sense of serenity as I took my fist step among the trees. The calls of birds seemed quite louder there, the buzz of insects did, too. This was my haven. This was where I truly belonged. I loved the woods.

My hands went out to my sides, and my fingertips touched the trees as I passed them. The feel of them was somehow magical. They had a slight vibration to them ... the trees. And if I stopped long enough

... touched them with enough conviction ... I could hear them. They whispered. Before my grandmother had passed away three years ago, she loved to talk about the souls of trees and how they forever longed to converse with people. "The Tree Huggers know," she'd say. "They know that the trees love them and actually want to be touched. The trees would hug back ... if only they could ... perhaps if we gave them time ... perhaps if only we had the patience they do."

The sentiment was beautiful ... as beautiful as my grandmother's soul. I loved her and oh, how I missed her! I thought of her smile ... her eyes ... her tissue-paper touch ... the stories she told with such passion. As tears welled in my eyes, I found myself falling to the ground in a heap. It was a momentary overwhelming sadness ... but even beyond the melancholy there was reflection and love. It was a bittersweet moment. Even through the tears there was laughter. She could be comical in her deep sincerity. She'd truly been an amazing woman.

"What are you thinking about?"

The voice startled me! I flinched in an exaggerated movement that I immediately felt self-conscious about. There was even a sort of strange little snort that came out of my mouth. I wiped the tears from my face and looked about. My self-consciousness only increased when my sight fell upon the red-headed stranger. There was a smile on his face and a brightness to his eyes. Nothing about him suggested that there was spite or malevolence in his words or intentions. "Umm ... oh ... ah, ah, ah," I stammered getting to my feet. Oh, he was beautiful and the butterflies returned to my tummy to swarm about in a tickling frenzy. I could only gawk at him, my eyes probably as round as saucers and my mouth hanging agape. It was only later, in a fit of self mockery, that I imagined how truly awkward and goofy I'd had to have appeared. My eyes traveled across the curves of his lips ... down his masculine chin ... athwart the slight rise of his chest ... into the steam of his sparse treasure trail. Why did it have to end at the waistband of those raggedy cut-off jeans? Oh, man ... that bulge!

"It must have been something good," he said. His voice was deep, mysterious ... like the drawl of a smooth, soulful country crooner. If the eyes and smile weren't enough ... the voice could melt the iciest of hearts. It was certainly doing a fine job of that on mine. He was standing several yards away just behind a tree as if he'd stepped out from behind it. One hand touched the trunk ... the fingers idly caressing the bark.

"Umm, I was just ... thinking."

"About?"

"My grandmother."

"Is she dead?" he asked ... not callously or gracelessly ... just matter-of-factly.

"Yes," I said.

"Mine, too. I miss her," he stated as he casually walked out from behind the tree and over to me. He had a slightly musky smell ... body odor and some kind of essential oil perhaps. It was oddly alluring. He was oddly alluring!

My mind searched its recesses for something to say ... something profound. I said, "Yeah." It was silly, and I felt foolish. I looked away from him to the forest floor and specifically focused on a large fern alive with new curls of growth. A dragonfly rested there ... its magnificent colors glimmering in the sunshine. I didn't want to look up at the other young man even as I was completely aware of his movement toward me. His feet moving among the undergrowth rustled and whispered, and it wasn't long before his toes were in my field of vision ... pale and dirty. All I could think of to say was, "So, you're with the ..."

It was his turn to say a shy and nervous, "Yeah." He was so close. His voice was low and there seemed to be an air of mischievousness.

"Must be fun," I replied.

"Not really," he said. "It's my mother's thing. She's been dragging me around to these ... gatherings ... ever since I was a little kid. Most of the people are like family ... you know ... boring. They get high a lot and act pretty stupid. That's kind of funny, I guess. You're a local?"

I nodded and still didn't look up from the glinting dragonfly. In my mind, I envisioned the red-haired stranger as something quite akin to that vibrant little creature ... his pale skin an extraordinary juxtaposition to the soaring gossamer wings fluttering out behind him. And he had tattoos adorning his body ... bright, brilliant and almost blindingly colorful. The smile remained the same ... the eyes forever emerald ... and his bold presence a joy to be in.

"Small towns can be pretty damn dull from what I understand," he commented. "There never seems to be anything to do in them."

"Warren is pretty boring," I said. "No, there isn't anything to do here. The old people seem to have an aversion to anything that would appeal to young people." I found myself pouring out a stream of consciousness rant that disclosed my exact feelings about my hometown and the prudes that ran it with iron fists. I went on and on and on until I finally realized that at some point I'd turned my attention up to him. He was smiling that Hollywood smile and those beautiful eyes were firmly fixated on me. I was immediately self-conscious, and the words spilling from my mouth faded away.

He huffed with amusement, "I wouldn't want to live in a small town. Don't get me wrong ... yours is beautiful and all, but I much prefer the city ... the sights, the sounds ... and there's always something to do."

"Where are you from?" I sheepishly asked.

"Portland," he answered proudly. "The greenest city in America," he announced and chuckled. "I was a winner of the Rosebud and Thorn Pageant three years ago when I was seventeen."

"What's the Rosebud and Thorn Pageant?" I asked.

"It's like a beauty pageant, you know. It's a queer youth spectacle ... the Rosebud being the drag queen and the Thorn being her male counterpart. It was a lot of fun, and I met a lot of great people."

I was utterly shocked by his laid-back nature and the casual way he just talked about this queer event he'd taken part in. I wished I could be as openly verbose about my own ... uniqueness. Even as he'd been quite open with me I still found it impossible to mention just how similar we were. Secretly, I hoped he'd already just guessed as much. That way I wouldn't have to come right out and say it. I sidestepped my own issue and asked, "Were you the Rosebud or the Thorn?" I was sincerely curious.

"Oh, the ever present elephant in the room, eh? In other words, you want to know if I'm a top or a bottom?" He laughed quite loudly and it echoed among the trees. A bird called out in response in the distance.

"What?" I asked genuinely not knowing what he was really referring to. I would eventually come to know, but at the time I was authentically out-of-the-loop. He took my naïveté as playful mockery.

He threw an arm around my shoulders and said, "Walk with me. Talk with me. Share with me!" And he pulled me along into a relaxed and friendly stroll. Well, relaxed perhaps for him ...

His touch set my skin afire! He continued to talk but his words were lost in the rushing sounds that filled my ears ... oceanic and profound. Storming bolts of electric emotion sprayed out from the touch ... the touch of his arm ... the touch of his torso against mine ... his hip ... his hip ... his hip! And the butterflies were raging inside of me once again so intensely that I thought I might actually get sick ... but I didn't.

Oh, but I might!

And it was wonderful. I found my eyes pouring over him ... and he was right there this time ... not just within reach but actually touching! I dared an awkward arm around his waist and held my breath anticipating a gruff protest ... but he didn't. And I held onto him practically digging my fingertips into his skin. He didn't seem to mind. My heart thundered in my chest threatening to race upward and perhaps escape into the very ether before us. I closed my eyes trusting that he would lead me though the forest safely. And in the darkness behind my eyelids I imagined him as that dragonfly crossbreed again as I ... myself ... transformed into a flurrying monarch with great, flamboyant wings that sent cascading clouds of dust in dance as they fluttered. We held onto each other in my thoughts ... and rose majestically into the air to flicker excitedly around the treetops ... turning ... turning ... turning so that we could look into each other's eyes. And when we kissed there were sparks of rainbow colors bursting from our touch!

Suddenly, I was pulled from my reverie as my handsome host pulled me to a stop. I opened my eyes and found that we'd wandered into an encampment ... clearly a Rainbow Family encampment ... and all eyes had fallen upon us. There was no judgment in the gazes ... there was only friendly smiles and marijuana clouds.

"Who's your friend, Crayon?" someone asked.

I could not help but smile as I turned my attention over to my newfound friend. He leaned over and whispered, "My name is not really Crayon. It's Justin." And then he directed a louder answer to the audience, "This is Butterfly ... he's a local."

I laughed and continued to laugh as he moved me toward his Rainbow Family and introduced me to everyone individually ... including his mother. She was incredibly sweet and wrapped me in a hug before I even realized what she was doing. I'd never before felt so welcome anywhere. I was asked to join them, and I accepted wholeheartedly even as I wished that my red-haired friend would politely decline for me and take me away to some secret and private place where I'd get my mythical kiss. But we sat with them in a Circle of Love and talked about Mother Earth, world peace and love ... love ... love. I was offered a soda, and I accepted it. I was offered a nip of booze but respectfully refused. I also refused the joint that was being passed around ... Justin did not. It wasn't long before his face flushed and his eyes grew kind of squinty. He never once pulled his arm away from me, and I was grateful. There was something so magical and secure in his embrace. I never wanted to be out of it. I found myself wanting to stay with him and his hippy family even as I knew it was about time to leave. The sun was setting, and it was sending rainbow colors across a darkening sky above. The forest was filling with shadows, and the sounds of the night echoed among the trees. I couldn't bring myself to announce that I really had to go but I didn't have to. Justin sensed that it was time to take me back to my mundane world. Everyone hugged me. Everyone said they hoped they would see me again. Justin's mother held me the longest and tussled my hair when I finally pulled away. My red-haired friend held my hand and led me off into the shadowy woods.

We talked as we went ... casual chit-chat ... nothing substantial. I still hoped for a kiss ... still saw him as a dragonfly hybrid in my whirling mind ... and still imagined us in fluttering flight about the treetops. At the edge of the forest I could see my family packing up all of our belongings into the car across the parking lot. We were going to be among the very last to leave. I turned to face Justin but found that my eyes were tearing up at the thought of actually letting his hand go ... actually having to say goodbye. I didn't want to do either. I felt stupid

34

and silly about asking if we would see each other again and even sillier about asking if we could stay in contact. Still the trepidation of rejection haunted me. He hugged me and whispered a sincere and sweet goodbye into my ear. My heart was sinking. He smiled and turned away ... vanished into the shadows. I had not gotten my kiss.

My family welcomed me ... my father, always the stern one, chastised me for being away so long without checking in, but there was really no harm ... no foul. I climbed into the backseat of the car and shrugged into a T-shirt before buckling my seatbelt. I was dead silent the entire way home. I wished so very much that I had been courageous enough to kiss him ... even if only on the cheek.

I was incredibly tired as I showered for the evening; my limbs were heavy and cumbersome. I had to will them to move at all. My bedroom felt lonelier than it had ever felt before. I turned off the lights and crawled under the covers dreading the next day ... dreading the rest of my life. Would I go to college? Would I just get some menial job? Would I ever see Justin again? Would I ever love? Would anyone ever love me?

I settled into my pillow, and there was a certain kind of comfort there. I closed my eyes ... dragonflies and butterflies danced there. I didn't even realize it when I drifted off to sleep, and when I awoke the next morning I did not remember what I had dreamed about. It seemed of little consequence. I ate breakfast leisurely remaining at the table long after the rest of my family had finished. I poured my dirty dishes in the sink and nodded to my mother when she asked me to collect any laundry I needed done and bring it to her. I shambled up the stairs and down the hall to my room. I began to gather my dirty clothes into a smelly bundle in my arms. At the foot of the bed were the shorts I'd worn the day before. I could still smell traces of pot on them. It made me chuckle. As I waded them into a ball to crush them in with my other clothes, there was a little glitter of white in the air. I must admit that it took me a moment to focus on it ... to even realize what it was. And when I did, I dropped my clothes onto my bed and leaned down to pick up the small scrap of paper.

It was a note ... a note from Justin ... signed Crayon, actually. And much to my surprise it was his phone number and address written in smeared blue ink. I closed my hand around it and pressed it to my

35

chest. It's only a crush, I told myself ... but deep down, I hoped it could be so much more.

NEIGHBORLY
By HL Champa

In all my years of going down the shore for my summers, the other side of my duplex was never rented by anyone remotely attractive. I was always stuck next to the world's worst summer neighbors. First, it was the young couple with the toddler that never stopped crying and apparently hated the beach. They took pity on me and deserted their lease half way through the season. I spent enough time around kids during the school year; the last thing I wanted to do was live next to one during my summer vacation.

For a few horrible summers after that, I was stuck next to the guy who loved to blare country music at all hours of the day and night, and his friends left chewing tobacco wads all over our shared driveway. He switched to hip-hop after a few seasons, but the result was the same. I did a dance of joy the day the older couple signed the lease, saving me from the constant noise problem. They didn't stick around, preferring a beach house in Florida to one in Long Beach Island, New Jersey.

After the summers of silence the kindly old couple provided, it was a steady stream of people who seemed hell bent on driving me crazy. I eventually got used to it, putting up with it all for the cheap rent and the view of the ocean from my deck first thing in the morning. Luckily, I only had to put up with them for three months at a time.

I had just settled in for my first days away from the grind of work when I saw him, walking down the path towards the vacant unit next to mine. My breath caught in my throat as I watched his tan frame move easily up the walkway towards the front door. He was the cutest guy I'd seen in a long time. I stared out my window, watching him haul boxes and bags into the house I sometimes wished would stay empty forever.

37

In that moment, watching his impressive legs flex and move with each step, I didn't care if he played horrible music and I didn't care if his friends were obnoxious – just so long as I got to look at that gorgeous body covered in tanning lotion lying in front of our house every day. I pulled up a chair to the window, so I could watch the show in comfort, sipping a beer as I took in the brief flashes of my new, hot neighbor.

I was mid-fantasy, picturing his tall frame stretched out naked on my bed when I saw her. A tiny blonde woman came bopping up the path, holding a shoebox in her hands. He met her half way, and he stopped to lean down and give her a long kiss. Of course, he was straight. My female friends always say all the hot ones are gay, but in my experience, all the hot ones who cross my path are straight. Really, really straight. I slumped back in my chair, letting out a deep sigh. Oh well, he'd keep my spank bank full for a while, anyway.

After a few days and nights of wonderful quiet, I awoke in the middle of the night to a strange sound coming through our common wall. At first, it was just a bang and a squeak. Then, it started. The unmistakable sound of a creaking bed and moans of pleasure. I looked up and stared at the wall above my headboard, as if it would help me see what was going on better. The sounds of my neighbor fucking his girlfriend grew louder, her high-pitched squeal outshining his low, steady groans. I should have been angry. Instead, I felt my cock stirring in my boxers, picturing him moving on top of her. I closed my eyes and wrapped my fist around my cock, envisioning the strong back he used to heft those boxes into his new place tense and relax as he fucked her.

I moved my hand in time with their vocalizations, not needing much warm up after the days I'd spent fantasizing about my new neighbor, hot from the sun and dripping with sweat. I pictured his face, contorted with pleasure, but instead of some silly blonde, he was pumping his hard cock into me. He was getting close, I could tell by the noises that were getting louder right behind my head. Even muffled, his voice was powerful. I was moaning myself as I came, hot spunk releasing onto my belly as the movie playing in my head came to a halt. Soon after I finished and my heart was slowing down, the two lovebirds next door shouted out their orgasms against the paper-thin walls of their house. I drifted off to sleep, everything quiet once again.

The next day, it was time to hit the sand and finally start relaxing properly. Sunday mornings were usually quiet on our stretch of beach, but when I walked out my door onto the cool sand, it was nearly empty. There were two older couples strolling by the water's edge, but the rest of the sand was gorgeously devoid of tourists. I had just plunked down in my chair and started to apply my sunscreen when I saw him. My new neighbor. He was even cuter up close, his tan skin already gleaming from whatever product he had slathered on before. He stopped walking; pausing to look me up and down before he spoke.

"Hey man. You're my neighbor, right? I've been meaning to come by and say hello. I'm Damien."

He moved closer to me and held out his hand. I reached for it, thankful that my sunglasses were hiding my wandering eyes as I took in every inch of his chiseled frame. The word straight kept running through my mind, but it didn't stop my cock from reacting.

"I'm EJ. Nice to meet you. How do you like the place so far?"

"It's nice. I've been looking for a decent place by this beach forever. It seems like I'm cursed when it comes to this stuff. One problem after another."

"Me, too. I live for the times when your house was unrented just so I could get some peace and quiet. Seems like everyone who takes that place has an affinity for making my life miserable."

"Well, I promise you won't have to worry about me. Oh, and on that subject, I'm sorry about last night. I don't know if you heard us, but Shawna can get a little out of hand sometimes. It won't happen again."

"No problem. Believe me, I've heard way worse."

I watched him as he ran a hand absentmindedly over his chest, as if he were still trying to smooth out his sunscreen. My eyes couldn't help but drink in his body, the tight muscle covered by gorgeous tanned skin. He was exactly what I'd always hoped my summers would be filled with. There was a reddish brown birthmark just over his right nipple in the shape of a strawberry. His imperfection made him even more gorgeous. Jesus, Mary and Joseph, he was hot. And, straight, I reminded myself once more. But, in the warm summer sun, that fact was the last thing on my mind. He seemed familiar somehow, but for the life of me; I couldn't place where I might have seen him before. It certainly wasn't during my summers on the beach. That was for sure.

"Well, it was nice to meet you EJ. Hey, I've been thinking about having a barbeque next weekend to break in my new grill. Maybe you'd want to stop by if you're not busy. Think of it as my way of saying sorry about last night."

I forced myself to look into his eyes as he spoke, but it took all my strength to do it. I found myself nodding, my brain barely even processing his words.

"Yeah, sure. Sounds good. Hey, Damien, this may sound weird, but have we met before?"

"No, I don't think so. I'm sure I'd remember if we had EJ."

His words seemed simple enough, but the way he said them made my cock harden a little more. He smiled, and then walked towards the water without another word.

# # # # #

Damien stayed in my head all week, my brain unable to turn off the vision of his body. I knew I knew him from somewhere, I just had no idea where. Plus, thoughts of him making those sexy sounds wouldn't leave my mind either. Going out for drinks with my friends didn't seem to help. There didn't seem to be any amount of alcohol that would drown him out. I took to the internet, in search of someone or something hotter to take Damien's place. My usual haunts were coming up short on new material.

I was on the phone with my friend Harley, lamenting my situation, but he wasn't very sympathetic.

"Damn, EJ. Leave it to you to fall for the straight guy next door. Could you be a bigger cliché?"

"It's not like I set out to do it, Harley. Trust me, if you'd seen him on that beach, you'd feel the same way I do. And, I'm telling you, it's more than that. I know him from somewhere. It's driving me crazy."

"You can look all you want, man. But, that's it. No fucking straight guys. It's my gay Golden Rule. You know that."

"Maybe he's not all straight. Have you thought of that, Harley?"

"Oh, EJ. Listen to you with your wishful thinking. He was fucking a girl, he's straight."

"I guess."

"Fine. Maybe he's not. In fact, maybe he stars in gay porn online. That's how you know him, EJ, since you watch so damn much of it."

Harley was laughing loudly at his own joke, but something inside my mind clicked. A vision of the birthmark on Damien's chest came crashing back into my mind. Harley started talking again, but I wasn't listening.

"Hello, EJ? Are you even still listening to me?"

"I have to go, Harley. I'll talk to you later, okay?"

I hung up, listening to the dial tone for a few seconds as I accessed my video files on my computer. Putting the phone back in its cradle, I clicked on the icons that stared back at me. My brain had finally accessed where I had seen Damien before. Except, where I had seen him was the last place I would have ever expected.

The videos clips were labeled George 1, 2 and 3. I clicked on the first one, and there in front of me on the screen was a guy who looked a lot like Damien. His hair was longer and streaked with blond, and he seemed a few years younger, but everything else looked very similar. As he leaned against a big, black headboard on bright blue sheets, stroking his impressive cock with his hand, I saw it. The telltale birthmark on the otherwise perfect chest. There, in that grainy footage was my new summer neighbor. His eyes peered into the camera, his bottom lip captured between his perfect white teeth. I could hardly believe my eyes, but my cock recognized him immediately.

As much as I wanted to keep watching, I clicked on the next link. I realized I had never finished watching all the videos the first time. Harley had sent them to me a while back. Some friend of a friend of a friend had made them, and Harley made me promise not to post them to the internet after he sent them to me. At the time, I had been too busy to give them a fair chance, watching a few minutes before filing them away on my hard drive. I had clearly seen enough to remember Damien. The second video was much less grainy, and the room was clearly different. Damien was laughing at the cameraman, but the guy's voice was too low to make out what he was saying. Then, there wasn't any more talking from Damien as he moved down the bed and looked up into the lens.

Suddenly, the cameraman's cock came into view, and Damien didn't waste any time taking it into his mouth, moaning as he let it slip between his puffy pink lips. His eyes were closed at first, until the muffled voice from off camera beckoned Damien to look at him. Dutifully, Damien looked up, his puppy dog eyes glassy and glazed with pleasure.

My cock was uncomfortably hard at the sight of him, the camera briefly panning over his naked body before coming back to focus on his sucking mouth. All my notions about my straight neighbor went out the window as he sucked that cock as if he knew exactly what he was doing. It was clearly not his first time, his technique better than I'd seen on some of the guys I'd been with. I couldn't stop staring, watching intently as Damien moved onto his hands and knees when he was told to.

A knock at the door brought me out of my reverie, scaring me half to death. Pausing the video quickly, I sprang out of my chair. I had to wait a few moments before I could approach the door, my cock still half-hard from watching the video.

"Just a minute. Be right there."

Once I had calmed down enough, I pulled the door open without looking through the peephole, only to find Damien on my steps. The sight of him threw my heart into overdrive, especially since he didn't have a shirt on. My face flushed, but if he noticed, he didn't show it. He smiled, before taking a step closer to me. I could hear the ocean crashing in the background, his body still smelling faintly of suntan lotion. It took all my strength to not reach out and touch him, his nipples begging for a good tweak.

"Hey man. I was just trying to fix the fan in the bedroom of my place, but I need a Phillips head screwdriver. Do you happen to have one? I didn't bring anything like that with me. I figured I wouldn't need that kind of thing at the beach."

His request was simple enough, but I could barely form the words. I stared at his face, scarcely believing that it was the same guy I just watched suck someone off on camera. Shaking my head slightly, I got myself together enough to answer him.

"Yeah, I think so. Let me look."

Damien moved towards my living room that overlooked the water, while I headed to the kitchen and pulled open my junk drawer. I knew I had a few tools in there, and I seemed to remember a screwdriver being in there somewhere. I rooted around the drawer for a while, but I was coming up empty. All too soon, Damien was heading towards me.

"It's a great view, isn't it? It's half the reason I rented the place. Hey man, if you don't have one, that's cool, I just thought ..."

His words trailed off as he stopped moving, distracted by what he saw on my computer screen. Ducking his head down to get a closer look, his face dropped when he saw exactly what I had been looking at before he arrived. I fully expected him to freak out or make a hasty exit, but instead he just stood up straight and finished walking into the kitchen. If I didn't know better, I thought he was going to hit me, but instead he pushed me up against my sink, the counter digging into my lower back. I thought I better start talking my way out of it, before he got even madder.

"Dude, I can explain that. My friend Harley sent it to me. But, I had no idea, I mean, I ..."

His whole face change the scowl replaced by a smile as he moved his hands around my back and pulled me closer to him.

"So, I guess you remembered where you'd seen me, huh EJ?"

I cleared my throat, trying to think of the best thing to say to him.

"It was the birthmark that gave you away, Damien."

He laughed, his big hands moving up my back before heading down again.

"I didn't think anyone was still looking at that old stuff. Lord knows it happened years ago. I should have known it was still making the rounds."

"I can't believe it's really you."

"Why?"

"Because, you're straight. Aren't you?"

"You know, I never know quite how to answer that question. Let me see if I can make it easier for you."

I opened my mouth to ask another ridiculous question, but I never got the chance. His mouth covered mine, his tongue diving right in. I held onto him to keep myself steady. We broke apart when both of us needed air, but my lungs didn't seem to be able to get any. His next words shocked the hell out of me, and made my cock grow even harder.

"So, which videos did you watch EJ? Did you see the third one yet? That's my favorite."

I sighed, his lips back on mine briefly, before he pulled back again.

"No, Damien, I only saw part of the first and second one."

"Too bad. They really are hot, if I do say so myself. Obviously, you think so, too, EJ."

He pressed his hips forward, grinding his hard cock against mine, making my knees go weak. Another crushing kiss made me even weaker, and when I spoke, it was barely a whisper.

"I do, Damien. I do."

"Good. How about I give you the live show EJ?"

"What about Shawna?"

"She's gone back home for the week. So, EJ, do you have any lube lying around here or what?"

He pulled away and I ran to the bedroom as fast as I could, grabbing what we needed from my night table. He took one last glance at my laptop before heading towards the door. I followed him, not knowing exactly what was going on. When we got outside, he grabbed a blanket that was draped over the railing by his front door as if it was waiting for this very thing. Hitting the sand, he spread out the blanket before turning back to me. It was dark all around us, only the lights from the other houses casting a dim glow. He reached for my shirt, pulling it over my head and tossing it into the sand. He drank me in with his eyes, and I hardened at his appreciative gaze.

"Very nice, EJ. I noticed your great body on the beach the other day. You know, this is the first time I've ever rented next to a hot guy. I was beginning to think it would never happen. Then I saw you. And I knew it was going to be a great summer."

"That's funny, Damien. I thought the same thing about you when you first moved in."

His hands rested against my hips, his forefingers slipped inside the waistband of my shorts. The oddest thought came into my mind, and I couldn't help but give it voice.

"So, why George? I mean, of all the names in the world."

He laughed, his deep voice getting a little lost in the crashing of the surf.

"Really? You don't see the joke, EJ? I thought you would get it right away."

"What's the joke?"

"The guy who filmed it picked it. He used to call me Curious George. Get it EJ?"

"That's pretty clever, Damien. But, you don't really think of yourself as just curious any more, do you?"

"Sure I do, EJ. I'm still curious. Like, right now, I'm wonder what your cock tastes like."

Sinking to his knees, he pulled my shorts and boxers down in one fell swoop, my hard cock springing forward right in front of his face. Just like he had in the video, he wrapped his gorgeous lips around the head of my cock, and began slowly taking me down his throat. My body tensed, my hips moving instinctively forward, pushing me further into his mouth. Damien left his hands on my hips, pushing and pulling me gently as he sucked. My toes dug in the sand, chilly by contrast to the warm night air. As if on cue, he looked up at me with those big brown eyes, and I buckled. No video could do that visual justice.

"God, Damien. You feel so fucking good."

He gave me one more deep suck down his throat before pulling his hot mouth off my cock and standing up; quickly removing the baggy shorts he was wearing. I thought he would just kneel back down, but instead he turned away from me, positioning himself on the blanket on his hands and knees. His ass, cheeks spread open and inviting, sat right in front of me, and Damien was looking over his shoulder.

"Well, EJ. What are you waiting for? You know you're curious."

I chuckled as I moved behind him, placing a hand on each muscled ass cheek. I ran a thumb over his pink pucker, watching it tighten slightly as I moved slowly around the perimeter. I couldn't resist a taste of him one minute longer and let my tongue trace over and across his asshole. He groaned so sweetly as I plunged into his hole deeper, his hips coming back against my face, forcing me inside a little bit more. I dug my fingers into his hips, rimming him slowly, enjoying his squirming and whimpering. His hand was working his cock, my own in desperate need of release. And, I intended to get it right now. Damien's shaky voice told me he had the same idea I did.

"God, I want you to fuck me, EJ."

I didn't back off right away, I was enjoying torturing him with my tongue too much. The whole scene was making me crazy. I'd always wanted to fuck on the beach, but I never thought it would be like this. But, when he begged again, I knew it was time.

"Please fuck me, EJ. I want it so bad."

Reluctantly, I got up and retrieved my lube and condoms from my shorts pocket. Damien didn't move, his ass still high in the air, waiting for me. He watched me roll on the condom and lube myself up. I squeezed some of the liquid onto his moist hole and worked it inside with my fingers. He opened up easier than I thought he would, his resistance mostly gone after a few deep strokes of my finger inside him. I added a second one, his hole gripping me tight as I moved. He was fucking back against my fingers in no time, groaning loudly. I didn't care if anyone saw or heard us by that point. I was too horny to care if we were caught.

He moaned his disappointment when I pulled my fingers out of him, but the insistent press of my cock head seemed to make him happy. When he opened up and let me inside, I let out a deep sigh, sinking slowly and steadily into his ass.

"Is this what's on the third video, Damien?"

"Yeah. Only his cock isn't nearly as big as yours."

I started pounding into him harder, my knees sinking into the blanket covered sand as I moved. He was sounding a lot like he did the other night with his girlfriend, only this time I didn't have to fantasize about him. He was right there in front of me, his tight ass clamping around my cock as I fucked him. Damien was pushing back into me, keeping pace with me, his hand moving furiously over his cock. I would have to remember to thank Harley the next time I talked to him, maybe invite him for a weekend to say thank you. And, tell him he was full of shit. His Golden Rule was well and truly broken. I slowed down just a bit, letting Damien do the work for a while, relishing each amazing sensation. I bit my lip to keep myself quiet, but then remembered there was no reason to be quiet as the pounding waves would cover most of our noise. Besides, it's not as if I had to worry about waking the neighbors. His voice cracked as he spoke in a broken staccato, his words the exact ones I wanted to hear.

"EJ, oh fuck. I'm gonna come."

Pounding with abandon, I fucked him deep and hard, watching with delight as he started to unravel. He cried out so loudly, his body shaking in the most delightful way. His ass squeezed my cock, pushing me right over the edge and sent my hot cum shooting into the condom that covered my cock. He collapsed underneath me, and I fell on top of him, both of us spent and sweaty in a heap. When we finally rolled apart, I stared up at the black night sky, trying to catch my breath.

"Damn, EJ. That was incredible."

"You weren't so bad yourself, George."

"Very funny."

We started to get dressed, Damien picking up and shaking out his blanket. He shocked me by kissing me hard, our mouths mingling so easily together.

"So, you wanna come in and see if we can find that screwdriver Damien?"

"No thanks, EJ. Didn't really need one. I just needed an excuse to come over and hit on you."

"Good trick."

"Maybe next time, if you're lucky, EJ, I'll bring my camera with me."

He left my arms and started walked towards his side of the house, but I couldn't let him go just yet.

"Good night, George."

"Night, EJ."

PIPE BLOWER
By R. Talent

Mikey was one of those ruggedly handsome twenty-year-old studs that loved his motorcycles.

You know the kind: Loveably dumb when it came to the books. Refreshingly savvy when it came to the streets. And yet, always ready to give the make and model of every bike known to man, even the foreign ones, in a matter of nanoseconds just by listening to the engine roar down the hot summer streets.

Mikey knew his bikes all too well. He was equally good at fixing them as well, which proved to be both a blessing and a curse working for my Uncle Marv at his auto body shop down in San Diego.

I say that because while my uncle was incredibly astute in hiring a gifted mechanic like Mikey to save his floundering shop, Uncle Marv secretly hated the tall, good-looking, high-yellow biracial guy because I was so enamored with him.

You see, when it came to family members that were cool, Uncle Marv was the guy to beat in our family full of strong-willed women. So after my dad passed away the previous fall and Uncle Marv losing his wife to cancer the following spring, flying out to California to console my favorite uncle seemed to me to be the most generous way to spend my summer vacation.

While I understood fully well that Uncle Marv was dealing with his loss just the same as I was dealing with mine, I didn't expect him to be so totally out of it. Different from the confident, laid back man that I had grown to love. First, it came off as if he was trying too hard to make everything be like the way it was. The way it used to be before my aunt passed. When I tried to indulge him in this way, in my attempt to meet him half way, he wanted to push me off on Mikey. When I thought I was giving him his space, he got irate because I was spending all of my time with Mikey, working on those crotch rockets.

The main problem was that Uncle Marv wanted to be my go-to guy for working on bikes. But even if he was in a better headspace, that wasn't likely to have happened. Uncle Marv was one of those mechanics that got his knowledge straight from the books and wanted me to do the same, as if beautiful Sunny California wasn't calling out for an eighteen-year-old kid like me. And while there was no question that Uncle Marv knew what he was doing as far as fixing bikes, there wasn't any real passion behind his work – other than running the shop – which happened to make every lesson that he wanted to teach me sound like some long boring lecture on the migrant pattern of snails.

Mikey, on the other hand, with his retro sideburns flaring out along his defined jaw line simply loved bikes.

He was just about a hair away from altogether worshiping the machine, if it wasn't for the fact that he clearly got the sense that it was a ferocious beast made for speed. Whenever he wasn't working on one or pointing one out in the streets, he was always riding a bike from his expansive collection off into the sunset with me riding bitch.

I honestly didn't give a shit about my position because when I was riding behind Mikey I was riding like I was driving, which was far more than I could say for Uncle Marv who wouldn't even touch a bike outside of working on one.

Don't get me wrong. Uncle Marv and I were still cool as only a favorite uncle and nephew could be ... just as long as I didn't mention Mikey's name outside of the shop. Something that was awfully hard to do because I spent every waking moment of my summer soaking up the aura that was Mikey Bobo.

I was in total awe of Mikey. He lived life by the seat of his denim with not a care in the world. He was a proud grease monkey that got his hands filthy by day and sweaty by night with some random chick that thought his exotic good-looks reminded them of some chic villain they saw in some cheesy C-rated movie. And because Mikey was just a few years older than I, he became the cool big brother I never had. He scored me a fake ID to join him at some of the local bike clubs in the outskirts of town. He invited over to his empty apartment where his landlady was insistent on providing him free alcohol in addition to free rent in exchange for a few sexual favors.

Mikey and I were hanging out at his apartment one afternoon after she had left when he decided that we should head out for a ride. Normally, that meant that we were on our way to the beach or to some biker dive or to the ramshackle house of one of his notorious weed suppliers. So when Mikey went into this new direction opposite of all those other places, I was a little unnerved when he pulled up to this dark warehouse in the middle of nowhere. My edginess about being in this strange place at night only intensified as he flipped on an overhead light and handed me a set of keys. The first key was to unlock the storage unit. The second key on the ring was to start the black and blue Suzuki motorcycle of my dreams!

Mikey waited until I manned up from blubbering like a baby to tell me that it was all mine. Uncle Marv had bought it off Mikey as a birthday gift to me. Mikey said that Uncle Marv bought it for me because he felt as if I had actually earned it. Given all the work I had one at his shop. Following behind Mikey and making his load lighter so he could get to more bikes in the shop.

"Man," I said, wiping away the tears. "Too fuckin' bad I can't ride my baby to night. Damn!"

"Why not?"

"Uncle Marv," I said, reminding him that even with such a generous gift, Uncle Marv wasn't a big fan of me hanging out with Mikey 'til all hours of the night, and it was pushing ten-thirty by then.

"That's what eighteen do for you. Besides, it sort of kind of the reason why he ain't here to give you this expensive gift himself." Mikey said showing off his crookedly goofy smile framed in a wisp of a connecting moustache and goatee. "Marvin kind of sort of figured that once you got your hands on this bike that you'd probably want to spend the night riding it. And since he never rode like that, I told him that it was cool if you crashed at my crib tonight, if you happen to tucker yourself out."

"Screw you, man," I laughed, moving his frisky hand away from my head.

It felt as if we rode the highway forever that night. But eventually we pulled into this dilapidated taco stand outside of Mexicali, where we were greeted by this gang of retired bikers and this plain-looking Mexican girl with long hair, big breasts, and an even bigger nose. She said that her name was Christiana, though I felt that was just her name for the night. Nevertheless, she proved to be the only ray of light for miles as she manned the whole place by herself, speaking to us in perfect English with a slight flare of her native Oaxaca tongue.

We first thought she was just being nice to us because we were the only two men in the place that weren't old enough to be her father, grandfather, or even a perverted uncle. Then, her tactics towards us became a little bit more aggressive. Not like she was angry at us or anything, but much more engaging, as if conversation between the sexes was a full contact sport.

Mikey thought she was flirty with him because of the way she threw her titties in his face. I thought the girl was flirty with me the way she kept on caressing my mannish neck and grabbing onto my well-rounded shoulders. (Even though Mikey was a few years older than I, I looked to be his equal, if not a couple of years ahead of him, being that I filled out my thickset five-ten quite handsomely.)

As it turned out, she was shamelessly flirting with the both of us. Mikey explained to me that like most girls she was turned on by the bikes out there, and that it didn't hurt that we were a couple of good-looking studs. But the thing that really caught our attention with her was when we got up to the counter to a pay our bill, where a lewd drawing of a voluptuous woman on the receiving end of two enormous cocks, one colored in black with a pen (to be me) and the other one left blank (to be him), slipped out from under the receipt.

Mikey and I could do nothing but study the simple yet enticing picture. And that was when Christiana let it be known that in less than an hour after she got off of work that she wanted to get off with a dick down her throat and a dick in her snatch.

I think it should go without saying that being both "heterosexual" men and all, Mikey and I helped her in any way would could to make sure that she locked up in a timely manner, from tossing the old geezers out to making sure that the place was spic and span from top to bottom before we left. As Mikey and I let her be to finish off her routine, I reached for the payphone outside to thank Uncle Marv for the bike. Before I thanked him for the umpteenth time, Christiana came out of the eatery with her stained tee shirt pulled behind her head shimmying her large braless knockers for the night to see. If that wasn't to get a horny teenager going, I left the taco stand feeling incredibly manly when she climbed on the back of my bike, grabbed onto me for dear life, and whispered sweet dirty nothings in my ear, driving to a place down the road where our threesome could commence.

After Mikey secured the room at the dingy roach motel, the three of us stripped down. Neither Mikey nor I were virgins (when it came to girls) nor were we virgins in seeing each other naked, as we occasionally indulged in jack-off contests while watching Guy Di Silva and Jake Sneed paint their respective dicks in soaking wet pussy juice in Mikey's apartment. And Christiana being the one that suggested the tag team obviously wasn't a virgin neither.

Being the youngest in the group, I felt I had the most to prove. So I took the lead in pulling her hair to get her to suck Mikey off properly while I grinded into her pussy. I then flipped her on back with Mikey keeping a steady hand around her neck, showing me a trick that sent her over the edge. It worked. She sprayed pussy juices to the like I had never seen before. By the time Mikey and I switched off it sounded like he was drilling into a well the way her wetness churned like a raging river rapid.

To make a long story short, Mikey got off twice while I was too nervous to even get off once. And with Christiana desperate to get back to the taco stand before her married owner-boyfriend found out that she closed up the restaurant for a couple of hours just to get laid, she couldn't stick around and wait. Though, she was sincerely apologetic that after I got her off so well that she wasn't able to reciprocate.

"I would've thought you would've been the first one to come." Mikey said, trying to be comforting. Not knowing that he was just making matters worse, as he grabbed the edge of the comforter to wipe his cum-stained dick.

"I know," I mouthed, grabbing the other end of the comforter to wipe away the spit and cunt sap off of my dick.

As that proved to be the first time that would ever happen to me, it certainly wasn't the last. In later years I would learn that I was growing into a very piggish dick.

At the time, however, I was beyond bewildered. It wasn't like I was getting off on the action as I just failed to get off. And because that was the first time I had sex in front of another man before, particularly one that I was in sheer wonder of, I chalked up my choking up as something that was destined to happen.

"I thought the way you were going hard in that broad that you'd be busting off like a firecracker, after getting a new bike and some fire-crotch to boot."

"I know." I said, respectfully annoyed by now, sitting on the edge of the bed.

"I mean you're not going to find too many girls that'll freak you and your boy off like that. That's a once in a lifetime opportunity, man."

"I know. Damn!" I cursed.

That was something out of character for me at the time yet enough to get him to back off.

"I'm sorry, man," he said after a few moments. "It's just that she may not have been something to look at in the face with that wiener nose, but she was a sweet fuck."

"I know," I said, feeling like I had to remind him that I was there.

"Maybe I can remedy that for you." He said confidently out of the blue, getting up from his laid out position on the bed.

"What?"

"Get up." He beamed, walking over to the television, playing with the hairy carpet over his hard chest and rippling abs.

"What do you got in mind?" I asked.

"Come here." He said, with me coming up to stand next to him.

He changed the channel, going through a series of barely playable station before he got to one full of squiggly lines that produced the slight image of a bouncing blond groaning her heart out into the lap of a man that I couldn't clearly make out.

"Jack off with me like we do back at the crib."

"You still got juice?" I asked in shock.

My dick never died down to begin with, not even after Christiana left, but Mikey came like a geyser the first time. And the second time, he shot like a bubbling stream that never seemed to stop running.

"Hell, yeah, you know me, man. A stroke a day keeps an ugly doctor away."

I said nothing to his last comment. I just grabbed my dick and stroked, regretting that we didn't ask Christiana if she had a weed supplier in these parts, seeing that we weren't bound to go anywhere without some much needed sleep first.

I swear. No more than ten minutes could've passed before Mikey was crying out another creamy load. Of course, I was mad as fuck, looking over to find a third load of dying babies dripping all over his sticky fingers.

Again, it wasn't like I wasn't feeling my dick. It just felt like I was far from oblivion in shooting out some milk. So I squeezed harder, stroked faster, think that speed was the thing to remedy my problem. After a few minutes of absolutely nothing, I started to worry that maybe my problem was that I didn't jack off enough like Mikey. Even worst, as I thought fearfully at the time, maybe my pipes were blocked and I wasn't going to skeet a nutt ever again!

"Whoa, slow it down, man! You might burn off some of those nerve-endings that won't allow you to come." Mikey commented, reaching over to put his hand just over my bellybutton.

I was pumping so hard that I probably could've started a forest fire down there.

"Relax and breathe." Mikey offered.

I did, slowing down my strokes as well.

"Let go of your dick, man."

I obliged.

"Now you know I'm good about busting a nutt, right?"

"Yeah," I said with a 'no-duh' attitude.

"You want to bust that nutt right?"

"Yeah," I answered.

"I got an idea. Close your eyes. Take a deep breath."

I followed his direction.

"Good," Mikey continued. "Now what I'm about to do is help you get your nutt, shouldn't leave this room, okay?"

"Okay," I said nervously, not knowing what he had in mind.

"Don't freak out, okay. Just keep your eyes closed. Remember to relax and breathe and let me take care of everything, okay."

Once again, I said nothing, trusting Mikey and not trusting him at the same time. Not knowing exactly what he had up his sleeve.

I waited patiently for something to happen before I felt him come from behind me and I felt his arm come underneath my arm, hitting the side of my stomach as his sticky-wiped hand reached out and clasped my swollen pipe.

I jumped at the touch of the new hand, but welcomed each new stroke that followed like an old dear friend. I started to leak just a bit – and then a lot. My dick drooled with so much slime that for a brief second I thought it was the lack of lube that had done me in. I settled in this thought before I remembered Christiana was drenching my balls with her pussy juices like nothing I had ever seen before.

I let his hand take me through the ropes of ecstasy. But much like before, it wasn't that I wasn't feeling anything spectacular as it was I just wasn't "arriving" at the place I wanted to go.

I had just exhaled my twentieth sigh, thinking that if I have into the feeling enough that I would be on my way to busting a good nutt or two, when I felt Mikey change hands and change positions., going from being behind me to beside me, sort of. I wasn't going to open my eyes, but was about ask what he doing when I felt a new kind of wetness on my dick. It was right on the head, encircling it. Had it been another girl in the room, I wouldn't have questioned what was going on. But Mikey had a dick just like me, so it couldn't have been what I was thinking. Mikey wasn't a fag. Mikey was a macho man who scored with a ton of girls. There was no way he was playing with me with his mouth.

Even though the feeling was unique, I didn't truly believe what was going on until I looked down and saw a very familiar face making a very familiar fish face in front of me. I nearly crawled out of my skin. It was already unfathomable to me that Mikey liked scrapping his knees. I was completely flabbergasted when he sucked it like a baby to a pacifier, consistently and relentlessly. I wanted to swat him away, call him out everything I thought he was. However, his mouth felt golden. He sucked dick better than any girl I had ever been with before. It was like his mouth was making sweet love to my dick. Or, at least, I thought he was when he began to choke on it a bit taking dick passed his trembling tonsils.

I stood there with my hands out to my sides, not knowing what to do with them, thinking that if I reached out and touched him that it was somehow going to make our friendship weirder.

Mikey reached up for my arms and moved my hands over to the top of his head like it was a game show buzzer. I used it to guide my dick further into his mouth as I slowly moved my hips forward. He scared me more than a few times when I heard the tone in his throat go from a lively gulp to a silent gag, which made me a bit tense. Yet, feeling his throat convulse around my dick in his mediocre retch felt incredibly wonderful.

I began not to feel so bad after he took my dick down to the hilt a couple of more times, letting me know that not only was he a good cocksucker but he was a very skilled cocksucker at that.

Although I should've felt relieved, I was angry more than anything else.

Angry that Mikey was a knob-slobber. Angry that I was letting him do this to me without so much a fight, angrier that I felt like I gave off this vibe that he felt free to do this to me.

I was just plain angry.

I wasn't expecting the anger to manifest itself, as I came to find that I was pulling on his head and jamming my dick down his throat. He was choking. I didn't give care. His face was my pussy. He was a smart enough cocksucker to keep his lips working over my dick.

I was so caught up in my emotions that it had to shake through me like a clap of thunder that I was about to come!

"Keep that up and I'm going to nutt up in your mouth!"

"Good." Mikey breathed, taking a quick pause. "You said you wanted to get that nutt. Go ahead. Bust that nutt in my mouth, if it's going to get you off."

It took me a few minutes, but after awhile I was losing my mind with lust watching those deep strokes drive in and out of his mouth.

"Yeah, that's it, suck my dick!" I said, adding some bass to my voice.

And as if it finally hit him, he began to go crazy, too, slurping on my dick like it was his life supply.

"I never thought I would say this to another dude, but you look good with my dick hanging out of your mouth."

He opened his mouth wider, giving it a loud slurp before he wrapped his lips tightly around my dick.

"Oh, yeah, Mikey," I said, grabbing a handful of close cropped hair. "Get ready for it. 'cause here I come!"

I ferociously pumped my hips, keeping his head steady. I went from feeling the friction of my dick to feeling my dick swell even thicker.

"Aw, man! Fuck!"

I grunted, but he grunted even louder with me barely pulling out of his mouth in time to shoot a long steady ribbon of cum straight into his open mouth.

I was exhausted and at loss for words, not with a sense of relief that my dick still worked but back to the original anger I had at Mikey, as if he purposely betrayed our friendship.

Mikey wasn't oblivious to this. He looked at me looking back at him. The angrier I got, the more of a smile he put on his face, licking his face of some of my runoff.

Over the years, Mikey has led to some satisfying jack off sessions, thinking about that night and the possibilities of the night thereafter if only I knew how to play my cards right. Even though Mikey still works for Uncle Marv out in San Diego and I have to come to fully embrace my sexuality over the years, Mikey unfortunately doesn't mess around like that anymore. As married life and his will to be faithful to his wife has consumed the handsome rotund ordained preacher on the side.

But, man, when Mikey was pipe blowing, he was definitely blowing pipe!

LIQUOR AND SUN
By Derrick Della Giorgia

Harlow dug out and discarded all the shrimps buried in the rice, elegantly vacuuming his paella. When he finished, he gulped down his third glass of red sangria and put his hand on my thigh.

"Why are you not eating, sexy?"

"Not very hungry. I think I'll get some fruit." My stomach was twisted like a corkscrew, and the rest of my body couldn't get rid of this low voltage electricity right under the skin. His hand made me feel safe and good, but the electricity wouldn't stop. It hadn't since he'd knocked on my door with his Burberry sun glasses on.

"Let's have a toast. To the beautiful night that's ahead of us!" The weight of his muscular arm transmitted through his glass to mine, and he stared at me like only he knew how to do. I swallowed the sangria and smiled back, trying to imagine what it would be like to feel his chest. The first three buttons of his black shirt were undone and when he leaned back on the chair with his elbow on the table I could see his left nipple, about two inches below the word 'pulcher' tattooed in black ink on his tanned skin. The first time I'd seen his tattoo I'd run to the computer and Googled that word, eager to discover more things about him before having him in front of me. Latin adjective for beautiful, gorgeous; 'pulcher' was the masculine, singular form. Nothing I couldn't have thought of myself, just looking at him.

"Do you wanna get some champagne?" The fruit hadn't helped either, but the conversation was slowly becoming easier and smoother, freed of the initial awkwardness that always accompanied my first dates. In my mind, I knew the perfect words to say and the most

61

appropriate things to make guys go crazy. Unfortunately, when the person in front of me really enthralled me, all that became confusion and emotion, and I ended up sounding like a quasi-loser. Him being a model didn't help either.

"Sure. That would be a fantastic way to celebrate your graduation." He looked very surprised when I told him that I had just obtained a full degree in chemistry. He pursed his lips in one of his sexy poses and then locked his mouth in a wide smile, with all his teeth showing like in one of those commercials for laser whitening. He thought I studied something like law or medicine, something "less unpredictable."

"Don't take me wrong. It's just that when I think of all those formulas, I imagine some weird guy, scribbling on a blackboard with his hair messed up."

"Come on."

"Yeah, and you instead look like a doctor or a lawyer ... you know, more structured."

"You are thinking boring, aren't you?" I laughed shaking my head.

"No, no-no-no!" He straightened up and raised both his palms to block my next statement.

"It's ok." He was so hot that I really didn't mind whatever came out of his mouth.

"You look like a very ... how can I say it ... distinguished guy. Aristocratic! That's the word." Smart observer. I had avoided my family history on purpose, and he had figured it out after merely two hours. I wanted people to get interested in me, before being awed by all the money my family had. Before seeing their faces dreaming about the life I led, or imagining how different my habits might be. Being the son of a duke doesn't count much when it comes to shoveling through yourself to find out who you are or learning to tame your emotions when you meet another person.

"All right, my family's a bit uptight. You got that right away. They are very formal. What about you? You look so positively charged and secure of yourself? But who's Harlow deep inside?" The waiter reached our table with the bottle of Dom Perignon and two flutes. He let us check the label and asked for permission to take the cork off.

"I'll take care of that. Thank you." His mesmerizing deep voice took over again and swept the young waiter away. He put down his cigarette and put both his hands on the neck of the bottle to prepare it for us.

"So? Champagne is not gonna save you from answering my question." The Dom looked so small in his hands. His biceps forced the cork out in a single stroke, controlling the power of the carbon dioxide with almost no effort.

"I write novels. I'm trying to publish one right now. But it's only a passion for now. You know. My job job is modeling" He filled my glass and then his, waiting for me to say something.

"That is so interesting. What do you write? Let's have a toast to your novel!"

His first novel was a science-fiction story about genetic engineering. In some near future, this company called Copyguy was specialized in cloning guys for the rich buyers that could afford it. The sick twist was that the guys were not meant to be adopted or anything like that. They were put into life, from a catalogue of cell donors that got paid for giving up their tissues, solely for the buyer's sexual pleasure. The main character was this rich banker that, with the approval of his wife, kept cloning a different guy every three or four years until he ended up with a copy of a son he had had with another woman, of whose existence he wasn't aware.

"Wow." I felt bad for thinking that, being so hot and sexy, he couldn't also be smart or creative. His attitude was studied to make you believe he was good in bed; everything else came after that.

"The book isn't about genetic engineering. I don't wanna be a Spanish Michael Crichton. It is about what way we are gonna choose to control our relationships and our feelings in the future. Because, you know things we consider fundamental today will have no meaning in twenty years."

"I'm speechless. I can't wait to read it." My second glass of champagne cancelled my stomach and the electricity under my skin. On the other hand, my desire for him grew stronger and wider every minute. I watched him swallow the contents of his glass and the protruding of his Adam's apple almost gave me a hard-on. The dark beard was accurately shaven and enhanced his strong features, which reminded me somehow of the model D&G used for that commercial on the boat. David Gandy! Damn ...

"I hope the editor likes the idea that much, too!" He lit another cigarette and blew the first cloud of smoke towards the sea, on our right. Barcelona was a labyrinth of voices that multiplied infinitely at that hour. People were just getting ready to face the long night, the peaceful summer heat. I loved my city and so seemed everybody else. I watched his smoke disperse in the air and then I felt it again. His firm hand on my thigh, going up to my waist, skimming over the hill formed by my sex.

I lived a couple of blocks away from the Sagrada Familia, but I asked the driver to drop us there, in front of the 'melting church,' as I had called it since I was ten. When I was little, my favorite past-time was to sit and count all the little holes, spikes and weird things growing on it. It was the Barcelona that best described me, the Barcelona I could totally relate to. My melting church. I had kissed my first boyfriend under its light, I had put the first cock in my mouth behind its pinnacles.

After I paid the taxi, I took Harlow's hand. He didn't take his eyes off Gaudi's baby and simply tightened his grip, bringing our arms closer to his body. He was four or five inches taller than I, his frame so much wider that he could easily hug me and completely hide me from the world. His cologne was stronger now and perfectly blended with the smoke of his cigarettes. He let me stare at him, at his sexy waist, his straight nose, his dark eyes, the beautiful collar bones that protruded at the base of his regal neck.

"Harlow ..."

"What's up, sexy?" He wouldn't use my name. I was 'sexy' to him. When I opened the door of my apartment, I had been sexy, when he wanted me to pick the table at Paco's he'd asked sexy, when it was time to decide what to do after dinner, there I was transformed into sexy again. Not awkward, not the chemical expert, not the duke's son, not the Spaniard with a dream, not the snob nor the aristocratic, just sexy.

"Nothing."

"Oh sexy, your nothing is everything ..." He fastened his hot arms around my back and sucked me into his embrace. My face was an inch away from his chin, making it impossible for me to resist the temptation. I innocently kissed it. I put my lips on his chin and landed a kiss on it, on the perfumed skin spiced up by the roughness of his beard. I smiled right after, and he pierced me with his eyes. I felt as if he was reading my life, unraveling and desecrating all my erotic refuges. "How about this?" He inserted his lower lip in between mine with an oblique move of his head and slid right out of my face. Then he came back, locked his mouth into mine, making pressure on my lower back and forcing me on the tip on my feet. He swam into me, starting a voyage that I had never experienced. The last thing I saw before closing my eyes was the highest tower of the Sagrada. After that, impossible to remember in what order, I tasted his tongue, his cheek, his teeth, everything wet that I encountered on my exploration of his face.

"Harlow." His chest was coalesced with mine, and his muscles felt like waves of wet sand against my skin and my hands. I put a hand on his hair and pulled him into me more, hoping to find out there was more to try. "You make me feel ..." I managed from the hunger of his mouth.

"How do I make you feel? Tell me, please." Even when we talked our faces were kiss close, nothing could be put between us.

"I don't know. Drunk. You know when you drink some strong drink in a sunny afternoon and your body lets go?"

"Yeah ..."

"That's how I feel right now. Like liquor and sun. You are liquor and sun to me." I laughed for the stupid thing I had just said and kissed him again.

"Nobody had ever compared me to liquor or sun. But it sounds good." He pulled my shirt out of the Dior pants I had selected from my wardrobe to conquer him and caressed my back, stopping at all the knots that my back bone created under my skin.

"Let's go to my apartment. Can you hold on your fire for two more blocks?"

"I don't know. But we can try."

When I slightly bent to put the key into my door, he blocked my hips and kissed my neck, reviving the electricity that had been my main enemy for the first two hours of our date. This time it was high voltage and intermittent, making me voracious for him.

"Stop that or you'll have to quench my desire in front of Mrs. Vela's door ... and I can assure you she won't like that! She is eighty-three."

"Come out, Mrs. Vela and watch how I do sexy!"

"Shut up ..."

I pulled him by his shirt and dragged him through my foyer, my red walled living room and directly into the kitchen. Next to the stoves, I let him go and grabbed a bottle of Dom from my black fridge. It was my signature, a bottle of champagne before making love. All the guys that had rolled through my bed knew that.

"The bedroom is next door to the right. Go get comfortable. I'll meet you and my glass of champagne there in five."

"Don't take too long, or I'll come look for you ..."

My mirror confirmed to me I was a little drunk, but I still looked decent. I took my shirt off and dropped my pants. My Hermes underwear looked like the perfect obstacle before getting to me. I rubbed some body oil on my abs, my inner thighs and my ass.

He was lying down on my king size bed, illuminated by my grandmother's Chinese lamp. His head rested on his hand, sipping champagne. His shirt was even more unbuttoned and his chest exposed and ready for me. He'd taken his shoes off and the white feet coming out of his black pants were where I wanted to start from. I advanced towards them and got on my knees. He kept sipping, like a master waiting for his slave. I licked his soles and put his toes in my mouth, moving my tongue in circles around them. Then he smashed them against my cheek and under my eyes, returning in my mouth only later.

He lowered a hand onto his bulge and rubbed it, roughly and rhythmically.

"Come take care of this." He spilled the fizzy liquid on his chest and waited for me to reach him, climbing up his body horizontally. He sank his hands into my hair and pushed me to his stomach, my nose surfing the groves of his muscles. "Lick it and swallow it." He brutally ordered.

Around us, the dense smell of my oil mixed with the champagne on his stomach, and turned every word of his into a potent drug. My whole body ached from the uncontrollable yearning that possessed me. Blinding me, his firm palm landed on my face as his other hand pulled me from my armpit. He wanted me on the sheets now, face up inches below the four pillows he was resting on.

"I hope you are ready sexy, because trust me, your pleasure will be more than worth this." He drowned into his pocket the eleven thousand Euros I'd left on the nightstand for him and downed the contents of his flute. He was the most expensive escort of his agency and was about to quench the void in my mouth and my ass. From the catwalk straight into my bed, my graduation gift to myself. Tailored to my most secret fantasies: the Burberry fashion, the writing passion, the "sexy" nickname. He modeled every detail for me as if it really belonged to his persona. "Now, make sure you keep your lips tight around it the whole time." He sat on my chest and freed his baton; the equine uncut member stretched skywards past his navel, menacing my face every time more blood was pumped to the head.

"Let me taste that foreskin, please." The complicated design of the blue veins, especially around his head made me salivate to the point that I started drooling from the corner of my mouth and my senses bounced off the walls of my heated bedroom. He grabbed the bottle of Dom and fertilized my oral opening, careless of my respiratory needs. Then he adjusted the inclination of his hips and forced his all-consuming flesh truncheon into my skull, repeating with manic precision to keep my lips pressed around it. I slid down his sweet head first, then encountered the velvety foreskin rolled up around his shaft. All my taste buds exploded under the weight of that passion instrument, as it proceeded forward pushing and making room into my throat.

"Good boy. It's ok, you can make it, just concentrate." He directed my head and my neck through my mild complaints and moaning until I felt his balls hitting the stretched skin on my chin. His almighty tool rested inside me like a sword in its sheath, initiating a rhythmic movement only when enough saliva lubricated thoroughly the flesh surface. "See how good you are?"

"More, please." I managed to mumble.

"I'll fuck your head like nobody has ever done before." He was so excited that it was truly hard to believe that all that was money-bought passion. He peeled his pants off his muscular legs and resumed his task. I could see the pleasure I was giving him on his slightly hairy and contracted abdomen, all the way up to his open mouth. I thought it was almost impossible before that night, but when he put his hand on my Hermes underwear, I had an orgasm and released so much cum that it seeped through the fabric onto his fingers. "This is better than the Dom, sexy." He smiled after sucking my juice off his fingers.

"Just do me."

His cock was still hard and hungry, only now it was also covered with my saliva and the precum that'd oozed out of his slit and cascaded down. He made me turn face down and spread my legs. Then he poured some of the lube I offered from under the pillow on the neck of the champagne bottle, massaged the bottle, poured more lube and massaged again.

"One always starts with small things first ..." He dragged the dripping bottle down my arched back and ended right above my hole. I felt the champagne and the lube forming a river and descending onto my balls, which made contract my ass blocking the bottle between my muscles. "Don't be impatient, here it comes." He pushed the dark green glass inside me, causing me to take in as much air as I could to relax. In and out, first slowly and then a little faster when my flesh dilated and didn't produce any resistance anymore. The so much talked about perlage irrigated my intestines, refreshing the fire that he'd built up. The alcohol got to my head in a heartbeat, yet when he abandoned the bottle and introduced his club inside me, it was like starting it all over again; the pain, the rigidity, the resistance and the craving for more. I let my head hang down, and on all fours I took it all in, until his skin banged against mine. He knew where my pleasure was. He was worth the money. With both his hands, he drove my ass where he wanted and suddenly switched to a rotating movement that didn't leave any inch of my insides untouched. I came like a baby, the second I heard his scream of pleasure and the white lava expanding on my back.

TRUCK STOP
By Logan Zachary

Everything told me to slam on my brakes, but I couldn't stop my truck now. I was enjoying the view way too much. As the red car sped up to pass me, I watched it peripherally, but when it pulled alongside of my rig's cab, I took a double take and all but slammed on my brakes.

The red convertible driver drove as fast as I traveled and kept even pace along side of me. Why wasn't he passing? Then I looked over. WOW! What a sight! A dark haired man with hairy legs and very short shorts rode along side, and his shorts were getting shorter. A massive piece of flesh slipped out the bottom of one leg and rested on the driver's seat.

My sweaty hands grasped the hot steering wheel. Despite the July heat, I had the windows open, enjoying the South Dakota breeze. From this high vantage point, I couldn't tell if the enlargement was growing or if more of it was showing? My glance switched from his lap to his face, and I saw him lower his sunglasses and wink.

Was he flirting with me at 75 miles per hour?

He tugged on his shorts revealing a full-length view of a third leg. I swallowed hard as he made it jump up and down. He was making it wave at me. My hands gripped the steering wheel trying to keep my rig straight between the lines, at least on my side of the road.

The red convertible's top was down, and the shirtless driver might as well have been pantless for how little the material covered. Actually, it covered nothing.

His right hand left the gear shift and grabbed his flesh stick. He rubbed the length of his shaft, and it seemed to grow a few more inches in the sunlight.

I licked my lips and wished for miles and miles with my new traveling companion.

The driver brought his bottle of water to his mouth and took a long sip. He stopped and poured a stream of water down his shaft. He stroked his erection and jacked it several times. He paused, turned his palm up and showed me his wet, open hand. The water and his body fluid slid along his cock as he worked it back and forth.

My jean shorts tightened as my groin swelled with blood and heat. My cut-offs were damp from sweat and humidity, but I could feel a wet spot soak through the blue material making it stain darker. I needed to open my fly and unbutton my pants, but I was afraid I'd never get them closed again.

The convertible driver maintained his speed and stayed alongside of me, showing me he knew how to pleasure a man and himself.

I looked at my travel log. Twenty miles ahead was a truck stop, and I knew I planned on stopping there for a quick bite to eat. I had been running ahead of schedule, so I had some time to play.

Sun beat down on me, and the humid wind blew across the South Dakota prairie at my backside. Pushing me along my way, I was sailing and making great time.

I squeezed my crotch. The sensation made me groan with pain and pleasure. My eyes shut for a second and savored the feeling. As they opened, the Road Runner sign announced it was twenty miles to gas, food, and showers. I pointed over to the sign.

The naked man followed my finger. He nodded and waved his hard-on at me. He tried to pull the silky fabric over it, but his stubborn member stood out and proud. He pushed down hard on the accelerator and pulled in front of my rig. His hand worked the cruise control and unbuckled his seatbelt. His legs pushed him up and brought his bare ass up and over the back of the driver's seat.

I pulled the rope, and my air horn blasted in the air.

He pulled the silk shorts down, and a perfectly smooth, alabaster bubble butt mooned me. He slapped his ass and sat back down. He waved over his shoulder and speed off.

My foot pressed the pedal to the floor, and my rig surged forward. The next twenty miles passed slowly. Waves of heat rose of the black surface. My balls itched, and my cock strained as my odometer ticked one tenth of a mile off at a time.

The Road Runner's sign loomed in the distance, and my heart beat faster. My directional blinked on and off on my dash as I veered off the highway and into the parking lot. I pulled into the first available spot and scanned the parking lot for a red convertible. I held my breath as I searched; no red car was in sight. As I stepped down and rounded the building, the car came into view.

I quickened my pace and entered the store. Walking down one aisle and then the next, the shirtless man in silk shorts was nowhere in sight. Where could he be? My full bladder suggested I look in the men's room.

A sweet air fresher filled the bathroom with a bubblegum scent. No one stood at the urinals. I quickly relieved myself and looked at the stalls. A silk pair of shorts hung over the door in the corner stall.

My footsteps echoed on the cement floor as I neared the toilet. I knocked gently on the metal door as it slowly swung open. He sat there with his legs spread and a thick bush of hair peeking over the seat. His cock aimed south into the porcelain. Mirrored sunglasses covered his smiling face. "You found me," he said.

I entered the handicapped stall and locked the door. Walking over to the toilet, I stood in front of him, peering into the stool. Ten inches of maleness semi-hung just below the seat.

"My name is Todd," he said, as he reached for my pants. He unbuttoned the fly, and my cock swelled. His fingers played along my shaft. The last few buttons tickled my testicles, and they rose. Precum milked out of me and soaked into my Hanes.

"You're happy to see me," he said, and licked his lips. "And I'm glad to see you." He pushed my shorts down. "What's under here?"

My body stiffened as he pulled me closer.

I penguin-walked forward as his hands squeezed my ass. I inhaled deeply and musky male sweat and semen filled my nostrils.

He leaned forward and opened his mouth, kissing me on the lips, darting his tongue inside. He licked over my stubby chin, down my neck, and between my hairy pecs. My briefs disappeared with one fast tug, and his hot mouth worked its way down my open shirt and swallowed my erection. He pulled me closer as I entered his mouth deeper. He slid his ass to the edge of the toilet seat.

My hips rocked as I slipped between his soft lips. My entire shaft entered and flowed down his throat. The solid piece of his flesh slid along my hairy leg. Thick and warm skin slapped against my knee.

My fingers combed through his windblown hair. I could smell the summer sun on it as I guided his head back and forth along my length.

His dick banged into my calf again. I closed my legs, brought my knees together and trapped his penis. He pulled back.

My cock slid in and out of his mouth. The tip rested on his lips, as a line of precum drooled out.

Todd thrust his pelvis forward, his dick swinging for attention as he swallowed me again.

My hairy balls hung low and bounced off his chin. His razor stubble pricked my sensitive skin as his mouth drew down on me, pulling me in deeper. His hand found and worked his erection faster as his tongue snaked along my aroused flesh.

He swallowed down hard on my cock, as he clamped down on his own. A hot wet cream shot over my hairy leg and ran down to my foot. His mouth milked me with more pressure.

My balls drew up, and I exploded. Cum flowed out of my shaft, and I felt the hot load fill his mouth as he sucked on me like a straw, working to get out every last drop.

His cock trailed along my knee and wiped more spunk over me.

A knock echoed on the stall door. "Are you almost done in there?" a male voice asked.

"Oh shit," I said, as I bent over and pulled up my pants without my underwear. My Hanes rolled into a donut in my shorts as I buttoned my fly. I raced to the door, pulled Todd's silk shorts off the hook, and tossed them to him.

He stepped into them as he moved to the door. "Ready?" he asked breathlessly.

"Here, let me get the door for you," I said, and wrapped my arm around his slender body.

Todd limped without putting any weight on his right leg as I helped him out of the stall.

A man in a wheelchair waited as we hobbled out of his way.

A blob of cum dripped off my leg as we exited the stall. The man's wheel rode through it and smeared it across the floor.

The scent of sweat and sex hung in the small cubicle's air. We made our way to the sink, and I turned on the faucet. The stall's door slammed shut, and the bolt slipped into place.

I peered at us in the mirror. "I need a shower, do you?"

Todd's mouth spread into a huge smile as a wet spot trailed out of the corner of his mouth. He wiped it away. "Me, too," he agreed, and squeezed my ass.

Without drying our hands, we raced for the door, forgetting all about his lame leg.

In the back of the Road Runner, shower stalls lined a wall, waiting for truckers to freshen up on their cross country travels. I pulled one door open, bleach and an industrial strength lemon cleaner hung in the air. The white tiles yellowed from time and abuse covered the walls and floor in the locker room. A private stall stood open, clean towels and a bar of soap sat on a wooden bench. Lockers lined the other wall.

I ushered Todd inside, and we both stood naked in seconds. His sun burnt body glowed. He flipped the deadbolt for privacy and stepped over our clothes discarded in a heap. I slapped his tight ass as his huge erection bobbed with each step.

My hard-on followed in sync. It brushed against his round, firm cheeks as he slowly stepped onto the wet tiled floor of the stall. We pushed the shower curtain out of the way and turned on the water.

Hot water sprayed out of the shower head. Steam rose quickly in the stall as Todd grabbed the bar of soap, individually wrapped. He pulled off the paper and held the bar under the water. He stepped closer and rubbed it on my chest. He circled my sun burnt pecs and lathered up my nipples. Foam rose and grew, flowing over my hairy chest and cascading down my body to my hips and legs.

As the water and soap swirled down the metal drain in the center of the tiled floor, Todd's hands worked lower. He scrubbed along my belly and lower. My thick, curly hair bubbled up as his hand brushed along my cock. Foam flowed down my legs and between my toes.

I shifted my body under the spray and rinsed the soap off.

Todd dropped to his knees and worked the bar up one of my legs and down the other.

My cock bounced up and down under his nose, and he inhaled deeply. His tongue slipped between his lips and circled the pink head of my dick. He puckered up his mouth and slowly drew me inside.

His hand worked the bar between my cheeks and soaped up my tight hole. His finger explored and circled the opening. The soap and water allowed his fingertip to slide in.

I rocked my pelvis. My cock slipped into his mouth, and I back up onto his finger.

He pressed deeper into me, the first knuckle slipped in and then the next, up to his knuckle.

My balls swung back and forth under his chin. Our rhythm quickened and my testicles rose up along my shaft. I could feel the wonderful pressure building, but my hands craved to touch his body.

As he finished my feet, I bent over, kissing him on the mouth and blindly searching for the soap. My hand clasped around his cock and slowly stroked the wet meat. He moaned as his tongue entered my mouth and tasted mine. Fresh mint tingled as our mouths devoured each other.

I released his cock and found the bar of soap. "My turn," I said, as I stood up and pulled Todd to his feet. His dick dueled with mine, as he tried to wrap a leg around me.

My hand rubbed the soap over his sculpted chest and circled around his erect nipples. He raised an arm, and my hand soaped up the hairy pit. Water washed it clean, and I worked over his other one. He threw his head back and my tongue licked the hairy bowl. Soap and water fresh with a taint of manly sweat teased my taste buds. I puckered my lips and pulled the hairy, tender skin into my mouth.

Todd's knees threatened to buckle.

I licked from his hairy pit to this nipple. The sharp tight nub rolled between my teeth as I soaped up his back. The small patch of hair between his pecs tickled my mouth as I worked to the other side. My hands slipped down his torso and found his bubble butt. The soap foamed up of the fleshy orbs of muscle and explored the deep groove between.

He spread his legs and planted his feet on the tile.

Kissing him hard and deep, he pressed his body against mine. We rubbed penis to penis. My hairy balls prickled his. I could feel precum ooze out of my cock, thick and rich, adding to the pleasure.

I stepped back and spun him around. I pushed his head down, exposing his ass to me. My tongue drilled into the groove and found the tight opening. I licked the pink bud and felt it pulsate with each lap.

He pressed back on it and opened himself to me. My tongue plunged in, filling his hole. He rode my tongue as I worked deeper into him. My hand reached around and found his cock. I soaped him up and lathered his balls. He humped my hand as more creamy soap splattered at our feet.

"Fuck me," he said.

I bent over and quickly pulled a condom out of my pocket of my shorts on the floor. My hand slipped it on my cock, which I lubed up with soap. I pressed my shaft against his crack and plowed forward.

Todd spread his ass cheeks wider and took a deep breath. My radar zeroed in on the spot and sought entry. His tight hairy opening resisted.

My hand jacked his cock as I pressed into him. Slowly, his sphincter relaxed as my girth entered. He clamped down on my shaft as I slid in, increasing the pleasure making me almost shoot my load in one stroke.

Todd rocked back and forth on his heels as my hand worked his dick. My pelvis pounded his ass, as our rhythm increased.

"Hard – er, hard – er," he demanded between slams.

Water sprayed everywhere as my body bore into his. My balls slapped his as they swung between my legs and then between his.

I increased my rate on his cock, as more soap and foam cascaded over our hairy legs. The suds circled the metal drain net and disappeared.

Todd pressed his hands against the wall, doing push-ups to match my thrusts. His low hanging balls slapped my hand as it neared the root of his cock. His ass squeezed down hard on my erection, adding more joy and waves of pleasure through my body.

Steam hung in the air, Todd shook his head and his hair sent a spray of water everywhere.

Soap and sex filled my nostrils as I felt his body buck. His torso went rigid for a second and then his pelvis pushed hard into my hand. A thick load of cream exploded between my fingers and hit the tiled wall. As the cum spread along his dick, my cock swelled and filled the condom. Orgasm upon orgasm hit as his tight ass milked me dry. He clamped down hard, and my body shuddered as I tried to withdraw. The pleasure was too much, and I collapsed on the stall's floor.

Todd landed on top of me, as the shower's spray continued to tingle our sun sensitive skin and rinsed the soap and cum down the drain.

We lay in each other's arms as our breathing returned back to normal. I turned off the water and walked to the wooden bench.

White cotton towels, soft and smelling April fresh, dried our bodies. Todd's skin glistened, golden brown from the summer sun. He slipped his nylon shorts up his long legs and flung his shirt over his shoulder. He looked in the mirror and combed his fingers through his wet hair. "That was hot."

"You're hot," I said, as I examined my cum-soaked Hanes and threw them into the garbage can. I stepped into my shorts, free balling.

Todd hesitated by the door.

"You know, I travel this route all the time," I said.

A sly smile played across Todd's lips.

"And I have a sleeper cab ..." I started with a smile.

Todd stepped into my arms and hugged me close. "I travel these roads for work, too, every day."

"I'm glad to hear that. This summer is heating up."

He kissed me, and said, "Look for me in your rear view mirror."

LIFE'S A BEACH
By A.J. Damian

"Hey Ed, why do you keep avoiding me?" That's Pete, one half of the comedy duo who haunts my life on campus. Walking away would be easy. It would be a breeze, but Pete and his friend always catch up sooner or later, and no one told me how hard it would be to pay off a debt from them. I learned the hard way with these two; they said they'd show me what paying meant. I felt I would pay, but not in the way I thought. With spring over, the promise of summer proved to be only a week away and I'd borrowed a sizeable amount of cash from Pete and Tom for my summer vacation. I worked two jobs to try and pay them back, but it still wasn't enough. I'm not the sort of person who borrows money from others. It seemed like a moment of madness came over me, and I decided to ask the two guys I thought I could trust to lend me it. They are loaded after all; both their dads are big city types.

"Ed, wait up!" Pete shouted again. I turned round watching him bound down the corridor. He, like his friend, was something to behold. His six-two frame complete with stunning biceps and hint of well-worked abs gave me a raging boner on days when I saw them. Some said they looked like twins; they shared the same hair color, ice-cream blond and straight out of a bottle. Both of them had amazing bodies though, and the most I saw of them naked happened to be in the summer. Once last year, Pete had a white cut-off shirt, open to show off his chest and ripped jeans, while Tom wore a white tee and combat pants he knew he'd get wet sooner or later at the beach and show every contour of his toned body. I needed to see more, but they had a reputation for only picking the cutest looking guys for their nights out. I'm decent looking, but not good enough for them. I never even got an invite. Maybe they don't like guys with stubble. Strange as it might seem, there might be a reason for this. I have to say I'm not the most popular kid in college. I'm not shy, but I'm clumsy and that's caused me enough trouble already. I've knocked over my fair share of drinks others have had the misfortune to get spilled over them, tripped up and fallen into strangers on campus when they were holding a stack of books that would rival the Empire State Building. You would think I'd get men that way, but you would be wrong. It doesn't help me get with the hottest guys on campus at all.

"About that money you owe." Pete had managed to catch up and seemed eager.

"I'll get it ... it's just taking some time that's all." I could sense he could be trouble, and I gulped, my throat dry as a bone.

"What's holding you up?" he asked, licking his lips. Whatever he had going on inside his head must have been bad.

"I work two jobs, and it's still not enough."At least I wasn't lying, but that didn't stop how nervous I felt.

"Well, me and my buddy have been having a think about this ... and if you don't come up with the cash in one week, then there'll be a forfeit to pay."

What kind of forfeit? I never got to ask him that question. Just watched him smile at me, you know, the million dollar smile rich kids like him had that made them stand out from the rest of us. Somehow, I don't think I can bring it on time to pay them. I just can't make enough in one week to satisfy them. It would mean me borrowing from someone else to give to them, which only an idiot would do. No matter how many times I lusted after Pete and Tom, or wanted to be a part of their elite group, it wasn't going to happen, so I had to suck it up, and pay them. If only it was that easy. As forfeits go, these guys had the ability to look intimidating enough to make me do it; they were good-looking and knew how to handle themselves. They were big guys who worked out on a regular basis, and, rumor has it the last one who owed them money ended up dangling by his legs from the Golden Gate Bridge, but it couldn't be the same Pete and Tom who did that, or was I too naïve?

Was I crazy? Did I even stop to think that working those long hours would make me enough? What made it worse? Well, one week from now I hoped to be stripped to the waist taking in some serious rays on a beach. The truth of it – the real truth meant the two of them might find me at any time and make me accept their forfeit, and trust me; their forfeits are not to be laughed at. They often took place in deserted locations, sometimes on beaches miles from anywhere. What the hell was I going to do?

I came to the conclusion I must be naïve to think the two guys I thought I knew wouldn't toss me over a bridge for the loss of some cash. If only they weren't so hot. Maybe I could think of them in a different way. If they were ugly sons of bitches, I wouldn't have a problem with the way I thought of them, but that would make me so shallow. I could go into hiding, but they would find me, and the result wouldn't be pretty. "Forfeit, what kind of forfeit?" I stuttered the words out, yet I should not be amazed at them hitting me with this. I guess in their eyes I deserved it for being so crappy at managing money that wasn't mine to begin with. I had an image in my mind of me waving goodbye to the sandy beaches, summer sun and nights spent with cocktails and sexy boys. As the image faded into the distance so did my hopes of a summer holiday.

"The sort of forfeit where we tell you where to meet us, and you come." Pete couldn't have been vaguer if he'd wanted to, then I remembered the guy before who had crossed them, a shiver running down my spine. Was I unlucky from birth or something? I tried to keep calm, sane in the face of Pete, the one Adonis I would give myself to if he wasn't acting so scary. His smile did not help, but neither did his heavy browed expression as he seemed to stare into my very soul.

"Where do I meet you?" Feeling nervous again, I wondered if he would meet me at a bridge somewhere no one came unless they were about to be murdered, or feeling suicidal. No ... not the bridge. Please, not the bridge.

"We'll let you know when it's time." That was great, just great. So there I was left in limbo, feeling as though I had a death sentence over me. The rest of the week went by silent as the grave, the look of the sunny weather outside should have lifted my spirits, but with the thought of my forfeit looming over me, it did nothing to help me try and get over it.

I spent some time with friends at the beach nearby, soaking up the rays I hoped for before, shades on, drink in hand, listening to Dave, James and Wil discussing the usual things, friends and girls.

"I can't believe Shelley's still dating Tim. I hear he's got girls in four counties and he's trying for a fifth." James had insider knowledge of others to back him up when these kinds of discussions turned into arguments, but most including me knew he got his information from Twitter, trust me on this.

"I've heard he knows nothing about Shelley's other guys besides Tim. Rumor has it she has three of her own at the weekends."

"What about them? Wil asked, sucking cola through a straw, his full lips inviting.

"She gets with them, they give her gifts, and," I had to save the best for last. "She sells them for big bucks on eBay."

"How do you know about that?" Dave sounded as bemused as he looked.

"Facebook." Shelley had a long history of using guys, and often thought in hindsight, I'd never be like that. While others took their lovers for granted, I still searched for mine, thinking the one man I wanted could never be the one I would end up in bed with. As quickly as he appeared, a guy dashed past me, stuffing something in my hand, then he was gone just as quickly – I never even saw his face. What was it, a note? Opening the crumpled piece of paper, I realized the kid had to be working for them:

Forfeit Boy

You're at the designated location. Go for a Popsicle, and you will see us.

Glancing over, I couldn't see them, but my fear increased, sweat forming on my brow, but not only from the heat. Taking a stroll, I ordered a mint Popsicle to cool me down. I hated to think how I would feel once they turned up. Not seeing them at college since had desensitized me from them for the time being, though the thought of them every now and then unsettled me.

"Hello there, Forfeit Boy," I gulped before I turned round, wishing I did not feel this way. The way a mouse feels when faced with a tom cat that hasn't had enough tuna. Thinking of my friends, I figured they would notice I'd left, but not worry about it. "Come with us." As if I had a chance. Kicking up the sand, watching everyone else having a good time on the beach I went off with them, trying to control my thoughts. What I experienced would be far removed from what I called fun. One look back made me think my friends were having a good enough time, but for me, death had come in the form of two of the sexiest guys in college. Pete and Tom wanted to take me as far away from the crowds as possible. I looked at the revelers behind me drift into the distance until they were specks on the horizon. Would the last moments of my life be spent in painful isolation with only my shades to hide how I felt? Scratching a nervous itch on the back of my shorts, I followed them deep into where no one came but the crabs and other smaller life-forms.

"On your knees!" Tom ordered, while I felt the intense fear wash over my whole body letting me knees sink into the sand in despair. I wanted to cry out, plead for my life, but also needed to preserve whatever dignity I still had, so I settled for an answer. "Why do you want to kill me?" Silence, so they wanted to make me wait, fine. While the last minutes of my life ebbed away, still nothing.

"Bow your head and close your eyes." Tom ordered, again. It is a wonder he didn't push a black bag over my head in true execution style and be done with it. So this was it, my last conscious moments before I got my brains blown out. As the sun and sand dunes were blotted from my vision, I heard a rustling sound, then nothing again, feeling so useless.

"Open your mouth." Okay, this was officially starting to sound weird. I did as I was told, my lips parted, feeling the press of something soft and smelling of musk and sweat on my tongue. There were two guys with me at the moment, Pete and Tom. Tom barked orders, which meant Pete – Pete had to be ... I had Pete's cock in my mouth!

"Who said we were going to kill you, Ed?" Pete pressed the slicked tip of his cock further into my mouth without complaint from me.

After all, I got my dream man in front of me with his shorts down and my fear began to subside. His smell filled my nostrils, his taste, the salt of summer sweat, heat, movement in denim shorts that showed his tight ass through frayed holes. I licked over the tip, feeling him juice in my mouth, eager to take more of him inside until he pulled out, teasing me. "There were rumors going around." I blurted out.

Pete laughed, then Tom. "We made those rumors up on purpose – didn't want any kids like you taking us for granted." I opened my eyes, and found I was staring at an uncut nine-incher. It bobbed up and down near my lips. "We also knew from your friends you have a thing for us, and the look on your face when I told you there would be a forfeit was too good to pass up, Ed." Relieved and calmer than before, I saw his hard-on plunge deep into my mouth, the feel of it made a tent in my shorts. His tip engorged, I licked over it, then the whole shaft went deeper again and stayed there as he moved his hips gently at first, then more urgent with extreme need, pumping my mouth, enjoying the feel of it being Pete's when he never showed me any interest before. As the pumping got faster, I felt him shoot a couple of jets of precum down the back of my throat. He filled my mouth with his long, thick shaft. I had to use my skills, so he didn't manage to choke me. Feeling him draw out, I pulled the foreskin over his tip, licking around the fat bulb, then underneath, waiting for the moans. While I continued to lick the tip, then down the shaft in long, drawn out strokes I felt hands run over my chest, lower, lower until Tom's palm stroked my hardness, his own cock rubbing against my ass in a brilliant three-way of sensations. Tom's thumb rubbed over my tip, releasing it, I heard the sound of a top being flicked open, then the feel of something cold and slick being stroked over my shaft. Nice, he certainly knew how to handle my cock, starting in slow movements, feeling me juice while I still tended to Pete's thick, impressive erection. Tom's handling of my cock started to get faster as I took a look at Pete's balls, hairless like he had them waxed, but weren't dwarfed in any way by his sizeable cock; these were full and round, and very, very large. Tracing a finger between them, I stroked in a W shape, and then grasped them, hearing a welcome gasp from Pete, and once he plunged his cock deep into my mouth again, another squirt of precum down my throat.

"This kid's quite good," Pete confessed. "But if he doesn't let go, I'm going to blow." I released my grip on his cock. Pete stroked his cock slow, still keeping it erect, while Tom pulled off my shirt, Pete dragged down my shorts, admiring the length of my cock even though it wasn't as big as his. Encouraging me to lie down on the sand, I stared at the sun through my shades, smiling inside. Maybe this was the vacation I wanted, away from college, and everyone else who went there. At last I lay there having a good time with the two best looking college kids around. On either side of me, I felt the sensation of Pete and Tom stroking me. Pete took a deep kiss from my lips while he pinched my nipple nubs, Tom spread my legs, feeling the same lube on my ass as I did on my cock earlier; he pressed deep, but slow so I wouldn't be shocked by the sensation. As I got used to his fingers being in there, he moved inside in gentle movements, my cock twitching from Pete's intense kiss. While Pete let his cock bob over my mouth, I felt the tip of Tom's cock against my entrance, the lube easing it inside, its girth ample, I felt myself clench, and had to let myself feel more relaxed. I let him do what he wanted, what I wanted. "Fuck me ... please. I want to feel you inside me, and Pete." He knew what I wanted; his cock in my mouth, fucking me at the same time, which is what I got; the three-way only dreams and porn are made of.

Who would have thought that I'd get this kind of action from these two? This was like an invite to some exclusive club most are envious to attend. As Tom plunged into my ass, Pete pumped his cock in a similar way, each time with Tom only an inch away from my prostate, and ecstasy. I shivered, my whole body in the grip of an orgasm, but held it off, knowing I needed Pete inside me, too. Tom pulled out, stroking his cock, the tip huge and swollen, it jerked with pleasure in his hand as they switched places. Pete got the lube, slicking his cock with it, from tip to the base of his shaft in long strokes, tempting me. "You want this, don't you, Ed?" His smile, one of his best features apart from his ass lit up his whole face enhancing his boyish good looks. He stroked his cock like he offered a lengthy Popsicle to me; it looked just as good, just as inviting.

"Yeah, I need that cock in my ass." I must have looked a real sight, laid legs spread from another guy, but he was the one I dreamed of most nights, stood over me, cock in hand, ready to fuck me while I decide whether to look at his six-pack or his cock, decisions, decisions. I chose his pecs instead noticing the sweat beads gathering there from his previous exertion in my mouth.

"I'm going to fuck you good, Forfeit Boy," Pete teased, lifting my legs, so he could lean forward to fuck me. I suppose that way; we were able to still kiss while Tom slapped his ass for full effect. Pete's cock felt enormous and took some getting used to, yet with Tom's earlier fuck, it didn't take me too long before I took it all in and at a steady speed, his hairless balls slapping my ass with every thrust. Pete was the sort of guy who thrust like he meant it, and my ass tingled, as he bounced off my body. I caught sight of Tom licking his lips behind him and had no idea what might be in store for me later. All I could do was reach for my cock, pleasing myself as best I could, in between hearing comical slaps from Tom. His ass must be stinging by now, for sure. I jerked, panted and held off another need to orgasm, enjoying the moment. Pete bucked harder against my body, his kisses tasted of my mint Popsicle I had before I found out I wasn't going to be killed after all. Instead I was laid with Tom and Pete who fucked me with relentless energy, sweat coursing over every muscle, nipples erect, skin glowing from the summer sun. This was one summer I would never forget.

As Pete pumped faster inside my ass, I knew he was ready. I was, too. My stomach tensed.

Thrusting my head back, I felt the final tingle in my prostate when Tom came to my side.

"Relax, Ed. let me." I let go of my cock, feeling his hand wrap around my shaft, jerking it slow, making me wait for release, the pain mixed with pleasure made me cry out, and as I did I felt Tom lick my tip, enhancing the pleasure, while Pete grunted, lost in delivering the hard strokes he gave me. "Feel my cum inside you, let me fill your ass up, Forfeit Boy." He taunted, giving out one last moan, long and loud as he shot his load inside my stomach, hitting the sides, the sensation enough to have me send a jet of cum above Tom's lips. I could feel Pete didn't want it to end there, he would have liked to carry on, but the heat of the day meant it had to end there for now.

"What about you?" I saw Tom looking unfulfilled even though he smiled. "You haven't come yet." Feeling there was still some lube on his shaft from before, I held his cock, pumping it with a rhythm that had him panting in seconds. Pete kissed me, then Tom, his tongue savoring the taste of his lover. It wasn't long before Tom threw back his head, moaning while his cum shot into the air and all over my chest.

"So what made you want to take a vacation to Hawaii? It's so unlike you." Pete said, letting his cock go down after such a long time fucking. I had heard that line before, but it's not like I am quiet, I'm as lively as it gets when I am around the right people, and my existing friends weren't up for it, instead wanting to travel elsewhere. I liked the idea of a road trip, finding nature, the great outdoors, but on my own I was sure it would suck big time. Hawaii seemed the best way to sample the sun, sea, sand and others, and still get laid. I laughed at my thoughts. Just thinking about it, I figured I didn't need all that, I was here laid with these two sex gods.

"Hawaii sounded a good idea at the time, and then I found out how much cash I'd have to spend getting there, plus the amount for a hotel."

"I hope there's room for more on your holiday, Ed." Pete rubbed more lube over his cock, ready to go again. I lay on my back, legs in the air, ready too – I couldn't miss out on that dreamy cock of his.

"As if I'd turn you two down. I planned on going along in the car and getting a room somewhere. I suppose we could share."

"My dad owns a five-star hotel nearby, so you're welcome to stay with u,." Pete said.

A few nights in a hotel with these two, wow. "That sounds great."

"Don't go getting too cocky, Ed," Pete said, eyeing me up with suspicion. "There's still the issue of your debt, which I want you paying in full – in installments of course."

"Oh, don't worry, I'll do my best." Now that I knew they were good guys, not hit men I felt at ease to be in their circle.

He pressed deep into my ass again, and I welcomed it, after all, I was paying my debt like a good boy should.

MIND FUCK
By David Connor

The last time Tyler Christian got an unintentional erection on public transportation it was on a school bus – in junior high! He glanced at the sweaty preppy across the aisle – argyle polo, hot body, white hair, suckable magenta lips.

"Look away! Twenty-two is way too old for subway stiffies!"

Two weeks 'til fall semester, Ty was headed home after a day in NYC. He had returned the day before that from Cape Cod, Mass. Forget spring break; summer 2011, one week in July especially, would be one to remember. It wasn't everything Internet porn sites said it should be – three straight guys and two gays – one college bud and three townies in a tiny ocean-side cabin, but secretly watching neighbor Mike Slocum, through the kitchen screen, bend over to wash his feet in the outdoor shower, flashing soapy things he'd freak over if he knew anyone was thinking about as sexual, certainly was! "Too bad there's no photographic souvenir." There were of other showers, and of dream boners – surreptitiously obtained, plus one of Billy sleeping like a baby, ass up, underwear down, after three beers too many. There were posed for shots, too, X-rated – Ty and his bud, Jack, mostly, but also one of college dorm mate Cris's jizz. "Mmm."

If the cop who rounded them up for drunk and disorderly had put them in a naked police line-up – Dude had a badge and a gun, fool he be for not – it would have gone something like this: Jack – been there, fucked that – was six-two. Tyler's mouth came up to his nipples. Convenient. Ty had wavy raven hair and thick, matching brows over sapphire eyes that sparkled and crinkled in the corners when he smiled. Beneath baggy shorts, everything was apple-round bitable in back and

91

bigger between his legs in front than his lack of height would attest, with plenty of body hair to prove he was legal. He wore a blue and white striped ski cap everywhere, except in the water, even in late July.

Grade school pal Johnny Doff, "Jack" to his buds, had that total "V" shape – broad shoulders and a smaller six-pack waist. He was always tan and his light colored body hair highlights sparkled in the sun, especially when wet. His green eyes had girls flirting mercilessly – little did they know – and were often droopy from copious amounts of weed. He was arrogant as all hell and dumb as a post. Not stereotypical fiction-jock-dumb – he majored in chemistry; he just laughed too loud, mostly at his own frequent not-so-clever sarcasm. Maybe it was the pot.

Jack started birthday-candle-wishing for a larger dick at thirteen. He shaved around it, now, to make it look bigger, but it still seemed incongruous to his mass. Truthfully, Tyler never had a problem with Jack's dick; he just sometimes had a problem with Jack.

Billy Whissel, known as Weasel, grew up three houses down. He had a wild head of dark curls, hazel eyes, and paper white skin – a perfect backdrop for bright pink nips and other sexy guy parts. He was tall and hairy – neat patches and lines on his chest and down his middle, wild coverage on his legs, thighs and ass – "Oh, God, his ass!" If Billy would allow, Tyler'd pet it like a bunny for hours on end. Tyler was a butt man. Tyler was a Billy man. He often dreamt of picking Weasel fur from his teeth after licking him head to ginormous foot, spending all sorts of time on the pink in between. Billy's ears were massive, and though science claims those, his long fingers, and large sneakers don't always equal big, floppy dick, Billy shows they sometimes do. Dude had a girlfriend, but things were stressed post trip. "Step off bitch!" was Tyler's opinion.

Mike Slocum had just turned legal. Back when Ty babysat him and his younger brother, pre-adolescent Mikey loved to be naked – for swimming in neighbor Nate's pool, or just because. Sadly, that changed. Mike was compact – though still taller than Tyler. His sinewy muscles were from work, not working out. He had a pale torso with thick, bronze forearms and dark skin on the back of his neck – a farmer's tan, only on the parts bared while he bent over the engine of his beat-up Cadillac – including, Ty noted, the top of his ass, exposed by up-riding shirts and down-riding jeans for sunning and viewing pleasure. Mike's dirty blond hair was close-cropped and facial scruff was a permanent feature. Redneck chic served him well – jeans and short-sleeved plaid or plain white tees. They didn't get to hang out much since Tyler went off to school, but they texted and emailed. Pure as the Driven Snow Mike, like most eighteen-year-old male virgins, was obsessed with getting a blowjob. (The others would be obsessed with giving one.) He constantly asked what it felt like to be sucked off. Maybe if he spent less time on plugs and pistons he could get some attention for his penis. Tyler offered to show him – often. Still, when Mike bared his grown-up cock – cut and floppy, average – "Perfect!" – definitely hotter once touching it wasn't taboo – Tyler Joseph Christian was a little surprised. Too bad, pun intended, he blew it. TJ wasn't all that good at sex yet, and though he enjoyed it, forget Mike living up to the Slocum moniker; slow was more like "Ain't never gonna happen."

Cristofer's smooth, Indian skin looked like chocolate milk powder. Ty wondered if it tasted as good. The chub was somewhat effeminate and often pantless. Even before seeing his long, slender, taupe dick out – Cris loved to converse while pissing, Tyler had a pretty good idea what it looked like, thanks to form-fitting boy shorts. Cris loved to cue up gay porn while they studied, alternately making "ick" faces and pantomiming the acts, frequently asking Ty if he had ever done that?! – followed by, "Do ya wanna?" with a laugh. Shy Tyler did want but was afraid to look the fool by making the first move. Duh! When he hit on Billy, Billy hit back. Once bitten – punched, actually, twice shy.

Gay Mecca P-town was amazing. Growing up redneck – hot rednecks, but still – in beyond rural New York, Tyler didn't really think men dressed in feathers and heels and walked around in daylight except on *RuPaul's Drag Race*, but there they were. Well, one. But 24/7 they ran across guys willing to buy college boys drinks to drop trou. Tyler's plaid cargos and wide-striped boxer briefs were around his ankles more than once. His favorite blow: a white haired guy – his grandpa's age!

"Ok, images of blowjobs and Mike's hole, not helping!" Tyler wondered if Argyle Cutie could tell he had a rager. Before he could even look up, he felt a palm on the thin khaki cotton covering his crotch, bumping over hard parts, gently groping softer lumps, fingers working the zipper. There was no flirting before. No conversation during. How could there be? It's hard to talk with a dick in your mouth.

Tyler moaned, quietly. His bedroom at home shared a wall with his parents. Quiet pleasure was well-practiced. He grunted softly as a wet finger found its way around the leg opening of his underwear, groping the sack, working the smooth underneath, then teasing his ... "Holy shit!"

# # # # #

"It was fucked bizarro!" Ty later told Jack. "I've daydreamed before, but Christ! I was feeling, man, not just thinking. And the guy across the aisle wasn't even ..."

"I left my damned cell in Provincetown!" Jack interrupted.

"What?"

"Which word was a stumbling block for ya, douche?"

"The one with," Tyler swallowed, "our dick pics, ass pics, cum shots ...?"

"Yup."

"D'ya call it?"

"Yeah. Some snarky-ass dude answered, all 'I ain't bringin' it to ya.' Fuckhole!"

"I got work all week." Jack wore just a towel. His tiny pud didn't hang; it stuck out, its cut tip nicely outlined – "Fuck!" – while Ty's tingled "Stroke me!" behind his zipper, inhibiting his will to converse. "Maybe road-trip it Saturday? God I wanna yank my meat! It'll be a bitch, in one day, but ... Now! I need a nap." Ty bolted up the stairs, before Jack could object.

Naked before the top step, hard before naked, Tyler tried to recapture the feeling of someone else on his wood when no one else was. It was hot – his mini stud body and massive crank both rigid. The bedroom was, too. With a grouchy, "I just wanna cum then sleep" huff, Tyler reached for the knob on the window AC.

He glanced outside. Jack was at the pool – naked. Unlike grown Mike, Jack tended to make himself at home a little more than he should in someone else's. Still, the visual was nice.

The jock snuffed his roach then started singing? "No. Talking to himself!" Tyler, who often had to mute his porn, lip read, "Yeah! Let me eat that ass!" The little biscuit almost came when, after saying it, Jack, who jerked with his right fist, pulled his left pointer out of his butt and licked it! Bottom Jack wouldn't rim at gun point – even Ty's mouth-watering pucker. Ty'd seen the guy finger himself a lot; he'd never seen him interested in how it tasted. When he did it again, Ty lost control, spunking shot after shot against clear glass. He rapped beside it, once empty, holding up "WTF?" palms, startling the stoned stroker. Jack ,dazed, looked for his ass-play apparition, then rushed inside.

"Dude! It was like you said." He grabbed Tyler. "Someone was touching me."

Ty broke free, swiped at his dick with an already stiff sock, then plopped to his bed, covering his sweat and cum damp stuff with the corner of the sheet. "You're baked."

"I've bong whacked a whole lot. Ain't never felt like that."

"Did your ass taste good?" Ty smirked.

"Like you don't know."

"Good one."

"Let me taste yours." Jack sat next to him, reaching under the sheet.

"I just milked. I need sleep!" Tease Ty turned bare bottom out. As Jack sulked off, settling for a taste of window white cream, he quickly drifted off.

Mike, blue jeans sagging, was under the hood. A strange man approached. He struck up a conversation – then they kissed! Mike was unzipped, mystery dude servicing him good, rubbing all up redneck front, under the wife-beater, then around, settling in the small of the back, rocking Mike, guiding his dick in deeper, then out. Unlike when Ty did it, dream-mind-Slocum was into it. Head thrown back, black, greasy hands grabbing at white hair, he made noises, happy ones, and quickly blew cum fire over Mystery Guy's tan face. It was a hell of a hot dream – not Tyler's, straight Mike's.

"Call Cris. Money Bags is still up there, solo. See if ..."

"Not even. The curry smelling rat kebab hates me. Mutual back."

Tyler pedaled hard uphill. "Oh my God, grow up!" he scolded. "Or get your own damned phone!"

"Eat cunt," Jack scowled.

Everyone had the summertime muggy morning grumpies. "Hi, guys." Except Nate. Ty's perky gay neighbor grinned and panted like his dog, for different reasons, as the hot, shirtless boy bikers, shorts conforming to squeezably damp, delicious asses, whizzed by. "Come use the pool while I'm at work."

"Thanks, Nate." Tyler smiled. "I'll bring Max a bone."

"I already got one," Nate thought.

Cris had set his book on unexplained mental phenomena – his favorite topic – on the table next to the futon they were about to fuck on. He offered himself to the man he had stayed behind hoping to meet. When the dick went in – "Jesus!" – wrong deity, but Cris thought it anyway – it was Heaven. He regretted, a little, not losing his virginity to Ty, but Ty, despite tons of hinting and opportunity, never made a move. Cris wondered if it was because he was fat. It was something he thought about often, bombarded by mainstream images in movies, TV, and certainly in porn, that fat and gay don't mix.

"Concentrate," the white haired man chided, thrusting so hard into Cris that the book, his keys, and Jack's phone, which he had taken from his pocket and set aside while stripping off, hit the floor. "It'll be as good as you imagined," he smiled.

Billy pulled up beside his buds, straddling his lucky, noisy quad. His milky shoulders and back glistened in the hazy sun, and when he raised an arm to rake a hand through his fro, a scent of spicy deodorant mixed with intoxicating man odor tickled Tyler's crotch. "We're planning a Cape run Saturday." He stared at the dark hair trail that disappeared into Bill's silky basketball shorts. "Wanna tag?"

"I'll have to check. I want head, I ain't better be pissing off Jess again."

"Ty'll blow ya, without ya havin' to buy him fucking tampons once a month."

"When you do ... that ... suck cock ..." Billy had to ask. "Do you ... Um?"

"Spit it out, Weasel." Jack barked.

"Funny you should say ..." Billy caressed his phallic handlebars. "Do you, Ty?"

Tyler's dick understood the question before his brain did. "Down, boy! Depends on the guy," he said, aloud. "I have rules, see: I don't kiss unless I like ya, but I'll blow ya if I think you're hot. Load lapping, that goes back to liking a guy."

As Billy imagined, TJ swallowing his boy batter, his cell buzzed. Fucking Jess's timing sucked – and when she did, she refused to. That sucked, too.

Saturday morning, after 1:00 a.m. Lightning flashed in the distance, sporadically illuminating Tyler's petit, half naked body in blue, briefly highlighting his rounded bulge, pronounced amidst a lot of flatness in tight, white boxer briefs. The voyeur liked.

Tyler blew out a sigh. He reached for his sketch pad and switched on a dim light. Flipping past the imagined nudes of his high school art teacher, he stopped at the first blank page. Charcoal in hand, rubbing over his own chest, gut, and fabric swathed, half-hard cock, when he went to paper, someone else's showed up. It wasn't Mr. Weiss, but someone older, equally enticing, the same muse who was controlling his hand.

Yanking his underwear over sweaty thighs, horny Ty scooched up the bed. His position, if anyone could see, and someone sort of could, left little to the imagination.

Tyler had been taught in class that things were easier to draw when broken into geometric shapes. The soles of feet pressed together formed a triangle, drawn up knees another. Yet a third appeared – firm butt-cheeks a slightly rounded base, inner thighs the lines, the imaginary point, where crack met taint, hidden by the balls.

Tyler touched his same spots, leaving a gray, creamy, boy sweat and charcoal mess, the texture of which he happily explored. He toyed with his hole as he drew the area on the man. Even it had triangles: the hair pattern, lines and crevices, though it just looked bumpy round.

"Who knew geometry was so fucking hot!" Tyler thought as he fingered himself. Next time he fired up porn he was gonna have to play that game – the one where you count the triangles, one within another – or maybe he could do it in person. "Billy – Mike – Cris, bend over!"

Ty wanted to suck his ass fingers, like he saw Jack do, but knew the black chalk wouldn't lend itself well to taste. The feeling though – Mother fucker the feeling! When it forced his eruption, cum-coating the drawing and his hand, charcoal or not, he could no longer resist taking some on his tongue. "Mmm." He actually spoke, gasping, panting, one hand in his mouth as he continued to streak his spent peen and asshole gray with the other. It was the best sex Tyler Christian had ever had – alone or with a partner!

He wandered into the kitchen hours later, his white, drawing coal streaked, practically see-through drawers inside out, the fly front straining, sometimes failing, to keep his long, thick, morning-wood-after-piss cock concealed as he walked to the fridge.

Tyler, Sr., sipping coffee, had something to say. "Umm, Ty ... You know I have no problem with ..." big daddy stammered.

"With?" Junior looked up from his milk and pulled his undies from his crack.

"You and John being together."

"Not even, dad." He took a swig of moo juice.

"Well, whoever it was, last night, it got a little loud, Ace. Your mom and I ..."

"Sorry, dad." TJ slinked from the room, ending the talk.

Pops, alone again, wondered which friend his son had fucked and why he painted himself like a zebra.

Jack picked Mike up last, at the library. Reading rednecks are hot! Mike reveled in books like *Harry Potter*, fantastical tales, even stuff about the occult. He climbed up front, still wondering if the dream he had and the boner he got looking it up along with "Gay sex positions" in the Adults Only section meant he was. Billy, who shared the rear with Ty, was thinking about sex, too. He whispered, just over Jack squawk-singing Jagger, "You, um ... know that, um, guy ..."

"Spit it out, Weasel." The phrase worked once.

"Jay Cruise?"

"The sportswear designer?"

Billy's face said, "No, you fucking idiot". His words said, "The old guy who fucks guys our age?"

"Gay porn a new interest of yours?"

"I just – accidentally ... Shut up."

"Fogey fucking?"

"Dude."

"Gay fogey in the butt ..."

"Dude!"

Mike and Jack turned around at raised voices.

"Eyes on the road," Tyler rebuked. "I've seen it," grinning, lower voiced to Bill.

"You think it's hot?"

Billy's words and breath in his ear was hot! "Sometimes," Ty said. "Why?"

"Just wondering." Beat. "You wanna suck my cock when we get to the cabin?"

Tyler's surprised, wide eyes hit Billy's bulge. He licked his lips, a silent, "You bet your ass, I want!"

"You like me," Billy raised a brow, "right?"

Tyler got a text from Jack's phone as they pulled in: Gonna b late. C U @ 4.

"Mother fucker!" Jack spat. "Why didn't he just leave the phone?!"

"Go hit that place you blew that dude," TJ suggested, "so I can blow Billy alone."

Not happening. Cris had left a 'make yourselves at home' note, which Jack obliged, drowning his anger in a – Click – Ssst – beer. "It's too fucking hot," he growled.

Billy leafed through DVDs. A crack of thunder and a sudden downpour made indoor activity a must. He tossed a few mainstreams and some pornos on the table, then a paperback book. A penis "I" dotted by a brain in the title caught Tyler's attention.

"Let's watch this." Bill held up *Strip Poke Him* – a cliché cards and sex flick.

"For real?" Ty's attention shot to him.

"We'll act it out," Weasel winked.

"Mike won't ..."

"I have a poker app on my cell." Mike said excitedly.

The three pocket adjusted wood, the two straight guys wondering what was happening, one gay in particular just thankful for whatever was.

"We're not really gonna play," Billy rolled his eyes.

"Poker or ...?" Thankful Tyler's face fell.

"Just sit!" Jack huffed. He fired up the DVD, assigning everyone a proxy. Ty wondered what was gonna happen if Mike's and Billy's turned out to be power bottoms. The first few hands were rather dull, except to Jack, who loved feet. Having Ty's flip-flops and Billy's stripped-off sneaks and socks in sniffing distance soothed his savage mood. Two more beers, some puff, and the prospect of a dick in his ass didn't hurt.

Mike's shirt was the first off. His chest and abs were scruffed, too – accented. New hair, Tyler thought, around brown nips, scattered over his tummy, concentrated in the middle, leading to the button on his jeans – a trail to hidden treasure. Ty hadn't seen Mike's torso in, like, forever, even when he blew him! He wondered when he got so shy.

"Let's get to the pants, mother fucker!" Shy One whooped.

Maybe it was a contact high.

Waist-up nude self-crotch rubbing, and Jack's improvised thong licking, froze as Cris's, "Hey, guys!" entrance hit Pause on real-life. "Deal me in!"

"You're him." Jack went stereotype, but Cris agreed, stripping down to match the ethnic guy onscreen who looked like he was hiding a salami in tighty whities. Cris's boxers had Bart Simpson on them, but his hard-on was in plain view, poking out the fly. Tyler wanted it in him. He didn't care where!

"Ok, I'm bored." Jack hit fast-forward.

"Oh God!" Ty panicked internally. "Don't frighten the skittish breeders!"

The DVD stopped on naked Tyler sprawled on the poker table. Real Tyler, egged on by Jack, Cris, and even Billy, stripped to red, clingy, cotton knit underwear that molded to his long, tubular, excitement-thickened, bigger-than-his-porno-counterpart's-even peen. He climbed up on the rough, weather-worn – on the cape, expensive doesn't always mean luxurious – picnic/kitchen table. "I hope no one lays their sandwich here," he joked, rolling down his undies, touching wood to wood.

Attached benches proved a convenient place to kneel while servicing. Cris, though his character wasn't the first at Table Guy, grabbed Tyler by his ski cap, yanking him upright, ramming his tongue down his pleasantly stunned friend's throat. He dropped him – "Ow!" – and moved further south, past Jack who was sucking Christian cock as Mike and Billy just stared at their counterparts on screen removing each other's pants.

"C'mon guys, dicks OUT!" Ty's last word was punched as Cris's tongue hit hole.

The heteros stood. Billy shrugged, "I will if you will," then struggled, after a nod, to get Mike's tight jeans over damp legs. A transparent, nervous-sweat-triangle showed the top of Mike's crack through his underpants. Their clinginess showed off his shape. He gulped, then bent over, pulling them down, showing all, as if twelve again – only not.

Ty gulped, too.

Billy revealed his altogether in short order. He kicked his shorts aside and his plaid, thin cotton boxers into the air. They landed on Ty's face. His pleasurable inhale was loud, his resulting "Mmm" unabashedly so, as he uncovered his eyes to look.

More triangles – obvious ones – the slanted lines down Mike's pelvis ending at the point of his crotch, a never been tampered with wild bush within. Billy's cock, not even remotely tubular, much wider at the base, roundy-pointy at the end, still did that pump and rise thing as triangle four got harder. As their porn versions stepped up, one on each side of Faux Tyler, the real one had other ideas. "Stand together," he demanded.

"The video ..." Mike started.

"Fuck the video! I wanna suck you both at once."

"Our dicks are gonna touch each other!" Billy and Mike moved slowly.

"Damned right!" Ty couldn't wait. He positioned the pair as close as two guys could get without being inside each other, squeezed their buddy boners into one tasty mouthful, opened wide, and, "Mmm." Jack's expert cock mouthing, Cris's rimming, the taste of Mike and Billy while he kneaded their asses and nosed one's underwear – Tyler was euphoric! "Jack, get off me!" he suddenly exclaimed. Cum-pletion was close and that would ruin everything!

So while DVD Jack was getting all sorts of attention – "I brought your pizza," from a delivery guy, bulging out of both shirt and pants with his own brand of "meat lover's" lunch, suddenly, genuine Jack was on his own – until, "I brought your phone."

Four naked guys jumped. Ty spit out Slocum sword and Weasel wood. Jack gasped.

"Hey, Randy." Cris, cool as cucumber, never let go of Ty's big as one. "Guys, this is Randy."

The white haired man set Jack's phone next to the lube and condoms he'd left, imagining them put to good use. He looked familiar to Ty, and to Mike, who, too stunned to think of where from, simply nodded, folding his erection up into his tummy, while Billy, as the man eyed his spit-shiny rosy cock-tip, flexed it, asking, "What's up?"

102

"Nakefy," Cris instructed. "Mini dick awaits." He nodded toward Doff.

"Fuck you!" Jack spat.

"Only if the brown guy onscreen does," Cris countered.

The two argued. Mike grabbed his pants. Billy lost wood. Ty nearly wept. The white-haired guy just smiled.

The size of the room amplified the sounds – the wet, slick slide of fists on dicks, the gurgling of mouths on others – Randy had rallied the shy.

Mike turned his back, only the real one; the movie dudes were just background noise, now. Uncertain, he put one leg up on the bench. Perspiration beads shimmered as he arched. "Holy redneck rectum!" Ty wet it, with his finger and some sweat, then went in with face. "Mmrgh!" Dude was an artist and a wordsmith, too.

Phone guy found himself bent over the kitchen sink, Jack on his knees behind him, not a half-bad first time rimmer. "Check!"

Cris moved to the table. He whispered in Ty's ear, his chocolate pencil dick poking him in the forehead. "I wanna ride your cock." He took "Mmrgh" for yes, then for "Shit! That feels good!" as he squat-lowered himself, taking Ty up inside.

"TJ, Can I, um, fuck you?" Not just asked for permission, as he tried to imagine it, simultaneous to other activity, Billy wondered if it was logistically possible.

Tyler bit butt. Mike squealed. Like a dream pinch test, "This is real!" the yelp was verification. TJ brought his legs up into two triangles, a third, a fourth, forming all in between. When lubed Weasel wood went in, only his third dick ever, bigger than the second, way bigger than Jack's first, he growled so hard everyone stopped and looked.

Randy was fucking Jack, two smooth guys glistening, shiny; Cris rode Ty as Billy thrust in and out of him, matted hair-beasts screwing. Mike, backing into hot mouth, pumped fast and furious 'til every part of him – trembling legs, neck veins, curled toes, said he'd be first to milk. "Let me." Ty turned him forcefully, pressing Slocum's about to meat to his chin, alternately licking at, and twisting the tip with wet palms.

Mike's eyes rolled back; his jaw dropped; his gut contracted four, five times. When his first shot, scorching hot, even against burning skin, hit the thin beard on Ty's cheek, they both whispered, "Fuck!"

Jack launched to upright next, throwing Who's It's off balance. With just a few short short-dick strokes, Jack Doff jack-off juice rained down on the older fox, who landed on his ass on the floor. Facing Ty, bouncing and huffing to the rhythm Bill provided, Cris was a vocal one, "Shit, yeah! Oh! Oh! Fuck!" His rounded brown tummy heaved as his warm cum trajectory hit Christian's chest, throat and mouth.

"Mmm."

Mike turned self-conscious. Spunk'll do that to a straight guy. "Hey, Mikey," Randy asked, sensing his discomfort, and also the answer to come, "ya ever fucked ass?"

Mike took a moment to shake his head side to side. Randy offered his. Hard again – still, virgin boy flashed back to the library books. Billy, with a sideways encouraging nod, flashed back on Jake Cruise.

Fucked with virginal abandon, the white-haired guy, as his cum hit the gritty floor, was surprised that, other than Cris, Mike seemed most easily ... Manipulated seemed harsh – but also apropos.

Tyler was envious, though not for long as that feeling, the fear of splinters, and, "Ho-ly fuck!" even silence training vanished as Billy grabbed his knees and increased speed, slamming warm, wet Weasel into all sorts of triangles.

He shook his curls, "I'm gonna cum!" raining sweat down on Ty's outside, as the heat of jizz in latex teased inside Christian space. When Billy stepped sideways, still stroking his condom covered rod, enjoying the spunk-as-lube sensation, Mike, without guilt, dumped his first ass, for an unfamiliar yet more familiar second. He found his motion quick. The virgin had skill.

As Mike fucked Ty, Cris grabbed his huge member, bathing it in sweat, lube, and the precum fucking and stroking had worked up. Ty grabbed Billy's fro from the back.

"Ow!"

"Get over here and give me your cock again!"

The little guy had no problem swallowing big Billy willie, and enjoyed – "Damn!" – beyond that even, the better than imagined thrill of sucking one besty while the other fucked his ass.

Jack joined in playing "this hot little piggy," sucking all ten Ty toes as the FILF licked nips. Tasty Tyler Christian was the center of attention, as he should always be!

He blew with a grunt, hitting each and every one, creaming mostly Cris's dark, coiled fingers, which the chubby Indian wiped in fluffy belly fur, then licked. Mike pulled out. He yanked off his condom, leaning in for a – "Wow!" – precum Slocum tongue kiss just before adding backwoods spooge to the mix.

Silence followed. Lying naked on a table post get-off can be a little awkward once inhibition turns back on. Ty suddenly felt exposed – Duh! – wet ass curls and all. He shifted, noticing the book, the penis and brain one, stuck to his moist, hairy leg. He picked it up, staring at the back cover. Gasp! It was him, the white-haired man he had drawn! The man from the subway, from Mike's dream. The man in the room!

"You wanna shower? I'll fix some eats." Randy wore a Cheshire grin.

Mike was already part way out the door, his clothes a shield against frontal nudity, his back left exposed. Ty looked, maybe one last time ever, as he tended to his sweaty face and drenched body with a huge wad of paper towels. "We should probably hit the road," he said.

The first blast of spray, though the outside temperature was eighty-plus with humidity at ick, sent a shiver through Billy. Soaping him up was like an instant bubble bath, all up his front, legs and gut, rubbing the dangling, pink-skinned, hot parts surrounded by it – all that hair lent itself well to making suds, Tyler's, too, whereas Mike had to be lathered first in sexy areas then soaped up and outward from them. They were hard again – Tyler, Mike, and Weasel – way quieter, more subdued than they were in the cabin's kitchen with porn as guidance and distraction. Mike was in charge of soap. When he dropped it, TJ took the opportunity to poke around his white, frothy hole, just the tip, at first, but then with the whole length of one finger.

Mike shifted uncomfortably. It was a new sensation, one he didn't altogether hate, he guessed, but not one he felt like sharing with a crowd, either.

Billy took to his knees. He rinsed, thoroughly, the stiffening, fat dick at face level. At least it would be one hundred percent clean. He licked it, tentatively, like trying a new vegetable, then placed his whole mouth around the fat head. There was no way, as a novice, he could swallow it all, but Ty seemed content.

Self-conscious as Mike, Billy smacked his lips.

Running water brought another urge. "I gotta piss," Tyler announced.

"Me, too," Mike said.

Billy pulled over and got out. All three let go of their flow roadside. It was erratic, to say the least, especially for TJ who was hard as a damned rock. As Cris may or may not have known all those times going in front of him, Ty found watching a nice cock put out pee hot as hell. He imagined the others' piss going wherever he directed, smiling as wide as Dr. Randall Hunt had back at The Cape, offering a silent "Thank you," to him.

"You pussies have problems," sulky Jack moaned as his buds climbed back in the car – Tyler moving his new favorite book to sit, Mike moving as far to the other side of the backseat as possible, Billy adjusting half-hard so he could comfortably drive. "We're thirty fucking minutes from home and you need a pit stop?"

"I can't believe you made all that happen," Cris said in awe, crunching chips.

"Well," Randy was modest, "your friends had to be somewhat receptive. The little sexy one must be well liked."

Dr. Randall Hunt made a lot more money off his Cape Cod rental dumps than he did his book. If only more people believed in mind control, like Cris did. When Hunt first laid eyes on Tyler's photo on Facebook, after searching the email address he made the reservation with, he couldn't help but dream about doing things to the boy. When he came across the other one's phone – the jPegs – while checking the cabin between renters, he couldn't help but dream of having at all them all for real. The renown psychic may not have gotten them to do everything he imagined, but that was ok. He felt as if he had, and even better, he knew they felt that way, too.

Tyler was up for the weekend, grabbing one or two more things to get him through the fall semester – including, hopefully, a certain book he lost. He was raking the first of the fall leaves for his dad. Mike was working on that never finished car of his, and Billy was arguing with Jess. The boys hadn't spoken much – even by text – about any of the weird sex stuff that had overtaken them toward the end of July. They liked TJ, a lot, but neither had ever, before that week, imagined fucking the guy. As far as Mike and Billy were concerned, it was a one-time deal, over and done.

Neighbor Nate walked the street with his giant black lab. As Max studied the grass at the edge of the Slocum's yard, Nate studied Mike's ass, licking it in his mind.

Mike brushed at his exposed crack, shooing a phantom bug.

Man and dog walked by Billy. "If that bitch don't appreciate him," Nate thought, "I sure would!" The bulge in Billy's long athletic shorts was begging to be rubbed. Nate imagined he was. Jess got pissed when Billy unconsciously grabbed it, thinking it was some sort of rude gesture.

And then there was Tyler. At least he was for sure gay. Nate would love to have at the kid just once – maybe twice. Tyler, in a tank, it was still a bit warm, raised his arms to resituate his knit cap, flashing pit hair and a bit of furry gut. Nate felt a twinge in his jeans. He imagined himself biting down on one of Ty's nips, outlined beautifully in his slightly sweaty top.

"Ow!" Tyler rubbed at his chest.

"Hey, Ty. Still warm enough to swim when you're done there."

"Sounds good, Nate."

Nate and Max continued on their way. Nate, wearing an ear-to-ear grin, pulled *Mind Fuck: Using Your Brain for Sexual Pleasure* from his pocket. He liked how the "I" was a dick. He had found it on the side of the road, well, Max did, where Tyler had dropped it while biking one day.

Nate noticed the boy still rubbing his nip. "Maybe Dr. Randall Hunt – whoever he is, isn't full of shit, after all. Suits optional," he sent to the boy's brain.

The hot summer was about to settle into an even hotter fall.

THE GUY DOWN THE HALL
By Milton Stern

I really dreaded moving out to a complex in the burbs, but after my upstairs neighbor shot her husband and missed sending a bullet through her floor and into my apartment, my friends convinced me it was time.

So, here I was in one of those secure buildings with 500 neighbors. That is 500 people who walk by you without smiling, who look at you strangely when you say hello, and who turn up their noses when they see your dog, even though it is a pet-friendly building. I always lived in bad neighborhoods, where people say hello because if you don't know your neighbors, you won't know whether someone is a gang member, mugger or a rapist. It is not that I was too poor to move; I was just too comfortable, paying a low rent and making excuses.

After a few weeks, I made up my mind that no one was going to say hello and that was just how it is with this "station of society" as Hyacinth Bucket would say on *Keeping Up Appearances*. I came back from walking my dog, who was in her twilight years, when the fire alarm went off. I never lived in a building with an alarm, so I scooped up my dog (she had gone deaf and partially blind by then, so in order to evacuate, it was better that I carry her), and we made our way to the stairs. I had moved to the top floor for obvious reasons (bullets tend to go down rather than up). Outside it was raining, and all I was wearing at the time was an undershirt and shorts. After fifteen minutes, we were given the all clear and made our way upstairs. The whole way, no one said a word. They didn't even comment about my dog and why I was carrying her.

Once on our floor, I put Lucille down, and we walked back to my apartment. As we reached my door, my neighbor from around the corner came around and said, "Hey, I see we had another false alarm."

I was surprised for two reasons. One, he said something to me, and two, he was wearing a sleeveless shirt and boxers. What a sight. He was a little over six feet, maybe a drop over two hundred pounds, with dark hair and eyes and the most fit build I had ever seen, or could see from what was exposed. He was also half my age at around twenty-five.

I had picked up Lucille at that point to keep her from running into him, being partially blind and all, and that made my bicep bulge. I should let you know that I am over six feet myself and close to two-hundred-sixty pounds and a professional trainer and competitive bodybuilder. Approaching fifty, when not in competition, I carry an extra inch or two around the waist, and that is all I will admit.

"False alarm?"

"Yeah, the burger joint downstairs tends to set off alarms all the time. My name's Matt, by the way."

"Nice to meet you," I said as I extended my right hand and shook his. I also put Lucille back down on the floor. "This is Lucille; she's pretty old, deaf and partially blind; that's why I picked her up, so she wouldn't bang into you." And then I shut up, realizing I was giving more information than was necessary and probably because this was the first conversation I had with anyone since I moved in.

"And, your name?" he asked.

"Oh, yeah. I'm Martin."

At that point he started staring at my arms, and my shirt was still wet from the rain, so his eyes glanced over my pecs as well. "Hey, my fiancé and I are throwing a little party tomorrow night around seven. Come on over. We're in five-eighteen."

"Sounds good," I answered and watched as he turned and went back to his apartment. I also hoped he never wore more than a T-shirt and boxers in the future.

As it turned out, I answered too quickly, since I already had plans the next night with a couple of friends to have dinner. So, the next afternoon, I bought a bottle of wine and knocked on five-eighteen.

Matt answered the door, dressed similarly to the night before.

"Hey, Martin, what's up?"

I handed him the wine and said, "I answered too quickly. I have plans tonight, and I didn't want to blow you guys off and just not show up. Here, this is a thank you for the invitation."

"You didn't have to do that," he said in protest.

"I insist. My mother raised me right," I answered. "Can I ask you a question?"

"Sure."

"Do you own pants?" I asked with a grin.

He laughed, and I heard a woman's voice in the background, "I'm so glad you said that." She appeared from another room, and was she gorgeous and a little thing about half his size. "I'm Gina. Thank you for the wine. I'm sorry you can't make it. He promised to wear pants tonight."

We laughed, and I said my goodbyes.

It was a few weeks before I saw him again. I go to the gym very early and am usually out the door around a quarter to five in the morning. I ran into him one morning as he was headed to his gym, and we exchanged pleasantries, and this became an occasional occurrence. Although beautiful to behold, I made up my mind after meeting his fiancé that he was off limits, and I was never into "flipping" guys anyway. I am too old to go around blowing straight guys, besides I never saw the thrill in that. I never said it out loud, but anyone can figure out I am a big fag from the rainbow Mezuzah on my door frame to the rainbow Star of David tattoo on my shoulder to the parade of flaming queens, who are my friends, who would drop by for dinner. Besides a fifty-year-old personal trainer/competitive bodybuilder is a dead giveaway.

One morning as I headed out my door to the gym, I saw a shirtless body walk by and noticed it was Matt. He was wearing very short, gray running shorts that were not unlike the ones President Clinton would wear early in his administration. I yelled at his back, "It is freezing outside. I just came back from walking Lucille."

He stopped and turned around, and I saw his bare torso for the first time. He didn't shave and had the perfect amount of dark hair and that theory about him having the most fit body I ever saw was confirmed. I immediately thought that if this guy has a big dick there is *no* God.

"They say it's seventy outside." He smiled that beautiful smile as I said this.

I walked up to him and got a better look and thanked myself for putting on a tight jock that morning. (I said I was not into flipping straight guys, but that didn't mean he couldn't turn me on.)

We walked over to the elevator and stepped in.

He hit the L and asked if I had an early client.

"No, just working out this morning," I answered.

"Cool, we should work out together sometime," he said.

And then, my odd sense of humor took over when I asked, "Can I pull one of your nipples?"

He looked right at me, smiled and said, "I wish you would."

And, I did. And he leaned in and planted his mouth on mine while simultaneously hitting the red button, stopping the elevator between floors. His tongue was down my throat before I could protest, and I decided not to protest and felt up that perfect body.

I finally came up for air and with a gasp asked, "What about your fiancé?"

"We're both bi," he said and proceeded to remove my shirt and pull down my shorts.

In the time it took for me to fully comprehend what he said, my jock was around my ankles, and my dick was in his mouth. He had pulled his shorts down and was stroking his cock while working mine, and I figured we didn't have a lot of time, and he figured we didn't have a lot of time, and he sucked me for points and knew I would blow any minute, and I tried to get him off my dick, so I could get at his, but he was insistent, and I just shot my load, and he swallowed every drop while jerking his and shooting between my legs and hitting the wall of the elevator. It all happened so fast, that I was still comprehending what happened when he stood up, pulled up his shorts, and I retrieved my shirt, jock and shorts, and he hit the button, and we stepped out of the elevator.

"Have a good run," I said as he took off.

A few weeks later, his fiancé went to visit her parents, and he came over, and we did it again. This time, however, we took our time. He has since married Gina, and their wedding was beautiful. And on occasion, he stops by for a little pre-run work out.

CLOTHING OPTIONAL
By Milton Stern

After a seven-hour drive through rural southwestern Virginia, a few miles across the Tennessee line, and down a very dusty country road, I arrived at the TimberBear Campground. I had read about it online and decided to try a different kind of vacation, but after being buzzed through the gate, if you want to call it a gate, and driving up to the main cabin, if you want to call it a cabin, I was beginning to rethink my idea of an alternative getaway.

Between the geezer who checked me in and the one who pointed out my cabin, there were a total of seven teeth. I drove down the hill to the far side of the grounds past what I assumed was the pool and bath house, a couple of campers and trailers, and spotted little duplex-like cabins lined up in a row. Mine was number 6–6B to be exact since it was a duplex of sorts.

It may have been late September, but the weather begged to differ, with temperatures in the nineties and not a cloud in sight. I heard they were suffering through a drought, and by the looks of the layer of dust on my 1975 AMC Matador Coupe, they weren't kidding.

What I didn't see were very many people. I guessed it was late in the season, which was fine, since I am not fond of crowds. I parked around back and unpacked my car. Being this was a clothing optional campground, I didn't have to pack a hundred outfits for a change the way I did for that miserable cruise my best friend talked me into taking.

"Nice ride," came a voice from behind me.

"Thanks."

"1974?"

I turned to face what appeared to be a post-op FTM transsexual wearing only cut-off shorts. "1975 AMC Matador Coupe Barcelona Edition ... it was my grandmother's."

He walked over to my car, and I hastily walked around front to 6B, opened the door and took in the décor. 'Early trailer park' would best describe the room, for the cabin was just that, a room. There was a bathroom with a shower stall, and that was about it.

I unpacked what few things I had with me then changed into my swim trunks to take in what little daylight was left in the afternoon. I don't know why I put on my swim trunks since they would be coming off as soon as I arrived at the pool.

I am a former powerlifter and have continued to work out hard since ending my competition days in the late 80s, which enables me to maintain my thickly muscled physique. I am not what you would call bodybuilder cut, but at five-eleven and over 270 pounds, I am a lot of man, and I have a pretty thick cock and big balls that swing nicely if I do say so myself. I am not self- conscious about my body, but I am aware that there are those with a lot more 'definition' and much prettier faces. The best way to describe my face is that it is that of a bouncer, which is what I do for a living, and my nose has taken its share of punishment as well as my jaw. I get my share of ass when I want it, but I have found that as I grow older and especially after 'a certain age,' I don't crave it as much as I used to. I figure I have done all I care to do in bed, so if I find myself rolling around naked with someone, it better be special.

I chose an empty chaise at the pool, which wasn't difficult since there were about four people there, and took off my trunks, lay down and took in what sun was left for the day.

I was bored already.

After what seemed hours, but was only about thirty minutes, I gathered my things and made my way back to my cabin.

I was kind of tired from the drive and having put in a long shift the night before, so I took a shower in the tiny stall and decided to take a nap.

I never realize how tired I was. When I opened my eyes, it was pitch black in the cabin, and the clock next to the bed indicated it was 2:11 – AM! I hadn't slept like that in years. I was sprawled out naked on top of the bed and sporting an erection that could hammer nails.

I got out of bed and looked out the window. There was no one around or lights on, so I opened the door and stepped outside, stark naked and still pretty hard. I stretched my arms and let out a big yawn, when I heard, "Hello." I just about jumped out of my skin.

I had a neighbor in my duplex. Standing at just over six feet, he wasn't a bad looking one either. He was around my age, bald, with a mustache, a nice muscular hairy chest – and everything else – and wearing boxer briefs. I immediately hid my cock with my hand.

"Hey, sorry about that ... I didn't think anyone would be out here."

"No problem," he replied then he turned his attention back to his cell phone. "I can't get any bars."

"Isn't it late to be making calls?" I asked while still standing there willing my dick to go down, which it eventually did.

"I've been trying to get a hold of our office overseas all day. Ahh fuck it," he said, then flipped his phone shut. "I guess I should just go to sleep."

"I just woke up from a nine-hour nap," I said with a laugh. "I think I'll see if the pool is open all night."

"The pool is closed, but the steam room and sauna are open all night. They're in the bath house right next to it," he said, obviously having visited here before.

"Thanks, either one sounds good right now."

He went back into his cabin, and I into mine. I brushed my teeth to get rid of the dead rat taste and hoped my breath didn't offend my neighbor. I grabbed two towels – one to sit on in the sauna or steam room and one to dry off with. I didn't bother putting on a pair of shorts and just wrapped a towel around my waist, and slipped on my flip-flops, grabbed a jug of water, then stepped out.

The steam room looked as if a sloppy orgy was played out just hours before, so I chose the sauna. After figuring out how to switch it on, filling the bucket with water to pour over the coals, I hung one towel on a hook outside the door, and slipped off the towel around my waist and laid it on the bench, sat down, leaned back, closed my eyes and relaxed.

I started to sweat almost immediately and took a healthy swig from the jug of water. I then wiped the sweat from my chest down my stomach and along my cock, which started getting hard again. I didn't care, figuring no one was going to come in at this hour, and if they did, whatever.

Wiping sweat across my cock turned into gentle stroking until it was standing right up again ready to do some carpentry work. I closed my eyes and continued gently stroking my dick.

I was starting to feel pretty relaxed and a bit horny when the door to the sauna opened. I opened my eyes and saw that my cabin mate had entered, and this time he wasn't wearing the boxer briefs.

He walked right over to me without saying a word, leaned down and planted his mouth on mine. We proceeded to make out and wrestle our tongues, while he reached down and grabbed my dick, and I switched my hand from my dick to his, which was also ready to hammer a few nails and had the heft to do so.

The guy was a great kisser, and he apparently thought I was to, which I am of course, but his moans didn't hurt my ego. When his mouth left mine, I missed it immediately, until he hopped up on the bench with his feet on either side of me, his hands on the wall behind me, and his huge cock pointed at my face.

I opened my mouth, let him shove it in, and grabbed his balls. He fucked my throat like a champ, and I didn't gag at all. When I could feel he was getting close, he increased his rhythm, then pulled out and shot a big load all over my face while I held onto his balls.

When he was drained, he hopped down from the bench, got down on his knees and swallowed my cock. It only took a few seconds for him to empty my balls into his hungry mouth. He then stood up, leaned in and licked my face clean before planting his mouth on mine again as we tasted our comingled loads in his mouth.

He then winked, turned around and left. I never saw him again.

GAYDAR
BY Milton Stern

Every morning, he jogs past me as I walk my dog. Then on the way back, he jogs by again and says hello. And, this happens every morning at 4:30 am.

I wonder about him, this man who jogs that early in the morning. I have been getting up that early for years to walk my dog then go to the gym. For months, he has jogged past me then back again in the other direction.

I want to say more, ask him his name, see what he is about, but who stops a jogger to have a conversation?

Then it stops.

I don't see him jogging at that early hour anymore.

I also walk my dog after the gym around 6:30 am. And, one morning he jogs past me? Does he jog twice, or have his hours changed?

Why am I so obsessed with him? Why do I care?

It is over 90 degrees, why doesn't he take his shirt off?

He always wears the same thing, blue shorts and yellow muscle shirt. It isn't even a tank top.

He doesn't have an iPod, so saying hello is no problem.

Where does his run stop, so I can approach him?

I need to get over myself.

I think of ways to get his attention. I have a wife-beater on under my T-shirt, and I am all pumped from the gym. It is hotter than blazes and humid, too, even at this early hour, so I take off my shirt as if I am just a little too hot.

There I am, walking my dog in nothing but a wife beater, all pumped and sweaty. This will get his attention.

He jogs past me again in the other direction – so predictable. He stares at me and checks out my body for more than a few seconds, then says something like have a good morning, or good morning, or nice seeing you this morning. And, he is up the street before I can respond.

He *is* gay. No straight guy checks a guy out like that. He was eyeing me from head to toe.

The next morning, he jogs by again. I walk my dog in nothing but the wife-beater, and I decide to take it off. Now I am pumped and shirtless, and just as always, he jogs by me again in the other direction.

But, this time he doesn't look, and when I say good morning, he mumbles.

That is what I get for being obvious. I immediately put the wife-beater back on.

Now, I have made a fool of myself, and I obsess about it all day.

I never see him again – not at 4:30 am, not at 6:30 am.

I guess that is the end of that.

A few weeks later, I am walking my dog at night. I see him walking toward me with a woman. The closer he gets, I notice the woman is pregnant, quite pregnant.

He says hello and introduces his wife and tells me he stopped jogging due to a knee injury.

I forget his name.

What does it matter? He's straight, married and expecting a baby.

My gaydar is all fucked up.

But, I'll go to my grave swearing he cruised me that one morning.

THE WINDOW ESTIMATE
BY Milton Stern

I hate being an apartment manager, and I only agreed to do it because my landlords promised me a fifty percent reduction in the rent for the four years they would be in Brazil. The worst part is that I have to listen to the constant complaining from the fat redneck, her drunk asshole of a husband and her future serial killer, slut daughter upstairs. I just wish the daughter would get it over with and kill them already, so I can clean up the mess and rent the place out to a couple of hotties. But, until then, I have to be the responsible one and that includes getting estimates for work that I would rather let go in the hopes the cast from *Cops* upstairs will leave in frustration.

Most of the time, these estimates are for things they have broken, and I know that the constant yelling and banging that goes on is the reason the frame of the large bay window in their master bedroom was cracked causing the glass to fall down into the wall, leaving a four-inch gap on the top.

I took my sweet time getting an estimate, but when the rain seeped in causing water to leak into my apartment, it became my personal problem, so I called a couple of window companies. I figured I would punish the landlords as well for sticking me with these assholes and get an estimate for all the windows.

Two salesmen had been here already, but they were so slick, I threw away their estimates before the door closed behind them.

On the day the third and final guy was to arrive, I pretty much didn't care anymore. I decided to work from home that day, so it was amazing I even bothered to shower, although I only wore a pair of gym shorts (actually cut-off sweat pants) and a wife-beater. I was totally engrossed in work when I heard a knock at the door.

I opened the door and standing there was what looked to be a teenager, wearing a loose fitting All-Weather Window Company polo shirt. He gave me the taillights to headlights three-second once over I tend to get from guys who see me for the first time, which doesn't even faze me anymore.

You see, I am an ex-professional football player (not that anyone remembers – third string center), and I am six-foot even, weighing in at around two-hundred-sixty pounds. At thirty-five, I still work out as if I am being paid to, and I won't deny I ever took a needle in the ass. We'll leave it at that. Now, I work as a bookkeeper for a nondescript company in a nondescript cubicle located in a nondescript building. I am one of the lucky few to have actually gotten paid to be a professional football player, but after almost five years on the bench, I got bored. I was told I was too nice, not aggressive enough, but the coach liked me, so I held onto my job.

Now, the kid in front of me may have played some sports. He had that college jock, too many frat parties body. You know the type – broad shoulders, decent arms, and remnants of the 'freshman forty' still around the middle. If they are straight, the paunch is there for life, and if they are gay, well, they wouldn't have taken on the freshman-forty in the first place. No gay boy in his twenties would allow such a thing to happen to him. This kid was definitely straight, which was fine with me as I don't like them young. I like them older, much older. I like being fucked silly by a big musclebear with gray hair. If this kid had a twelve-inch dick, I couldn't have cared less.

"Mr. Kennedy?"

I let him in, and he introduced himself as Allan. I showed him all the windows upstairs and downstairs in all the apartments. Of course, the redneck had to butt in and say what she wanted in a window, but I shut her up immediately and continued to follow Allan from wall to wall while he measured and wrote on his legal pad.

When we were done, we returned to my apartment, and I had to ask him his age.

"I'm twenty-three. I couldn't find a job in my field, so I took this sales job, which has made my college education a waste ... can I ask you a question, a personal question?"

I said sure.

"I can see you work out ..."

He could see I work out. He was brilliant. My arms relaxed are eighteen inches around. My pecs are so huge, I can't see my feet, and he can see I work out.

"I've been trying to lose this gut since I graduated, and nothing I do works. Should I do more cardio?"

"You should quit drinking so much beer," I said and raised my eyebrows. I may let a quack doc shoot what is probably horse piss into my ass to get huge and ripped, but I never drank or did drugs. Yeah, I know, what I do is just as bad. Whatever. You'd fuck me if you had a chance, especially if you saw my rock hard and huge bubble-butt.

"Yeah, I guess you're right."

"So, how long before I get an estimate?" I asked.

"Oh, I can have one for you this afternoon. I'll email it to you."

And with that, he was gone.

I went back to work and took a mid-day break to go to the gym because I have body dysmorphia or manorexia or some other psychological shit because I think I'm fat or skinny and have deep emotional issues. Please. I know what I look like. I look like a fucking freak, but I like the freak look, and the old musclebear dads I let fuck me like it, too. Don't assume you know guys like me.

After I returned from the gym, I was mixing myself a protein shake when there was a knock at the door. I was back in my cut-off sweat shorts but not wearing a shirt anymore. I opened the door, and it was frat-boy window guy.

"I decided to hand deliver the estimate," he said as he handed me the envelope. "I can explain it to you if you like?"

I gave him my best you think I am a dunder-headed muscleboy with the IQ of a baboon look.

"Oh, I didn't mean it like that ... uh, I mean I like to explain why we may be higher than most anyone else," Allan recovered.

"I may look mean, but it takes a whole hell of a lot to offend me or piss me off ... believe me, kid, I haven't lost my temper in years," I said with a smile as I motioned him inside.

What, you say? A juiced-up freak who hasn't had a roid induced hissy fit? See, you read too much. I have never been a hot head. That is why I sucked as a professional football player. I'm too easy going. The only side effect I ever got from the juice was shrunken balls, but I can still come a gallon of spunk.

I offered Allan a protein shake, and he accepted. As we sat there drinking our whey concoctions, he explained all the window crap, and I pretended to listen, but I couldn't get over how he was avoiding looking at me. I was shirtless, pumped from the gym and sitting no more than two feet away from him. Although I had showered at the gym, I hadn't bothered putting on deodorant, so I had a light musk about me, which some guys like.

When he finally looked up, I could tell he was enthralled by my pumped pecs and my nipples, which I pulled on constantly. They stick out a good inch even now.

"You want to touch them?" I asked.

His eyes bulged.

"Look, it won't make you gay. Straight guys always want to touch my muscles to see what they feel like. Are they hard, soft, will they vibrate?" I said with a chuckle and a smile.

"Sure," he said as he slowly reached over to kind of poke a finger at my bicep.

I flexed it for him, and he then caressed it a bit before taking his hand away. So, I was wrong about him. He was a big ole fag. I grabbed his hand and put it on my pec while I made it bounce.

"Damn, they are hard as a rock," he said.

I was not turned on by this. He just wasn't my type. Yeah, I know, get over it.

"Now, about this estimate. What can we do to get you to come down by at least ten percent?" I may have been pissed at the landlords, but I was still a tightwad at heart, and I wasn't going for the obvious scene you are expecting here.

"Become my personal trainer," he said.

I sat back and looked at him. He had potential and a good frame. And that gut he complained about wasn't really that bad, just a little soft.

"Take off your shirt," I said.

He stood up and without hesitation removed his shirt. His shoulders were broad, and his biceps a nice size, too. However, his chest was a surprise as it was huge, which made me make a mental note to suggest he wear a tighter company shirt, and it was covered with hair, curly blond hair that trailed down to his pants.

"You'll have to shave that," I said pointing to his chest.

"Really?" he said as he ran his hand seductively down his torso.

"But not until after you bend me over this table and fuck my brains out. The condoms and lube are in the drawer behind you. If you want me to train you, you better be ready to do what I say at the drop of a hat," I said without stopping to take a breath. Then I stood, dropped my cut-off sweat shorts revealing my hard five-inch dick. Yeah, I know, everyone in these stories is hung like a horse. Well, I'm a bottom, and I may not have a lot of dick to play with, but I certainly have enough muscle to make up for it. Besides, little dicks get hard, stay hard, and shoot nice creamy loads. So, get over it.

I also know that I said he wasn't my type. But, I wanted that estimate lowered, and my hole filled at the same time. He was there; I was horny; do the math.

I then bent over the table, while he fumbled around with his pants.

"Hurry up, I don't get this horny often, just grease it up and plug me," I said over my shoulder.

I then felt the cold lube dribbling down my crack. He sort of rubbed it all around, and I could tell he was nervous. I then heard the condom wrapper being opened; he cursed himself while he tried to roll it on. I clearly had him flustered.

"Are these the largest ones you have?" he asked.

I turned around and saw what looked to be a good ten thick inches of circumcised dick sticking straight out at me. There you go – a horse-hung top in a porno story. Are you happy now?

"Look in the back of the drawer. They must have slid back. There should be some extra-hungs or whatever they call them," I said as I marveled at his heat-seeking moisture missile, which is a friend's nickname for huge cocks.

"Found them," he said with delight.

"Good, slip one on and fuck my brains out," I said as I again bent over the table. "And, don't bother eating me out or fingering me, just stick that barbell up my chute ... I hate foreplay."

He did just that. All the way in, no apologies, no hesitation, no finesse, no bullshit, and I loved it.

"Now, reach around and pull my nipples as hard as you can while you fuck me."

And, he did just that. He reached around and pulled my big nipples, no apologies, no hesitation, no finesse, no bullshit, and I loved it.

He practically pounded my huge muscular ass over the moon (excuse the pun) and pulled my nipples another inch. I was in heaven. He was having a pretty good time, too. Or, he was good at faking it because he kept telling me what a hot ass I had and what a sexy motherfucker I was. And at one point, he started nibbling on the back of my neck, and that did it.

I cried out as I came. I wasn't even touching myself since I was using my hands to hold onto the edge of the table while he pounded me for points. And, right after I came, he filled that extra large rubber with his own load and yelled out loud what a "man slut" I was, and amazingly, I came again – hands free.

When he recovered, he apologized for calling me a man slut and gave me ten percent off on the windows in addition to another ten percent for the hot fuck.

I never told him, but calling me a man slut was the best part of the fuck.

The windows look great. And Allan? He is a muscle freak now, too.

I love being me.

THE EDGE OF OBSESSION
BY Milton Stern

I had waited a long time for this.

David had been the object of my affections for years, several years. I first saw his profile on Bigmuscle right after I joined up. I don't know why I became obsessed with him. Maybe it was the fact that he would tease me; say he would call; sometimes call; say he would go out with me; had dinner with me once; say he meant to call me.

We would run into each other on the street, and he would give me that "I could eat you for dinner look." He would tell me he would call. I would tell him I erased his number from my phone because I had given up on him. He would smile, wink, then promise to call. A month or two later, he would. Then nothing.

This went on for almost a decade. I don't know why. In that time, I dated other guys, got plenty of action, but I continued to obsess over David. It wasn't like he was something all that special. He was cute – very cute – a prematurely-gray haired Italian who was five-four if he was an inch, compact with just the right amount of muscle, and a smile that would melt your heart, or at least mine.

He was the opposite of me. I stood one foot taller, still had more black than gray hair, hardly compact but muscular nonetheless. David, you wanted to squeeze and cuddle. Me? Well, I had been described as intimidating, imposing, pushy, loud, etc. I am not the guy you want to squeeze. I am the guy you want to fuck. I am also the guy you want to throw you down and fuck you into the next zip code.

The problem is I am not really any of those things. I look like those things, but I am just a big, furry, Italian Teddy bear. And, this was the problem. David was probably scared of what would happen if he did end up in the bedroom with me. Little did he know.

# # # # #

I am still trying to figure out how it happened. As I said, it had been over a decade of trying. I remember running into him at a Pride festival in Annapolis of all places. We had our usual flirty chat, then he went on his way while I continued to staff our booth. Around five, or was it six, what does it matter? We were breaking down when he walked up to me and told me that his friend who drove him there left with a trick and would I be able to drive him back to town. I no longer lived in the city, so I told him I could drive him to my home and put him on the Metro from there. You see I drove my 1953 Willys Aero that day, and I didn't want to drive it into the city on a Saturday night.

Off we went.

We talked a bunch of nonsense in the car, and for once, I didn't flirt or even intimate that I wanted him to come inside. He offered to help me bring all the booth decorations into my house, and I didn't refuse.

Once we were done, I offered to walk him the two blocks to the Metro, and he said he would rather just hang out a bit. I said that was cool, but after standing in the heat for nine hours, I needed a shower, so I gave him the remote and walked back to the bathroom to shower.

I was facing the showerhead, rinsing the last of the soap from my face when I felt a hand on my waist that moved to my stomach, then down to my crotch and another hand reach between my legs and grab my balls. Needless to say I was hard in an instant.

After a decade of waiting, I was also ready to shoot in an instant, so I turned around quickly. He had that smile on his face that always got me. I grabbed the soap and proceeded to lather him up all over. Then I rinsed him off. We never said a word.

I handed him a towel, and we dried ourselves off in silence. Then, I led him into the bedroom. I picked him up and placed him on his back on the bed. I then straddled him, reached down beside the bed and grabbed four restraints, and before he know it, he was bound at all four corners.

I expected him to fight me off, but he had a look of trust in his eyes.

I bent down, brushed my lips over his and whispered, "You trust me. I can tell. Just relax. I am going to give you pleasure like you never had before." I then softly kissed him and gently let him have my tongue. He was extremely receptive, and when I ran my hand down that sexy torso, I found a nice hard cock waiting for me.

I stroked it lightly, and when I rolled my thumb over the tip and gathered a good amount of precum, I brought to our lips, and we both savored the taste. By now, I was generating quite a bit myself. Between the two of us, there was enough to generously lubricate our cocks, and lubricate them I did. I rubbed them together, and he started moaning and streaming more and more of the tasty stuff.

I then licked his neck slowly and worked my way down his sternum. My hand continued to stroke us gently and both our cocks were hard and throbbing with pleasure.

I licked my way over to his nipple, and he shuddered when I found it. I gently tugged with my teeth then worked my way to his left armpit. I love armpits, and his were sexy as hell. I licked and he loved it. I felt his cock harden even more, and I realized he was going to shoot, so I let go of our cocks. He whimpered.

I then ran my tongue over to the other side, grazing the right nipple on the way then tasting his right armpit.

I placed my hand on his cock again and found a puddle of precum on his belly. I used that and mine, which was dripping all over his cock and balls, to stroke us again. By now, he was writhing on the bed. Again, he was getting close, so I halted the stroke. He whimpered.

My tongue was back on his neck, and I worked my way up his throat. Once my mouth found his again, I slipped my tongue in. He tried to go for a heavy bit of making out, but I was in control and kept it gentle and delicate. This drove him wild. His cock was on fire, and the precum was flowing like syrup.

He whimpered as I left his mouth and worked my way down his torso again. I made a slow and steady trail with my tongue to his navel and oh so sexy belly. I love a muscleman's belly. There was also plenty of love juice on his belly to lap up, and lap it up I did.

I then found the tip of his cock with my mouth, and I gently sucked on it. He whimpered.

Then I took it all in, slowly, but steadily, and it pulsed in my mouth, so I slowed my suck to a crawl, so to speak.

"Let me come."

It was the first words he had spoken.

I released his cock, looked into his eyes and winked.

He whimpered.

I then proceeded to lick down his left leg. There is nothing sexier than a compact muscle guy's legs – except for every other part of him. He was just delicious. When I got to his foot, I looked up, and his dick was just as hard, and I wasn't touching it anymore. I took one toe into my mouth and sucked on it. He whimpered. I then tasted all his toes very slowly.

I still had not made a sound. This was all about him. But, my cock was hard and making a mess or precum on my floor. I didn't care. I had him where I wanted him.

I then worked my way up his right leg after savoring those toes for a long time.

I didn't know how much time had passed, but I guessed maybe an hour or so.

I reached his crotch and took one full ball in my mouth, and his cock jumped. He whimpered. Then I took both balls in my mouth, while my hands gently stroked his thighs.

I released his balls after getting them good and wet and licked up the length of his throbbing cock. I knew it must hurt from being hard so long. I know mine did.

I found the head all wet with precum and a huge puddle on that sexy belly again. I licked it all up then took his cock in my mouth again. He whimpered.

By now, my hands were working his balls, and my mouth was gently stroking his cock while my tongue found that sweet spot where the head meets the shaft. You know that spot where all the nerve endings meet.

He yelled, "Oh God."

He shot.

I swallowed.

I shot without touching myself.

I licked him clean.

He thanked me.

I untied him and gave him directions to the Metro.

He refused to leave.

I was happy.

SUNNYSIDE UP
By Landon Dixon

I wasn't exactly overjoyed when my parents suggested I spend the summer on my uncle's farm. But I had no job, no idea what I was going to do in the fall – work? college? travel? – so I decided to go along with the idea.

Apparently, my cousin two times removed, Jake, was going to be there, and we were around the same age. He could, presumably, show me the ropes and provide some companionship, because at five-foot-ten, 140 pounds, I wasn't really built for the rugged life of farm work.

But things turned out better than I ever expected – much, much better.

Jake was a big, blond, sunbrowned guy with twinkling blue eyes, a handsome face, and a muscular body. He had a fun-loving, magnetic personality. For my first day on the job, my uncle had me and Jake baling hay.

It was a hot summer prairie day, and even though Jake and I got an early start on the work, by 10:00 am we were sweating rivers. I was huffing and puffing and taking every break I could to catch my breath, while Jake was working smooth and efficient as that hay-baling machine. He pitch forked the bales off the belt and heaved them up into the open barn hayloft three for everyone I struggled with.

"You just got to get the rhythm right, Mark," he claimed, a huge, white grin splitting his face.

"Yeah," I gasped. "It doesn't help to be built like a brick outhouse, does it?"

135

The grin spread even wider. Jake planted his fork in a bale and stripped off his shirt, showing off his muscled upper body. His smooth, brown skin glistened with sweat. "Doesn't hurt," he said, picking up the fork and the hay bale, pitching the bale up and away in a strong, practiced motion.

I stripped off my T-shirt, feeling the heat now something fierce. My slim torso paled – figuratively and literally – in comparison to Jake's. "I'll be buff as you," I bragged nonetheless, "after a summer on this place."

I went to pitchfork a bale of hay and found them all gone.

"Okay, boys, that's enough work for awhile," my uncle said, coming out of the barn. "We don't want to burn out this city slicker all in one morning," he added, looking at me and smiling. "Why don't you take a break 'til after lunch – go for a swim or something? Jake, give me a hand unloading these fence posts, will you?"

I didn't have to be told twice. I grabbed up one of my uncle's fishing rods from inside the barn and headed off down the trail that led to the creek in back of his property. Instead of just lollygagging around swimming, I'd catch my lunch and maybe theirs, too.

I arrived at the burbling brook and stood on the bank and licked my lips, staring at the cool, rushing water. I set the rod down and dipped my face into the creek. Sweet nirvana! Cooled down some, I then cast my line in and stretched out on the bank, sunning myself now without all the hard labor to go along with it.

I quickly fell into a doze, thinking about home, this girl I knew back home – Amy. She was blonde and stacked and bronze. I'd traded kisses and tongues with her, but hadn't progressed from there.

I folded my hands over my chest, crossed my ankles. The fish were biting, but my brain was jumping. Only now I was thinking of Jake – blond and built and bronze – the big guy's body shining in the sun, his handsome face and sparkling eyes and lush lips filling my mind's eye. And the hard-on that Amy had raised, Jake built harder and higher.

I gulped. I liked girls. At least, I think I did. Though, when I'd accidentally stumbled onto that hardcore gay video on YouTube, before they took it down, I'd gotten kind of excited at that, as I recalled.

Two muscle studs were kissing and Frenching, naked in each other's arms. And then one had gone down on the other, sucking the guy's huge cock into his mouth and wet-vaccing it. And then the other guy had returned the favor. And then the bigger guy had shoved his fat cock right into the other man's ass, had started fucking him, banging his thighs off the guy's rippling cheeks, churning his prick ...

Holy shit! I had my own cock in my hand, stroking the pulsating member through my jeans. I was getting off on those guys!

I blinked my eyes open and looked around. No one and nothing but the trees whispering in the wind and the babbling creek. I swallowed, hard. Then I got up and skinned off my jeans and T-shirt, stretched back down on the warm bed of grass, in the sun; nude, lewd with my bare cock in my bare hand. Figuring I might as well enjoy nature while I had the chance, knowing I was well isolated from the rest of humanity.

And when I took up my prick again, recommenced the heated stroking, and closed my eyes, I thought about Jake – no denying it. I pictured his body, naked, his huge cock, standing out right in front of me. And it was me on my knees, taking his dong into my mouth and sucking on the turgid appendage, enjoying every sensual sensation of having another man's beating cock in my mouth.

The male body could be just as beautiful as the female, I mused, no doubt about it, my hand gliding up and down my towering erection, my body flooding with delicious heat. I brushed my left hand over my chest, making my nipples stand up and take notice. I pinched a swollen pink bud, rolled it, did the same to my other nipple, stroking long and hard.

The sun bathed me in dazzling heat, the wind and the water soothing me, the outdoor openness of it all heightening the erotic sensations of jerking off. I kept my eyes shut, thinking of sucking off Jake, playing with his balls, mouthing his sack; as I felt up my chest and nipples and tug lovingly on my prick.

Jake wanted my ass, he said so. He wanted to stick his big cock in my ass and fuck me. I'd played with my anus before, a few vegetables in the bathroom acting as phallic replacements, and I knew what marvelous emotions getting your chute pumped could elicit. I reached down with my left hand and clutched my balls, squeezing, twisting, arching my butt off the ground, my cock higher in the air and my fast-moving hand.

Then I heard a twig snap. And my mind wasn't far behind.

I popped my eyes open and looked up. Jake was standing there, naked as I was, his huge cock dangling semi-erect from between his sturdy legs. It was my worst nightmare – getting caught jacking off; and my dream come true – seeing Jake in the buff.

"Fish aren't biting," he said, "so you figured you'd try a different pole, huh?"

I stared up at him looming over me, at that hanging man-bait of his, totally embarrassed and totally turned-on. I willed my cock to soften in my strangling hand, but that was a no-go. If anything, it grew, surging with blood like the rest of my body, naked Jake so close, the hot air crackling with the tension of my possible homosexuality, possibly my first man-on-man contact.

Jake looked down at me, his keen eyes gliding all over my laid-out body, focusing on my swollen erection. Then he dropped down onto his bare knees, straddling my head. His shaven balls touched down on my hair, his tremendous cock shadowing my face, hood brushing my lips. "Nice view from here," he quipped. "Wouldn't you agree?"

I was speechless, on fire, smelling the man's musk, feeling his hot, heavy meat. I tentatively stuck out just a little of my tongue and touched his bloated hood. His cock jumped above me.

"Now you're getting the hang of country living," he said, crowding up higher, pushing his cock down lower. He eased his hood in between my lips, into my mouth.

I'd never tasted, never sucked a man's cock before. My head spun, body tingling wickedly. It was all instinctual, natural. I simply opened wide and let him shove his meaty hood into my warm, wet mouth, and a good third of his swelling shaft. Then I sealed my lips around him and sucked, tugging on his dong with my mouth.

"You got the rhythm now," Jake groaned, bobbing up and down on his knees, feeding me more and more of his beef.

It felt incredible, sucking on that pulsing cock, feeling it slide back and forth in my mouth. I reached up and grabbed onto Jake's mounded butt cheeks, and they jumped, clenched in my hands, as I moved my head up and down, hoovering his prick.

Until he said, "Hey, what kind of host am I? You're the new guy here. I should be showing you the ropes." He got up, his cock oozing out from between my clinging lips.

As he walked around my prostrate body, I thrilled at what I'd done to the guy. His tremendous member was standing straight out, glistening with my spit.

Jake kneeled down in between my legs, picked my own hard-on off my stomach and squeezed it in his big, hot mitt.

"Oh, God!" I gasped, spasming. I'd never had another guy touch my dick before.

His hand enveloped me in warmth. He shifted it up and down, stroking my dong, and I just about fainted with the shimmering sensations I was feeling. He stroked easily, strongly, quickly, stretching me out even harder and longer. My body vibrated, my cock consumed in his hand, his fingers swirling expertly around and over my mushroomed hood.

"Yup, you're one healthy young man," he stated, grinning at me glaring at his pumping hand. "Let's have a taste."

He dipped his head down and brought my cock up and swallowed my cap in his mouth.

"Yes!" I yelped, writhing with delight, clawing at the grass. "Suck me, Jake! Suck my cock!"

I could hardly believe what I was saying. But I could hardly believe what I was feeling, either. Jake enveloped my hood in velvety heat and wetness, his soft lips surging around my knob, sucking. I arched up into his mouth, his wet-hot tug driving me wild.

He easily took more and more of my dong into his mouth, lips sliding lower, tongue cushioning. Until he had me sealed tight in his molten maw almost right to my fuzzy balls. His brilliant blue eyes looked up into my desperately blazing eyes, and he pulled his head up, pushed it back down, sucking long and hard on my raging prick.

It was too good, too much, too soon. Precum leaped out of the tip of my sucked cock. Jake vacuumed it up, hummering the length of my boiling appendage. I was ready to blow, totally overwhelmed by it all.

But the big guy was obviously an experienced hand at this kind of manual work, too. Because he pulled his head all the way up, lips sliding off my cocktop with a pop, forming the words, "Let's get a taste of your lazy ass, huh, Mark?"

He let go of my prick and it hung in the air, buzzing with electricity. Then he gripped my thighs and rolled me up, bringing my butt up to his mouth. He spread my cheeks with his strong fingers and speared his hot, wet tongue into my pucker.

"Oh my God!" I cried, jolted by the impact.

Blood rushed to my head, none of it from my cock, which was a twitching length of steel. As Jake swarmed his tongue all over my asshole, licking my rosebud, lapping my crack.

It was totally insane and totally amazing. Why had I waited so long to experience this? Who cared if it was a man or a woman? As long as it was Jake. The guy's tongue dragged up and down my butt cleavage, flooding me with raw delight. He spread me even wider and rimmed me, stuck his sticker deep into my bung and tongue-fucked my ass.

Jake bobbed his head up and down, plunging my buzzing chute. Tears streamed down my face and sweat dewed my trembling body, the man plugging my anus with his tongue. I knew what was going to happen next, and I wanted it so, so badly. Out there in the open, me out and loving it – getting ass-fucked by another man.

"Stick your cock inside me, Jake! Fuck me, Jake!" I implored the beautiful stud.

He pulled his tongue out of my butt and licked his lips. "My sentiments exactly. I like a quick learner."

He stood up, his massive dong rising with him. He gripped one of my thighs with his left hand, bending me over even more, my virgin bumhole his for the taking. He gripped his huge schlong in his right hand, the tool of ultimate sexual pleasure still slick with my spit, like my butthole was slick with his spit.

Then he drove his hammerhead downwards, against my browneye. I jerked at the touch of his hood to my pucker, was jolted to my very soul by the surge of his cap through my ring and into my chute. He'd popped my anal cherry! I whimpered, as he sunk his thick, veiny shaft into my anus, swelling my butt and myself.

He didn't stop until his balls kissed against my trembling bum. The man's cock was buried in my ass. It was weird, wicked, wild. He pumped his hips, stroking my anus, and I discovered heaven on earth.

"You're tight," Jake gritted, churning my ass. "First time?"

"Yes! God, yes! Fuck me, Jake!"

I grabbed onto my own numbed cock and tugged on it, in rhythm to Jake pumping my butt. His balls bounced off my upended cheeks, his cock rocking me faster and faster, sawing my burning chute.

I couldn't take it – his big body crushing down on me, huge cock cleaving me in two. I pulled frantically on my dong, and then I exploded. Jets of white-hot semen burst out of my dick and rained down on my face and chest. My mouth opened in a silent scream, and I tasted my own sperm, gulping it down, shooting more and more into my mouth. As Jake pounded into my ass, blowing me apart.

"Oh, boy!" he blurted. Then jerked, muscles tightening up all over his chiseled body.

Sizzling jizz scorched my bowels and seared my chute, the big guy coming and coming and coming in my ass.

It seemed to go on forever, but was over far too soon. Jake pulled out of my anus and fell down into my arms, helping me lick my own sperm off my face, his spent cock squishing up against my cock. We kissed and Frenched, no denying my manly feelings anymore, an aching need already redeveloping in my painfully empty butt.

It was the longest, hottest summer on record. For yours truly. I was a real experienced hand when it was finally all over.

CRACK DOWN
By Landon Dixon

I adjusted my string tie, my flat-brimmed hat, squared my broad shoulders in my tan tunic. Then I snapped off a stiff salute at the mirror. I was all ready for another day on duty – keeping Canada's parks safe and clean and recreationally friendly.

I strode out of my one-man log cabin and into the well-maintained wilderness. It was a sunny day, warm, a few clouds up above, a good crowd down below.

The campsites were just about full. I marched in and out of the main one, picking up carelessly discarded trash as I did so, chiding the occasional camper for a still smoldering fire. The park was designated alcohol-free, and I inspected for signs of liquor everywhere I went in the piney playground, found nary a drop. I inwardly grinned at that. I didn't like a drop spilled on my tour of duty, but darn it, I'd spill it if I had to – right down the shower drains.

I walked out of the woods and onto the open beach that fronted the largest lake in the park. There were plenty of kids and adults here, too, enjoying the bright sunshine and warm, blue waters. I scanned for crafts infringing on the swimming area, found none. But there was a pod of teenagers out by the floating dock, splashing around just a little too aggressively for my liking.

"Take it easy out there!" I commanded through my bullhorn. "Cut down on those shenanigans!"

There were fish and ducks to consider. It was their lake first, after all. The teens cooled down, one giving me a bird that was no waterfowl. But I wasn't there to make friends. I was there to enforce

143

the rules, conserve the environment for the enjoyment of all four-legged, two-legged, and finned creatures.

A kid tugged at the razor-sharp crease on my shorts. "Hey, Mr. Ranger, I just had an ice cream cone. Can I still go into the water, or should I wait 'til it disgusts?"

I almost broke out a grin. "Digests, you mean."

The kid's stomach was distended with more than that one ice cream cone. Childhood obesity was a sad thing to see – especially in swim trunks. "Certainly," I responded to his question. "I would suggest a brisk twenty laps out to the dock and back. How about it?"

He looked dubiously out at the wooden platform bobbing off in the distance, the pizza sauce smear on his cheek crusting in the sun. "Uh, well, maybe I'll go in later – after lunch."

I tousled his hair, handed him a pamphlet on Type 2 diabetes, then half-turned and headed off down the beach.

I reached the end of the sand, veered off onto a cedar-chip path that led into another wooded section of the park. I nodded at hikers, ticketed a couple of bikers. I was writing up one such ten dollar summons, when I heard a snort, saw a black body pass through the brush about twenty yards up the trail.

"Holy shit! It's a bear!" the fast-peddler hollered, hauling his ass on out of there.

I stood my ground. The black bear meandered out of the brush and onto the path. A bunny rabbit hurriedly hopped forward, through the hairy wicket of my legs and out the other side. The bear rose up, pawing at the air.

He was a big one – Buster. I'd dealt with him before: encroachment, defecation, destruction of private property and public garbage. He'd even chased Lori, our greenhorn Ranger, up a tree.

He knew me, too, recognizing my six-foot-two stolid frame blocking his path. I held up a paw of my own. "Back in the bush, Buster!" I ordered. "Where you belong."

He snorted and dropped down onto all four pads, lumbered forward, quickly closing the distance between us.

"You want another dart in the butt? Another ride out to the middle of nowhere?" You could do it with bears, but try it with a human and you'd lose your job on the police force.

Buster considered what I'd said, stopping and wagging his shaggy head back and forth. He was already a two-time loser. One more serious incident and he'd join the great bears in the sky, labeled a nuisance and expendable.

He turned, started to trundle off.

"Better," I gritted with satisfaction.

He turned back, charged me.

He drove like an express train, four hundred pounds of furious furry muscle. Testing the resolve and training of two-hundred pounds of rugged man.

It was no contest. I flash-drew my canister of pepper spray and let fly.

Buster took it square in the muzzle, as I danced out of his path. He skidded, roaring, blinking his eyes and blowing his nose. I gave his furry rear-end the toe of my boot, sending him scampering off into the bush in search of easier prey.

I continued on my rounds, down the path, through the forest. I emerged out onto the sunlit bank of a shallow, twenty-foot wide creek, spotted a man stretched out on a flat rock in the middle of the babbling brook, downstream.

He was a good distance away, just a blurry form and a thatch of blonde hair. I unholstered my binoculars, pressed them to my eyes. And the guy leaped up in front of me, naked as the day he was born, built along all-adult proportions.

He was laid out on a blue air mattress on his stomach, his bare body shining in the sun, glistening with oil. His hair was blond, all right, cut long, his shoulders wide and muscled, torso tapered, legs smooth and long. His curved feet were propped up on one end of the air mattress, his mounded butt dead-center. His cheeks achieved great heights, his crack a curving dark spot on his otherwise illuminated form. His long arms were folded in front of him, chin resting on his hands.

I blew a hot breath. This guy was flaunting it big-time, absolutely flouting the park's ban on full nudity. My spine snapped straight, and I went rigid to attention, staring at the powerful man through the powerful lenses, tracing every smooth, curved, striated, oiled inch of him.

And then my eyes just about popped out the glass of my sight-seekers, when the guy suddenly rolled over, turning face-up. He laced his fingers in behind his head and stretched out his legs, his cock stretching out to a prodigious length on his flat stomach. He was now full-frontal under the glaring sun. It was a breathtaking violation of the park's code of conduct.

I swelled with indignation. Then almost burst a few blood vessels, as the blond in-the-buff sunbather reached his right arm down and gripped his hard cock in his big right hand, started stroking it.

"My God!" I blustered.

He swirled his tan hand up and down the swollen length of his smooth, tan cock, stroking slow and sure and long. He slid his other hand out from beneath his head and down onto his chest, long fingers latching onto a puffed-up nipple and pinching, pulling, rolling.

The binoculars shook in my hands, the citations piling up on the beautiful man – lewd and lascivious conduct now tossed into the mix. Maybe he thought he was all alone. That was no excuse. How many other men, women or children were currently watching him with binoculars or their bare eyes? He couldn't be sure.

But that didn't bother him in the least. He kept right on stroking, rubbing his cock with his palm and fingers, twirling his nipples. His erection gleamed like the rest of his body, greased to protect against the sun's harmful rays, to lubricate his intimate hand gestures.

He arched up off the air mattress, pulling harder, faster on his prong, the impressive appendage seemingly growing another half-inch in length and width. He dove his other hand down underneath his shaven balls, cupping, squeezing the heavy sack. His lush mouth broke open, the man moaning, groaning.

Things were about to get way out of hand. I had to act.

I tore my binoculars from my face and tossed them aside. There was no time to lose. I jumped into the creek and started running, splashing ankle-deep in the clear, cool waters.

I yelled at him to stop, risking the further disruption to nature. The blond man froze in mid-arch, mid-pump. He stared over his handled cock at me racing towards him. I was on top of him in half-a-minute.

"Just what do you think you're doing, sir!?" I gasped, jumping up onto the flat, bare, hot rock with him.

He lay there, squinting up at me with his green eyes, a quizzical expression on his dimpled-chinned face. His cock was flopped back down on his stomach, hard as that rock, nowhere to hide it.

"Hello ... Ranger Todd," he said, reading my nametag. "My name's Evan. I was just, uh, taking in the sunshine, and the peaceful surroundings. Did I do something to rub you the wrong way?"

I snorted, drawing my citation book and pencil, beginning the write-up procedure. "You were engaged in activities best left back in the wilds of the city," I responded.

He responded, climbing up onto his knees on the mattress and placing a palm against my cock in my shorts. "Your lips say one thing," he breathed, "but your dick says another." He rubbed my beating hard-on with his warm, soft palm.

My knees buckled. My body flooded with even more heat, my cock a pulsing length of sensation under Evan's shifting hand. He gripped, clutching me with his fingers, pumping with his hand. My pencil and pad shook like my legs.

Evan cupped my balls with his other hand, squeezed them through my shorts. They tingled, tightened, my rod surging in his shunting mitt.

I tried to put lead to paper, but the nude blond beat me to the punch, pulling down my bursting zipper, bursting my swollen penis out of my shorts and undershorts. He took the bare appendage in his bare hand and rubbed up and down, clasping my hairy nut sack.

I had to drop my instruments of reprimand, to grab onto Evan's head, to keep from tumbling back into the water with the force of the scorching hand-to-cock combat. His hair was soft and fine, downy as a newborn duckling's. He pulled my boner down straight and slid his lips over the bloated cap.

"Mmmm!" I was forced to admit.

Evan's plush lips spread over my hood and down my shaft, swallowing my throbbing inches up in his hot, wet mouth. He gripped the base of my cock, reaching up and under my tunic with his other hand, capturing a buzzing nipple between his fingers and spinning it.

I held tight to his shifting head, the man sucking on my cock, feeling up my chest. It was impossible to resist, best that I take it in order to successfully diffuse the charged situation to everybody's ultimate satisfaction. This guy could suck the bark off a birch tree, his tight mouth gliding back and forth on my rigid pole, almost right down to the fur line and back up again, over and over.

The sun beat down on me, my eyes blinded by the glittering blond, my senses broadsided by his vigorous wet-vaccing. I thrust my hips forward, moving in rhythm to Evan's sucking, churning his mouth, my balls boiling inexorably to the blow-off point.

He pulled back, his timing impeccable, a natural amongst all that nature. He disgorged my glistening member and noosed it at the base with his fingers, staunching the flow of bubbling semen up my shaft. "Fuck me, Park Ranger Todd," he breathed all over my straining erection. "Fuck me in the ass!"

He sprawled down onto all-fours on his air mattress, thrusting his bottom up into the air. His cheeks were round, flesh thick and pliable. I plied them with my hands, filling my sweaty paws with their smooth, hot fullness and squeezing the pair, kneading them. Evan groaned. My cock bobbed, pointing at his crack.

I wrestled with his golden rump cushions for a good long while. Until he planted his face in the mattress and reached back, gripping the lush pair himself and pulling them apart. His crack blazed pale before me, his pucker winking pink. "Fuck me!" he urged.

My hands were greasy with the tanning oil I'd rubbed off his cheeks. I rubbed my cock with my greasy hands now, oiling the long, hard stake. Then I crouched down slightly and drew a bead on the man's asshole, shot cockhead up against his starfish.

We both jumped at the burning hot intimate contact. My cap squished against his elasticized opening, anxious to pop through. Evan thrust his bum back. I thrust my cock forward. I exploded into his asshole, breaking the seal and surging deep.

"Yes!" we exhaled.

I plunged my entire erection into the man's velvet anus. Then stopped, staring at his tapered waist and flared stretch of back, his smooth neck and blond head; at his ripe, round butt cheeks where my cock lay buried, my balls squeezed up against.

Evan rocked, urgently sucking on my cock with his ass-walls. So I pumped, grasping his brown hips and bouncing off his bronze buttocks, fucking the man.

He moved faster. I moved faster. His cheeks shuddered against me. I spanked them again and again with my thighs, watching my shaft plunge in and out of his gripping bung.

Our breath got ragged, rushed, Evan's body glowing with moisture, sweat pouring down my face and sides, coating my bare legs and arms. The crack of hot, wet flesh against hot, wet flesh filled the sizzling air.

"Fuck, that feels so good!" Evan grunted, his voice jumping to my joltings. "I-I'm going to come!"

He had his cock in his hand, was frantically fisting it.

I wanted to time it just right, punctuality being one of my many bugaboos. I increased the pressure, torquing up the speed, pistoning Evan's chute with a choppy urgency. He cried out, his body shivering in front of me. I dug my fingernails into his flesh and pumped like a madman.

I spasmed, muscles locking up all over my body. I sprayed, blowing my balls out inside Evan's asshole. I shook like he shook, the both of us coming at the same time with a fearsome ferocity that had to impress even any wildlife watching.

I let the man off with a warning: to be sure to be back there the next day.

MEN OF THE OPEN ROAD
By Landon Dixon

I was only a mile out of town when the first car stopped.

It was a Benz, the driver a businessman in a flawless pinstriped suit and flashy pink tie. He had rings on his fingers, his white hair perfectly coiffed, soft and flowing, his green eyes smiling into mine. For a guy over fifty, his face was smooth and young-looking, tanned a golden brown.

"Where you headed?" he asked, as I filled the open passenger side window with my blond head and broad shoulders. He ignored the ringing of his cell phone, looking me over.

"West," I responded vaguely.

"Then get in. I'm headed out to my cottage. I can take you about thirty miles down the road."

"Sounds good," I said and pulled the door open and slid into the leather bucket seat next to him.

His cologne was a little on the heavy side, but I put up with it. He went on and on about the pressures of his job, how his trophy wife was a royal pain in the ass, and I put a stop to it – by placing my hand over his crotch.

He'd had a bulge down there in his pinstripes ever since I'd gotten into the luxury car. And now I covered it with a warm, smooth palm, worked his erection bigger and thicker by rubbing up and down. He groaned and gripped the steering wheel, looking over at me with slightly glazed eyes.

"My wife ... I don't ..."

"Sure you do," I said, gripping his dick through the expensive cloth and stroking. "Fuck your wife. She's nothing but a pain in the ass, anyway, remember?"

He forgot all about his wife and the pressures of his job, as I rubbed the rather impressive length of his hard-on. I had one going in my own tight jeans that he couldn't help but notice. He reached over and reciprocated, as I knew he would, grasping my bulging cock with a manicured brown hand and squeezing and stroking.

I leaned back in the padded seat and groaned. I like older men, like them to do things to me, like doing things to them. And this aging pretty boy knew just how to show a kid a third of his age a good time, with his hand.

We had our cocks out and cuddled in our bare fists two more miles down the road. The silver fox introduced himself as Roger, as he introduced me to a pulsating erection as smooth and slick as the man himself. He liked my eight inches of meat, too, judging by the way he clutched and pulled.

The white lines whizzed by, Roger's foot pressing harder and harder on the gas, as we tugged faster and faster. His prick throbbed like the motor in my hand, just as hot. I swirled up and down his length, over top of his handsome hood, as he jacked my dong with his tongue hanging out and his eyes off the road. He wanted to two-hand all of my cock, but I told him not at that speed.

We pumped, fisted. Our breath came in ragged gasps, our chests heaving, loins thrusting up into each other's hands, pricks spearing palms. It was a four-lane, separated highway, and we barely kept to our side of it.

"Fuck, Danny!" Roger gasped, his cock jumping in my pistoning hand. "I'm-I'm going to ..."

He came, cum rocketing out of the tip of his jacked cock, adding more pinstripes to his business attire. I milked him fast and tight and hard, and the sight of the silver-haired guy shooting sperm, his hand convulsively clenching my dick, jerked me over the edge.

"Yeah!" I grunted, bucking, jetting.

He almost forgot his own orgasm, staring at the white-hot semen geysering out of my ruptured dong. I coated that walnut dashboard and the leather seat.

"My wife won't be coming out for another day or so," he said, when he came to the turn-off to Eagle Lake. "You can stay with me – swim, boat, fish ... you name it."

It was a tempting offer, the lake the exclusive domain of the city's elite. But I had miles to go before I slept ... with anyone.

# # # # #

A couple of women stopped for me, intrigued by my skin-tight white T-shirt and blue jeans, my smooth, young, sun-bronzed body filling out the form-fitting duds. I gave them the brush, went on walking.

It was half past two and the sun pouring gold down upon me, when I was picked up by my next ride.

He was a trucker, said his name was Stu. He was driving a company big rig, his face and body grizzled from years and years on the road; a lean, hungry-looking fifty something with an iron-grey brush cut and pale blue eyes. He stubbed out his cigarette as soon as I climbed aboard, didn't waste any time putting it into gear.

"Lonely on the road, huh?" he said.

"Yeah," I returned, liking what I saw, not so much what I was hearing. I wasn't about to become anyone's buggy buddy.

Stu was wearing a red plaid work shirt and a pair of blue nylon pants. His veiny hands on the wheel were large. That was another good sign I just couldn't ignore.

We blew through a small town at the blink of an eye, and I leaned over, unzipped him, pulled his cock out of his underwear and pants. And was not disappointed. The guy was packing a second stick shift, his meat huge and heavy in my hand even semi-erect. Older men always seem to be hung.

153

I stroked Stu, staring into his eyes. "How 'bout we take it off-road," I offered, "park this rig of yours in my ass?"

He shook his head, gripping the wheel with whitened knuckles. "Sure'd like to, kid. But I'm on the clock, and the GPS. Can't make any stops except authorized ones."

I shrugged and leaned right over his lap, licked his gaping slit with a slurp. "No problem. Just drive," I said. I swirled my wet, pink tongue all around his bloated knob, then poured my plush lips over top of it.

He groaned, giving it gas, the truck leaping forward, his cock jumping harder and higher in my hand, and mouth.

I dug his hairy balls out, gave them a lick. Then I gripped his sack with one hand, ringed the base of his fully-erect prick with the other, and dove my mouth straight down his pole until I kissed up against that second hand. His meat filled my mouth and flooded my throat, hot and throbbing, like my dick in my pants. Stu bucked on his air-cushioned seat, thrusting deep into my throat full-throttle.

I bobbed my head in rhythm to his hip movements, sucking on his shaft, tongue velveting up and down, his cock plunging my mouth and throat. I was as hungry as he looked, smoking his pipe. He gave me a long, hard ride; then growled, and spasmed, heated salty sperm spunking my throat and mouth.

I gulped as fast as I could, not spilling a drop as Stu redlined his engine. He gave me everything he had, and then more, when I released his prick in a gush of spit and hot, humid air and he gasped, "Your turn to drive."

He knew his way around the inside of that cab like he knew his way around a man's cock. We shifted positions in no time flat, me holding the big rig steady on the road, he holding my hard-on in his hand, then his mouth.

He admired my pulsing length and breadth with his rough, sure mitt for awhile, pumping slow and sensual, quick and exciting. Then he did the lean-over, inhaled my hood. He sucked hard on my cap, ravenous for meat, and more meat. His head sunk lower, right down into my lap, my entire cock buried in his wet, hot maw.

I blew the horn a couple of times just to let him know I appreciated his skill. He showed me more of it, working his tongue out, over my balls. I squirmed in the seat, locked down in the man's throat, his tongue lapping at my nut sack. Until he pulled his head back up, plunged it back down, high-dive deep-throating me.

I clutched at his gristly hair with one hand, keeping my other sweating hand on the wheel, the road humming beneath us. He gripped my thighs, moving onto his knees on the floor now, sucking hard and long on my pipe, shifting my semen into high gear. The suction was just too intense; I couldn't hold back.

"Fuck, I'm going to come!" I warned. Then came, bucking in the driver's seat, blowing Stu a mouth and throat full.

He took it like the hardened road-dog he was, still sucking as he swallowed, and swallowed, and swallowed.

Only afterwards, when I'd softened, did he soften again. He went off on another jag about how lonely it was on the road without having anyone to ride along with you. I dropped off his rig when he slowed for diesel at a station. I wasn't looking for a long-haul.

# # # # #

A carload of young flamers skidded to a stop alongside me a few miles further up the road. But that wasn't my speed, and I gave them the wave by.

Then a white van pulled off onto the shoulder, and I jogged on over to it. New Deal Ministries was stenciled on the side of the vehicle, and a man of about fifty or so was behind the wheel. He looked kindly, with his beaming brown eyes and wavy, graying hair. He had a ripe, full mouth and an angelic face, a slightly chubby body dressed in black pants and jacket, a clerical collar.

"Need a lift, my son?"

"Sure do," I responded, licking my lips.

He started in with the preaching soon after we'd exchanged first names. Father Todd was part New Age and part Old Testament, counseling me on the roads that led to righteousness and the paths that led to damnation.

I stopped his proselytizing with a quick kiss to his fine mouth. His lips were soft and lush, wet from talking. He stared at me, his eyes registering official shock and condemnation, something deeper and darker in behind.

"Danny, I'm going to overlook that as …"

I kissed him again, harder, longer, speaking in tongues inside his mouth. When I broke away this time, he was panting, his face red. I told him to pull over to the side of the road, so I could fuck his ass in the back of the van.

He'd had his lust frustrated for too long. He jerked the wheel over to the right and stomped on the brakes.

The first bench seat in behind was as good as any pew to worship at the man's ass. And he had a ripe, round one – smooth, pale, fleshy cheeks that quivered warm and willing under my groping hands. I smacked one, the other, and they blushed, Todd groaning and arching his butt up at me on all-fours on the seat.

The windows were tinted just dark enough so that the cars and trucks whizzing by couldn't see me baptizing the holy man's ass with my palms. I spanked him so hard that he rocked back and forth, whimpering; punishing him for his transgressions, the greater transgression yet to come.

I unzipped and pushed down my jeans, pulled out my cock, crowding in behind Todd's upraised bottom. I smacked his ass with my dong. One cheek, the other, the crack of cock-flesh against butt-flesh filling the stuffy confines of the vehicle. I bent my head down and clutched his buttocks up and bit into the right one, the left one. The guy really did have an amazingly meaty ass, and I just couldn't get enough of it. When I licked his crack, he almost jumped right out the window.

I spread his cheeks wide and lapped at his butt cleavage, stroking wetly from his balls to his tailbone, over and over. He moaned, cheeks quivering. I speared into the delicate pink pucker of his asshole, squirmed my tongue around inside, and he begged me to fuck him with my cock. He'd seen the length and the width, and his eyes had lit up with glorious anticipation.

I pulled out the tube of lube I travel with, oiled my cock. Then I slipped two slippery fingers in between Todd's thick cheeks where my tongue had just been, scrubbed his crack even slicker. He groaned, then howled, when I plugged those digits right into his anus and pumped back and forth.

The guy was tight, hot. But I was making him looser, hotter. I plowed his butt with a piston-like motion, bouncing my fist off his buns. Then I yanked my fingers out and grabbed onto my cock, pushed my cap inside.

"Oh, God!" Todd yelped. "Stick it in me, Danny! Fuck my ass!"

I sunk shaft deep into his chute, slow and steady and sensuous. His cheeks swelled before me, his anus bulging with cock. He was oven-hot and vise-tight, and I rutted around on the end of his ass, buried to the balls. He rotated his overstuffed bottom up against me, reveling in the wicked sexual sensations as much as I was.

A police car slowed down, drove on by. It was late-afternoon. Time was getting short. I had miles to go before I slept the sleep of the truly fulfilled.

I gripped Todd's waist and drew my hips slowly back, gliding my cock out of his anus. Then I lunged forward, plowing right back in again, full-length. I pumped, fucking the man's ass.

He gripped the seat cushion with his hands and teeth, his butt cheeks gyrating under my onslaught. I torqued up the pace even more, drilling his ass, plundering his chute. My thighs smacked so hard and so fast against his buttocks that they rippled non-stop, the sound blurring into one continuous crack.

The van rocked with our passion. Todd tore a hand off the seat and grabbed onto his cock, pulled. He bleated pure joy, instantly jacking ecstasy out of his prick and all over the seat.

I clutched his hips and pounded into his hole, my balls tattooing his butt, cock splitting his anus. I reamed him unmercifully, adding another wild orgasm onto his own. Sperm spewed out of the end of my sunken, shunting cock and doused the man's bowels with my superheated bliss.

I pulled out of his ass when he started crying. I pulled out of his van when he started pleading with me to stay.

I walked across the road and stuck out my thumb, looking to catch a ride or two back into town. You see, I'm never actually trying to go anywhere. I just like getting picked up by older men and taken for rides. It's the most satisfying form of travel I know.

OFF SEASON
By Mark Apoapsis

We changed into our bathing suits in the car. It meant rubbing shoulders a lot – less so for Gary, who had the back seat to himself – but none of us wanted to waste any of the daylight hours remaining in our first day of Spring Break by checking into our hotel room.

As an afterthought, I pulled on a brightly colored T-shirt. We'd each bought one at a souvenir shop on our way into Santa Cruz.

"That's a good idea," Kevin said. "It's better not to get too much sun the first day. Hand me mine, Gary."

Gary, who had already opened the rear door, leaned over and got Kevin's shirt, but instead of handing it to him, he raced off toward the beach, waving it overhead like a captured flag. Kevin cursed softly, climbed out and ran after him. I was left to lock up the car and take Kevin's keys.

By the time I caught up with my two buddies, Gary had soaked Kevin's shirt in the surf and was using it as a whip, playfully fending the bigger man off. I jumped onto Kevin's broad back while Gary grabbed his hairy legs, and together we managed to bring him down. Before we could get him pinned, Kevin succeeded in getting my shirt off. He started to put it on, though it was a Medium and he wore a Large, but I grabbed his wrists, which wouldn't stop him for long but at least slowed him down.

Suddenly Gary stopped laughing and raised his head. "Uh oh. Is that guy a lifeguard?" He might have pointed, but his arms were trapped between Kevin's legs. I did see a well-tanned pair of smooth but obviously male legs approaching. I tried to raise my head from

159

Kevin's hairy chest to get a better look, but Kevin had me in a headlock. He released me, and I saw that the legs were attached to an even more obviously male body with a whistle bouncing against his smooth, tanned chest.

We were still disentangling ourselves when the lifeguard reached us. We froze. He was, after all, an authority figure, never mind that he looked no older than we were. He was probably a student himself, or more likely, he'd dropped out to devote his life to the beach, judging by his tan chest, his sun-bleached blond hair, and his well-defined abs and respectable other muscles. He was built more for swimming than wrestling, though. Kevin alone could have mopped up the floor with him, but I hoped he wouldn't try anything stupid.

The lifeguard dropped the large beach bag he was carrying and took off his stylish sunglasses, revealing large, soulful brown eyes that contrasted with his blond hair. "Hey, guys!" he said with a disarming smile. "What's up?"

"Sorry, sir. Were we being too rowdy?" I asked.

"It's cool, dude. Don't worry about it."

"We thought we might be breaking the rules or something," Gary said.

"Maybe if you were roughhousing in the water, but on the land is a totally different story. I only have to worry about the safety of swimmers. On the land, you're not swimmers, right? Just a bunch of guys doing what guys do. Besides, I'm going off duty. See?" He removed the whistle from around his neck. "Just a regular guy." He put it back on for a moment: "Lifeguard ..." He took it off: "Regular guy."

We laughed. His warm smile was irresistible. It occurred to me: if he was off duty and hadn't come over to reprimand us, then why approach us? On a hunch, I said, "Quick, while he's a regular guy, we should grab him!" The lifeguard barked a laugh. I grabbed his ankle and tugged. It was suspiciously easy to throw him off balance. As soon as he flopped down in the sand, I said, "Grab his whistle, so he can't change back into a lifeguard!" The lifeguard laughed in delight, and Kevin snatched it from his hand and held it out of his reach. I grabbed the lifeguard's shoulders as he tried to rise. He rolled on top of me, and we grappled playfully, rolling over and over each other, laughing. He

160

was stronger than he looked and soon was sitting astride my chest and pinning my wrists over my head. Meanwhile, Kevin managed to get Gary face down in the sand, sprawling on top of him to hold him down with the weight of his own prone body while pinning his wrists above his head. When Gary submitted, he let him up, and they finally came to my rescue, lifting the lifeguard off me and dragging him away from me by his ankles. He started scrambling back to me on his belly, using his elbows, somehow managing to drag both my friends along. I was amazed at how strong his abs must be to do that. Kevin threw himself onto his back and grappled with him, and even then, the smaller man seemed like an equal match. Gary chose that moment to switch sides and gang up on Kevin. That didn't seem fare, so I took the rare excuse to wrestle with Gary.

Finally, the four of us lay exhausted in a tangle of limbs, covered with sweat and sand. Kevin's chest hair was caked with it, and it was clinging to what little body hair Gary and I had, and coating everyone's skins. Eventually, Kevin and Gary ran into the surf to rinse off. I stood up to follow.

"Aren't you coming?" I asked our new friend.

"Nah, I have to put my stuff in my locker," he said with a warm smile, picking up his beach bag.

"Hey, I'll be glad to watch it while you take your turn."

He looked at me as if I'd offered to look after his life savings. "Dude, don't take this the wrong way, but I hardly know you. I'll catch you guys later."

# # # # #

An hour later, as Gary and I were beating Kevin at an unevenly matched game of beach volleyball, I caught sight of the lifeguard wandering along the beach. He had put on some ragged stone-washed cut-offs and sandals, with an unbuttoned shirt that flapped in the ocean breezes.

"Yo! Lifeguard dude!" I called out.

He trotted over, giving us a winning smile. "Hey! What's up, dudes?"

I realized I didn't know his name. I introduced myself and my buddies.

"I'm Boyd," the lifeguard said. I offered my hand, and he gave my palm a friendly slap instead of the handshake I'd expected. Well, it was what you do when playing volleyball.

"Want to help me out here?" Kevin asked. "Even up the odds?"

"Sure!" Boyd quickly stripped off his shirt and kicked off his sandals, leaving them lying in the sand as he trotted up to stand beside Kevin.

He turned out to be really good. He and Kevin immediately began trouncing us. I might have guessed that a guy who looked like he spent his entire life on the beach would have had a lot of practice at playing volleyball in the sand. He did tend to fall on his face more often than the three of us put together, but he made up for it in power and accuracy at slapping the ball back over the net. He also had a showy way of serving, balancing the ball on his finger.

By the time the sun set – not into the bay, as I'd expected, but the opposite direction – we were once again covered in sweat and sand. We called it quits and ran into the surf together.

"Next time, I get Boyd," Gary griped.

"You'll have to fight me for him," Kevin said, playfully dunking Gary under the water.

"Watch out, the lifeguard will see you," Boyd said facetiously.

"What lifeguard?" I countered, grabbing him from behind. "I don't see a whistle," I pointed out, running my hand briskly along his smooth chest.

Boyd ducked under the water and threw me over his shoulder. He was very strong, as I'd noticed when wrestling him on the sand.

"What are you guys doing tonight?" he asked, after I came up sputtering.

"We're going to find a bar somewhere and try to pick up some babes," Kevin said. "Why don't you come with us?"

"Yeah," Gary and I agreed enthusiastically.

"Sure. I've got nothing better to do. My buddies are all out of town for Spring Break, chasing tail." He looked across the bay, in the general direction of Monterey, with a longing look that made me wonder what had kept him from going with them.

"We'll give you a ride," Kevin offered as we walked ashore.

"Let me make sure I have enough cash," Boyd said, fishing his wallet out of his discarded cut-offs and fumbling it open. "Cool. Over a hundred dollars. And my fake ID. I'm all set."

# # # # #

We gave Boyd a ride to his apartment, checked into our hotel, and met him at a nearby bar within walking distance. As usual, Kevin immediately attracted a lot of female attention with his ruggedly handsome face, broad shoulders, and abundant chest hair peeking out from his partially open flannel shirt. Gary's a good-looking guy and I'm told I am, too, but we didn't stand much of a chance with our buddy around. Sometimes, I wondered why we always hung out with him.

Then Boyd arrived, and I swear that every female eye near the door was immediately drawn to him. He looked right past them, his gaze sweeping the bar, and gave us a warm smile when he spotted us. Brushing obliviously past a gorgeous brunette and a busty redhead, he made his way over to us and slapped our shoulders in greeting.

He took the stool between us we'd saved, and ordered a margarita. He turned out to be a good conversationalist. He didn't want to talk about himself, like most guys would have, but instead seemed interested in hearing about our lives.

"You guys students?"

"Yeah," Gary said. "We go to San Jose State."

"What's your major?"

"Communications."

"Kevin and I are Computer Science majors," I said, since Kevin was completely occupied with the two women on either side of him. "Gary is Kevin's roommate."

"Yo! Boyd!" someone called. "How's it hanging, dude?" The stranger was a strikingly handsome dark-haired guy in his mid-twenties, his shirt unbuttoned halfway to show off a swimmer's build similar to Boyd's.

"What's up, dude!" Boyd responded warmly.

The guy set down his drink – I'd have taken it for Scotch, except that it came in a salt-rimmed glass like the margarita – to slap palms with Boyd. "Looking for some female action, of course! It's springtime, dude."

"Whatever." Boyd shrugged.

"No, really, dude, they're easy around here! Not like the girls back home." He gave Boyd's shoulder an affectionate slap. "Why else hang out here, huh?"

"Well, there's music, cable TV, booze, video arcades ..."

"Whoa! Check her out. Later, dude!"

"See you in a couple of weeks," Boyd muttered. "When you come back to your senses."

"So are California girls really easier?" I asked him. "I was born here, so I've never had a chance to compare."

"Who am I to argue with the Beach Boys?" Boyd shrugged, wrapping both hands around his margarita glass and lifting it to his lips.

But if this was "easy," I'd hate to try my luck in the Midwest or East Coast or wherever these Boyd and his friend were from. Gary succeeded in buying a drink for one chick and was beginning to get his hopes up, but then her boyfriend showed up – a big bruiser who towered over him. Gary picked up his drink and came back over, squeezing in between me and Boyd as though seeking protection.

"Better luck next time, dude," Boyd said, slapping his back companionably. He was a naturally friendly guy, as uninhibited while sober as most guys are when they're drunk. Now he'd had a few drinks.

A while later, Kevin walked over to us with a hot babe on each arm.

"I don't supposed those are for us," Gary muttered to me.

"I hope you two losers weren't planning to turn in for a couple of hours. I need the room." He left without waiting for an answer.

Gary sighed. "Next time, you and I are getting our own room no matter what the cost, man. It's bad enough getting kicked out of my dorm room all the time, but at this rate, I'm not going to get any sleep this whole break."

"That's always the way it is," Boyd commiserated, his voice slightly slurred. "Guys like him get all the females. What's the point in us even trying? It's not like they're even worth it."

"Damn straight," Gary agreed, raising his fourth or fifth beer in a toast.

"Think they'll be done before the bar closes?" I wondered.

"Do you guys need a place to crash?" Boyd asked.

"You wouldn't mind?" I asked hopefully.

"I need someone to hold me up on the way home anyway."

Gary and I laughed, but when Boyd stood up, we actually had to grab his arms to keep him from losing his balance.

"I wasn't kidding, dudes. It doesn't take much to make me unsteady on my feet."

We put our arms around his shoulders and staggered out of the bar. "Kevin took the car, of course."

"It's not far, and I can use the walk. I need the practice, apparently."

# # # # #

Boyd's apartment was tiny, but he had plenty of floor space since it was very sparsely furnished. He had fewer possessions than I'd brought with me to my hotel. I revised my impression that he lived here year-round.

"I'll take the floor," I told Gary. "You can have the couch."

"My bed is easily big enough to hold at least one more guy," Boyd said.

"I couldn't ask you to do that," I protested.

"Come on. Why sleep on the hard floor when you can sleep in a real bed like a human being?"

He opened the door, and I saw the bed was a California King – all three of us could have slept in it and had almost as much elbow room as I would have had alone in my dorm bed. So I agreed.

I took leak first, and noticed that Boyd had the odd quirk of collecting toothbrushes instead of throwing out the old ones when he replaced them. He'd accumulated about a dozen.

After closing the bedroom door, Boyd stripped to his boxers. "Man," he commented, shaking out his shirt, "the sand gets into everything, doesn't it? I changed clothes, and still ..."

I was going to climb into his bed in my street clothes, but I took the hint. What the heck, we'd been wearing no more than this when we'd met.

Once we were in bed, Boyd rolled against me, rested his cheek on my shoulder, and whispered "I'm glad I met you guys."

"Me, too," I said sincerely but uncomfortably. "Good night."

To my horror, he began gently nibbling on my shoulder.

"Cut it out, dude!" I said. "I'm not into that kind of thing."

"Then why do you have a boner?" he whispered, rolling on top of me.

"What the hell are you doing?"

"Relax, dude. Let's just sleep like this." He pinned my hands over my head and relaxed his smooth, compactly-muscled form against me.

Our bodies were pressed together, skin-to-skin along their full length, with nothing between us at all, except the thin layers of cotton separating my crotch from his. I could tell he had a hard-on, but that might not really mean anything; like he said, I had one too for some reason.

Close up like this, his skin smelled of the ocean, mixed with his own musky scent, strong but not unpleasant. His face was about an inch from mine, and there was no cruelty in his soft brown eyes, just yearning and trust and maybe a hint of mischief. I stopped struggling and relaxed under his weight. He tucked his head into the space between my shoulder an my ear. I fought back an urge to lay my arm along his bare back and stroke his silky blond hair.

Gary stormed in through the open door, wearing only his briefs. "What's going on here?"

"Get him off me," I pleaded. I'd almost decided to try to sleep in that position instead of arguing, but that was out of the question now.

Between the two of us, we managed to roll the strong lifeguard off of me and hold him down.

"OK, I shouldn't have done that," he said contritely. "Sorry, dude. I'm a little drunk. I was just messing around."

"I'm going to sleep on the floor," I said.

"No way! I'll take the couch," Boyd offered, "and you guys can sleep in here. It's the least I can do."

So we locked him out of his own room, and Gary and I stretched out in his bed together, side by side.

Impulsively, I rolled close to him and reached across his chest to lay my hand on his shoulder.

"What?" he murmured.

"I − I just want to thank you for helping me out, man," I stammered.

"Any time. What are buddies for?"

I leaned closer to him, close enough to be enveloped by his own, more familiar scent. "You won't tell anyone, will you?"

"Don't worry, buddy. It could have happened to anyone. I won't even tell Kevin."

"Thanks, man!"

"Now go to sleep." He gave my shoulder a little push, and I realized I had rolled halfway onto him. I guiltily moved to the edge of the bed.

# # # # #

Boyd was gone when we woke up the next morning. We had breakfast on the wharf and called Kevin from a payphone, which was easier to find in those days, to arrange to meet him on the beach. Meanwhile, we found Boyd at his lifeguard station.

"Hey, guys. Sorry about last night. I was a little drunk." He removed his cool sunglasses to look down at us with his soft brown eyes.

All the harsh words I'd been rehearsing in my head disappeared. I could no more stay mad at him than I could kick a puppy dog with a similar "did-I-do-something-wrong?" expression on its face. Instead, I said, "Forget it. I guess I overreacted a little. We've all done some embarrassing things when we were drunk. Anyway, thanks for letting us crash there in the first place."

"Yeah, man, sorry you wound up having to sleep on the couch," Gary said.

"Actually, I slept on the beach."

"Now I really feel bad!" I said. "We had no right to kick you out of your own room."

"No, it's cool. I sleep on the beach all the time."

"Well, I just wanted to make sure there were no hard feelings ... um, bad feelings between us."

"So can I hang out with you guys when I get off-duty?"

"Absolutely!" I said, relieved. "We'll be over there, where you first found us."

"Awesome! Later, dude."

# # # # #

Boyd hung out with us all afternoon then took us to his favorite sushi restaurant.

The day after that was his day off, and he spent the whole day with us. We decided that four guys was a good number for sharing seats on the amusement rides on the boardwalk. Despite being a local, Boyd turned out to have a childlike enthusiasm for the rides.

"I wasn't allowed to go to places like this until I was grown up and on my own," he explained as we sat eating fish and chips and looking at the ocean.

"Over-protective parents?"

"Totally. My mom never let me out without my coat. Anyone want my chips?"

"Where I grew up," Kevin said, "the boardwalks were made of boards, not concrete. You could make out under them, between the beams."

"Like the wharf here," Boyd said.

"Uh, yeah, except not underwater."

"He means at low tide, stupid," Gary told his roommate.

Apparently, it was also impossible to get cotton candy where Boyd grew up, judging by the delight with which he consumed it.

# # # # #

Kevin decided that there's nothing so good that it can't be improved by adding beer. The morning of the fourth day, we bought a cooler and a few six-packs. As I helped Kevin lug the thing onto the beach, I regretted that we'd felt it necessary to dump the whole bag of ice into it. The whole bag, that is, except for the dozen cubes the three of us had stuck down each other's shirts.

We'd each had two or three beers by the time Boyd came by. "Watch out," I said facetiously. "He's wearing his whistle. Don't let him see the beer."

"Well, yeah," Boyd said easily, "it's officially only allowed up on the boardwalk. But don't worry." He removed his whistle. "My shift just ended. I'm officially in regular-guy mode."

Kevin fished out the two beers remaining from our second six-pack, holding them up by the white plastic rings that had attached them to the other four. "Is Bud okay? We've also got – What?"

Boyd was glaring at the beer as if it were a viper. Strange. He'd just said it was okay.

Finally he relaxed and accepted the beer. "How long you guys here for?"

"Through Sunday," Gary said.

"Great!" Boyd said, glancing up from his task of prying the tab open, to favor us with that winning smile of his.

We made small-talk, right up until Kevin helped himself to another beer.

"Dude!" Boyd cried. "What do you think you're doing?"

"Don't worry, there's plenty more. You ready for another one?"

"I mean the yoke."

"Huh?"

"The plastic thing." Boyd pointed to the six-ring yoke that Kevin had casually left lying in the sand. "You should put it back in the cooler, so you don't forget to throw it away."

"Now you're the litter police? I thought you were in regular-guy mode," Kevin chuckled.

"It's not funny, dude." He snatched the yoke from the sand and began stretching each of the rings until it tore. Then he stalked off to a trash can a hundred yards away to throw it out. We looked at each other and shrugged.

When we got up to leave, he discovered the yoke from the first six pack the three of us had shared, lying forgotten in the sand. He almost started a fist fight with Kevin over it. Later, in the bar, I asked Boyd what the big deal was.

"Those things are deadly, dude."

"Deadly?"

"Have you ever seen a ... a marine mammal strangling in one of these things? No? I have. I've personally tried to rescue three of them." He stared down at his hands, flexing his fingers. "One of them ... didn't make it. The other two were scarred for life. They're even worse than plastic bags."

"Plastic bags?"

"Dude, they look just like a nice tasty jellyfish when you're underwater."

# # # # #

Boyd didn't hang out with us much for the next couple of days. Then, one day, we noticed he wasn't at his lifeguard station. We didn't see him again for the rest of Spring Break.

We had a great time even without him, for all that Gary and I complained about Kevin always getting laid and leaving us to fend for ourselves. A typical example of his exploits was the afternoon we spent pretending to watch some seals in the surf beneath the wharf, when really we were watching three babes in bikinis on the beach who were watching the seals. It was the perfect excuse to pass a pair of binoculars among us, as long as the ladies didn't notice exactly where we were pointing them.

Finally, Kevin declared that it was time to make our move. We walked down the beach to the three women, and by way of an opening line, Kevin said, "It must be mating season for the seals, too."

The women looked him over appreciatively – he was wearing nothing but swimming trunks, as were Gary and I – before one of them replied, "Actually, harbor seal mating season ended a few days ago."

"It sure looks like they're still going at it, out there," Gary pointed out.

"I doubt it," the same woman said. She was attractive enough, I suppose, though Kevin was focusing most of his attention on her friends, both of whom had much bigger breasts. "Those are all males out there," she explained. "They've already mated. Or a few lucky ones have, anyway. Probably that big one."

"But they're rolling all over each other," I protested.

"Just playing," she replied, sparing me a brief glance before returning her gaze to Kevin. "They do that after mating season. It's sort of the phocine equivalent of a Super Bowl party, only it lasts for months. By the time the females start giving birth and caring for the pups, the males have lost all interest in them."

"Wow. How do you know all that?" Kevin asked, finally deciding to pay some attention to the one who actually talked.

It turned out she was a grad student at UCSC, studying marine biology. Kevin lent her his binoculars, leaning close to her when she pretended not to know how to work a focusing knob. An hour later, he strolled off with all three women, leaving me alone with Gary. Again.

# # # # #

Spring Break had been so awesome that when we finished the school year, we returned to Santa Cruz in June, planning to spend as much of the summer there as we could jointly afford.

I was happy to discover that Boyd had resurfaced. I ran up to his lifeguard stand. "Good to see you! You never said goodbye."

"Sorry, dude," he said, reaching down to slap my hand. "I sort of forgot you guys when my roommates got back in town, to tell the truth. And I won't be here full-time, like in the spring. I'll be hanging out with them, and we may spend a lot of time out of town. But I'm glad you're here."

And sure enough, about the only time we saw him was when he was on lifeguard duty. A few times, we saw him headed onto the wharf to change – that's where the lifeguard headquarters were – but never managed to catch him on his way back off the wharf. We didn't even get to meet his roommates. We stayed in his territory, though – not just talk to him while he was working, but because unlike the other lifeguards, he let us roughhouse as much as we wanted, even the time Kevin managed to get both our bathing suits off underwater. I saw Boyd watching our horseplay closely, as usual, and was sure he knew that our manhood was exposed under the concealing water. We managed to beg them back from Kevin and change underwater without anyone nearby figuring it out. Those were really good times, when I think back.

Then one day it happened. It was about a week into our summer vacation, a bright sunny day like any other. The waves didn't look particularly big or choppy. Kevin and Gary and I had gotten tired of our horseplay in the surf and gone for a swim. We were all strong swimmers, and we'd ventured a good bit further from shore than anyone else, with Kevin in the lead.

The first sign of trouble I noticed was when Kevin turned back and started swimming rapidly in our direction. The strange thing was he wasn't getting any closer. It looked like the distance was widening, if anything. Then he started treading water and yelled at us, "I think I'm caught in a riptide!" I could hear the uncharacteristic fear in his voice.

"Hang on, buddy!" I called. I swam toward him as fast as I could. Stupid, now that I think about it. Loyal, maybe, but stupid.

He was weakening by the time I reached his side. I slipped my shoulder under his arm, realizing that I wasn't going to be able to keep both of our heads above water for more than a few minutes. I looked toward the shore and panicked when I saw that it looked about ten times as far as I thought we had swum. We were definitely getting carried out to sea.

"Gary! Don't come any closer!" I yelled at my remaining buddy. "We've got to swim back to shore!" I let go of Kevin and gestured frantically.

Kevin's head slipped under the water. I grabbed him under the armpits and kicked hard, then slipped my arm around his hairy chest. His heart was racing.

"We've got to swim for it."

"I don't think I can make it!" he gasped.

"If I can make it, you can," I assured him, trying to sound confident.

I saw that Gary was struggling back toward shore. I couldn't tell if he was making any progress. I also noticed that Boyd's lifeguard station was empty. He'd been there a minute ago. I hoped he was attempting a rescue and not just off buying cotton candy.

"Come on," I said encouragingly. "I'll be right here by your side." I started swimming. Kevin followed, obviously running on his last reserves. My own arms were aching, too, and my lungs were burning from the effort. When I stuck my head up as I crested a wave, it looked like we were further out than ever.

I heard Kevin calling my name, and looked back to find that he'd fallen way behind me. I stopped, treading water. "Come on! Hurry! I'll wait for you."

Watching his weak strokes as he fought his way closer to me, I realized that he was doomed. And whatever slim chance I had to save myself was slipping further away every second I waited for him. Looking toward shore, I thought I caught a glimpse of Gary's head and arms, but I didn't think even he was going to make it.

When I looked back, I couldn't see Kevin anymore. I peered out to sea, hoping he was just hidden in the trough of a wave, but he never reappeared. I stifled a sob. At least I hadn't had to watch him drown. I resumed my own futile struggle against the riptide.

"Dude! Grab this," said a voice as I came up for air. It was Boyd, treading water several feet away. He was wearing a wetsuit, halfway unzipped down the front. He tossed me the end of what I took to be a rope, zipped up his wetsuit, and dove underwater. The rope turned out to be kelp, that ropy seaweed that I'd seen washed up along the beach, but it felt strong enough. The end I was holding looked like something had chewed through it. I felt myself being towed rapidly. I was surprised that he was towing me not toward the shore but parallel to it, and also at how fast we were moving.

After a few minutes, he stopped and resurfaced. His wetsuit was open again. "We're out of the rip current. A sandbar gave way this morning down there. There must have been a minor earthquake."

"Gary's still out there, and ... maybe Kevin. Can you find them?"

"You guys are kind of hard to miss, struggling like fish in distress. You're lucky there aren't any sharks this side of Monterey Canyon today, or you'd totally be lunch by now. Can you keep your head above water a few minutes while I go after your buddies?"

I nodded, not wasting breath or time on questions. I could probably even reach the shore now, exhausted as I was. But I didn't have to. While I was catching my breath, I saw two men on shore launch a motorized inflatable life raft. Presumably lifeguards. One was blond, but I could tell even at this distance that it wasn't Boyd; both men were wearing only swim trunks. As they were launching, I saw Gary's head and shoulders moving parallel to shore so fast he left a wake. He stopped directly between me and the shore, and Boyd's head popped out of the water next to his. He only stayed a few seconds before diving again. A few minutes later, the two lifeguards on the raft reached Gary. Once my buddy was safely aboard, I waved my arms to get their attention, and they sped toward me. I'd never felt anything as welcome as the warm human hands that grabbed me and hauled me onto the raft.

Gary and I clutched each other tightly without speaking for a full minute. Then I asked, "Where's Kevin?"

"Boyd said he was still looking for him," Gary said bleakly.

"We're launching more rafts," one of the lifeguards said grimly. "We'll do our best."

# # # # #

Before the sun had set on that horrible day, it was clear that their best hadn't been good enough. They didn't find Kevin, or even his body. I asked about Boyd. Rumor had it he was fine but had taken a leave from his job.

Gary and I stayed in Santa Cruz hoping for some news. The only news we realistically expected was too horrible to think about but would at least have provided some closure. Our hotel room had two beds, one of which Kevin had claimed as his own, just like spring break, forcing Gary and me to share the other. We never discussed it, but neither of us could bear to take over our dead friend's bed, so we left it empty. We were too proud to cry in public, but we spent half of each day staring out to sea, sitting close together, and every night we drank until we couldn't see straight and then staggered back to our hotel room, holding each other up. We would collapse into bed and fall asleep, crying on each other's shoulders where no one would ever know. Sometimes still fully clothed.

# # # # #

We hadn't seen Boyd since we'd left the water. I hadn't had a chance to thank him for saving my life and Gary's, and I needed to see for my own eyes that he hadn't drowned trying to save Kevin. As soon as I felt up to it, I went to Boyd's apartment. Gary still didn't feel like doing much beyond sleeping, drinking, and watching mindless TV in our hotel room, and he was currently going through a phase of being angry with Boyd for rescuing him before going after Kevin, who'd been in much more immediate danger.

When someone answered my knock, for a split second I thought it was Boyd, but no, it was another handsome browned-eyed blond surfer, shorter than Boyd but with impressive arm muscles shown off by his tank top. He studied me warily. There seemed to be a noisy party going on behind him.

"Oh. Does Boyd still live here?" I peered past him and saw the apartment was full of guys. I recognized one of them, Boyd's dark-haired friend who we'd run into at the bar during Spring Break. He happened to be on the floor at the moment, in the middle of wrestling a much bigger man who had him pinned down and had pushed up his T-shirt in order to tickle his well-tanned, hairless belly. The larger man, a browned-eyed redhead, had his shirt half open to show off a smooth chest with impressive muscles.

They stopped when they saw they had company, and the smaller guy on the floor said, "Hey, I remember you. One of Boyd's tourist buddies. Let him in; he's cool. How's it going?"

"Not so great, actually. Is Boyd here? Uh, sorry to crash your party."

"No, it's okay, dude, we're just hanging out," said the blond who'd opened the door, now smiling warmly. He stepped aside, his body language inviting me in. One guy hastily closed the bedroom door, and I briefly wondered whether Boyd was hiding out in there, but just before the door closed I caught a glimpse of naked flesh and realized I'd been hearing bedsprings squeaking in the background. Obviously someone had a girl in there, and the guy was giving them some privacy. Certainly there were no girls out here, and it looked like a very informal party. Besides the guys wrestling on the floor, there were three guys playing a video game, two shirtless and one in a tank top, two more shirtless guys standing around with their hands wrapped around bottles of José Cuervo, and a third, with his shirt hanging open, focused on using a bottle opener to get the cap off his own bottle. There were no snacks laid out, just a table full of plates that looked like they were left over from lunch. Socks were scattered all over the floor – several days' worth, certainly more than the number of bare feet at the moment – along with shirts and several black or gray heaps that could only be wetsuits. Except for the wetsuits, it looked like a lot of dorm rooms I'd seen, but you'd think whichever of these guys lived here would have cleaned up before having this many friends over.

"Boyd's not here, dude," said the dark-haired guy, struggling to his feet as his buddy released him. "Hey, are you okay? Anything I can do for you?" He'd ignored me in the bar last spring and had been perfunctory with his friend Boyd, but now he was suddenly warm and solicitous. He must have heard about Kevin and knew I'd been close to him; that was the only explanation. I'd better get used to that kind of sympathy from strangers, real or otherwise.

"I just was hoping to talk to Boyd."

"I haven't seen him lately. Anyone seen Boyd?"

"No. Not here in town, anyway."

"He's usually here all year round, isn't he?" someone said.

177

"Maybe he's tired of us already," someone joked.

"This early in the summer?"

"Tell you what," the dark-haired offered, "when I see him, I'll tell him you guys are looking for him." Behind him, one of the shirtless beer-drinkers had set down his beer and snuck up on the giant redhead still kneeling on the floor to throw an arm around his neck from behind. The redhead easily threw him onto his back and began attacking his ribs. Like all of the bare-chested guys here, the man now laid out on the floor was as sleek, tan, smooth, and muscular as Boyd. I'd never seen so many great abs in one room.

"I wanted to make sure he was okay," I said. "Are you sure he didn't drown in the line of duty?"

They all looked at me and laughed, all except the guys engrossed in their video game or bottle opening. "No, dude, he didn't drown. Trust me on this one." He slapped me on the shoulder. "Hang out with us. Have a few beers."

I really didn't feel like being around a lot of people just then. Still, he came surprisingly close to convincing me.

# # # # #

Gary and I found we weren't in the mood to mix with the happy vacationers. The bar on the beach had live music, and everyone else was drunkenly singing along to "Margaritaville," as if it weren't a depressing song. That was Boyd's favorite drink; I wondered if he could cheer us up if only he were here. Next they played "José Cuervo," which the guys in Boyd's apartment had been drinking with more than a little salt but no lime.

We moved to the Boardwalk, but that was also too upbeat for our current mood. We tried the crowded beach, but neither of us could work up any interest in cruising for babes. So we started walking aimlessly, side by side, along the top of the cliff above the rocky shoreline. That suited our mood better, and we spent the next couple of days doing that. There was an inaccessible beach or two far below, but mostly just water. Some mornings, we saw more sea lions and seals than people.

Then one day, over a week after the tragically incomplete rescue, Gary stopped suddenly in his tracks.

"What?" I asked.

"Shh! Did you hear that?"

"No. What?"

"I don't want to say it. It couldn't be what I want it to be."

I listened carefully, and thought I heard it. A man's voice, calling for help. And to my desperate ears, it sounded a lot like Kevin.

# # # # #

It was coming from somewhere below the treacherous edge of the cliff. The one the signs warned us not to go near. There had been signs warning about rip current, too. So we were extra careful at first: I lay down on my belly, spreading my weight as I peered over the edge, and Gary gripped my calves out of fear the rocks would suddenly crumble. But they felt solid under me. I shouted down over the edge. To our amazed delight, it clearly was Kevin's voice that responded.

With Gary bracing my trembling calves, I crawled forward enough to get my shoulders over the edge, then a little further, to lean over. The cliff face turned out to be concave, forming a narrow cove that rose up close enough to where my head was hanging that I was able to look straight down at Kevin.

He had a week's growth of beard and had lost what few traces of fat he'd had, and looked a little less beefy; I could count his ribs. That much was to be expected. But I didn't expect the rest. Someone had provided him with several gallon-sized jugs of spring water. A clear plastic trash bag held two crushed empty jugs and several containers of the kind the supermarket sells sushi party trays in, what might have been a bottle of sun block, and something green.

His hands were bound in front of him and tied to a choke collar around his neck. Apparently that was to prevent him from untying the bonds around his ankle, which tethered him to a rusty boat anchor that lay on top of the sand. Either that, or just to humiliate him. Whoever had done this to him had also taken away his swim trunks.

When he saw me, he hefted the anchor awkwardly and walked closer, his chest and arm muscles flexing as carried the anchor with him. He let it fall when he'd reached a point almost directly below my head.

"Who did this to you?" I asked, shocked at seeing my strong, swaggering friend reduced to someone's helpless prisoner.

"Who the hell do you think?" he sobbed, holding up his bound, raw wrists. I saw that the material binding them was in fact a tangle of white plastic that had obviously come from six-pack yokes.

"Boyd?" I asked in disbelief.

# # # # #

We didn't think we could safely get him up the cliff face by ourselves, so we called the authorities. Poor guy; it must have been humiliating enough to have his buddies find him stripped and tied up, without strangers coming down to cut him loose and winch him up to freedom. At least they got him wrapped in a blanket before the local paper snapped his picture.

The rescue was completed before Boyd returned. He had been visiting a few times a day – entering from the water, not climbing down – to check Kevin's bonds, feed him sushi and limes, replenish his water, and generally gloat over his naked prisoner and do whatever he felt like doing to him. Kevin refused to reveal the details even to his best friends.

# # # # #

Boyd looked very small and lost in his orange jail uniform. He wasn't a little guy by any means: almost six feet and 160 or 170 pounds, none of it fat. But his powerful swimming muscles were hidden under his loose-fitting jumpsuit. His swimming muscles weren't going to do him any good here.

"I don't know what to say to you, man. You saved my life. Probably Gary's, too. I'm grateful for that. You even saved Kevin's life, no question about that. But what you did to him afterward ..."

He gave me his kicked-puppy expression. "It's not like I hurt him or anything."

"You held him prisoner for over a week!" I said hotly. "Do you know how humiliated he felt? Now maybe you'll see what it's like."

"Yeah, well, it was almost worth it. Bringing a big alpha male like him down a peg. Dude, I had him totally at my mercy."

I shifted uncomfortably, remembering how good it could feel when Gary and I would gang up on Kevin and pin the big guy down and tickle him until he begged for mercy. But that was just playful roughhousing. Boyd had taken him against his will.

I changed the subject. "Orange really isn't your color, man."

"Hey, if it was good enough for Aquaman ..." he joked feebly. "Besides, I don't get to wear this as much as you might think." He glanced at the prisoners who were talking with their own visitors. They were huge guys. If they were all standing on their feet, they would dwarf Boyd.

"Oh," I said simply. Somehow, I didn't think Boyd spent a lot of time standing on his feet with these guys.

"Not that I'm complaining. It's totally not the worst thing I've eaten here. The seafood in the cafeteria stinks."

I laughed nervously at his brave humor.

"Seriously, dude, the thing I hate the most is being caged up here. I used to have nightmares about being taken captive, but somehow I never pictured being trapped indoors. I really miss my freedom, dude."

It hurt to see him like this. He should be sitting by the ocean, staring out to sea as the warm wind ruffled his blond hair and the sunlight gently baked his smooth chest to a golden brown. Why'd he have to get arrested? "Look, if there's anything I can do ..."

"Actually, there is one thing. I left my stuff in my locker. They'll cut the lock off at the end of the season. Could ... could you keep it safe for me? I don't trust my lawyer with it. Would you do this for me?"

"No problem. I owe you that much. I mean, you saved my life!" And Gary's, which had become more precious to me that I cared to admit.

He swallowed hard, fear and trust warring in his soulful brown eyes, and told me the combination.

# # # # #

His locker proved to contain only his beach bag, which in turn contained his sunglasses, towel, wetsuit, and whistle, and sun block. I zipped it up and took it home, where it sat forgotten in the back of the closet in my dorm room.

Kevin talked for awhile about transferring to some school a thousand miles away where no one knew him, but he never did, and he roomed with Gary again their junior year. The next summer, the three of us rented a house off-campus for our senior year. Kevin took the master bedroom for himself and his succession of one-night stands, and Gary and I shared the other bedroom, which had twin beds.

I drove a couple of times a year to the state prison to visit Boyd, still feeling that I owed him something. He seemed so lonely and out of place. I also wanted to convey to him how shattered Gary and I had felt when he'd made us think Kevin was dead.

"I don't know how I could have made it through that week, if it hadn't been for Gary. He was all I had left. The only thing that made life still worth living."

"Dude! You should tell him."

"Tell him what?"

"How you feel."

"Not really. He might get the wrong idea, if you know what I mean."

"Is it the wrong idea?"

"What are you talking about?"

"You've got to be true to your nature, dude."

"What are you insinuating? That I'm – Look, Gary and I are just buddies, all right? Maybe you're being true to your nature, stuck here with all these guys and taking it ..."

"No way," he interrupted. "I don't belong in this place. Not that I'm complaining about the sex, particularly. It's the only exercise I get these days."

"You don't look so good," I observed quietly. He'd gotten pale and scrawny over the past couple of years. What I could glimpse of his chest through his half-buttoned work shirt wasn't nearly as muscular as I remembered.

"The seafood here's even worse than in jail. And I've never been into running or weight lifting, so ..."

# # # # #

He lost even more weight each time I saw him, and seemed to have aged ten years in his four years behind bars. He was always pathetically glad to see me. I felt guilty for not visiting more often, as stupid as that might seem, given that he was in here for kidnapping one of my best friends.

"Kevin bought his own place," I told him on one visit, a couple of years into his imprisonment.

"Bummer," Boyd said.

"He can afford it now, with all those stock options from his dot com. He doesn't need to share the rent with us anymore."

"At least you've still got Gary. Have you told him how you feel about him?"

"Look, I don't know what you think is going on, but Gary's got a steady girlfriend now. They're even talking about getting married."

"That means he'd live with her year-round, right?"

"What? Of course!"

"Dude ... you're making a big mistake if you don't at least talk to him."

"I don't know what you're talking about."

# # # # #

I finally persuaded Kevin to pay a visit to Boyd, if only for the satisfaction of seeing the pathetic state his erstwhile captor had been reduced to.

"You know," Kevin said after his visit, "I actually feel sorry for the poor guy."

"After what he did to you?"

"He held me prisoner for a week. As punishment, he's been a prisoner for years. How fair is that? I'm sure he would have let me go in a few weeks."

"And he didn't leave you to rot," I agreed. "He brought you water – or was that for himself?"

"No, it was all for me. He never even took a sip. He did eat some of the sushi."

"And he provided sunscreen, right? Otherwise you'd have been brick-red all over by the time we found you."

Kevin's face now turned that color.

"What?"

"My hands were tied, remember?"

"So how did you put – oh."

"It wasn't the most humiliating thing he did to me." He hung his head in remembered shame.

"You okay?" I asked gently, putting my hand on his shoulder.

"It was a long time ago," he said, brushing my hand away. "And after his years in prison, he's been paid back many times over."

"He's miserable in there. If you think he's paid his debt, is there anything you can do for him?"

"Well, the guy did save my life, right before he stranded me and then came back and tied me up. I'll call my lawyers."

# # # # #

Whatever Kevin's lawyers did must have worked. Boyd was released two months later, and Kevin gave him a job as a live-in servant. Meanwhile, Kevin had bought a new house with a swimming pool, explaining that he'd always wanted to host pool parties, and that the profit on the sale of his first home made it easy to afford the down payment on this larger investment.

I didn't see that house for a couple of months. To tell the truth, I was avoiding Boyd. I'd been looking for that beach bag I'd promised to keep safe for him, and I couldn't find it anywhere. The last place I remembered seeing it was my dorm room.

Then Kevin threw a big beginning-of-summer party and invited all his friends. I had no excuse for missing it.

Whatever Boyd's usual duties as Kevin's houseboy might entail, his job during the party seemed to be to provide entertainment. He spent the whole time in and around the pool, showing off his swimming and diving prowess, wearing only skimpy new Speedos. He looked great: tanned and very fit. I'd have sworn he was several years older than I, well into his thirties, if I didn't know better; but he was still an incredibly good-looking guy.

After a game in which the guests tossed a beach ball into the pool for Boyd to swim after and bat back to them, Kevin finally let him take a break, and sent the caterer over to him with a tray of sushi. I went over to join him.

"Dude!" Boyd greeted me. He stuffed a salmon maki in his mouth and embraced me – getting my shirt wet, but I didn't care.

"You look great, man! You happy here?"

"Sure beats the hell out of prison. I only have one guy to keep happy, and I can spend most of my time swimming, especially when Kevin has one of his women over."

I hoped that didn't mean what it sounded like it meant.

He went on, "I've been trying to reach you, but Kevin said he didn't have your phone number, and I don't know how to use email. Or type. Do you have the stuff from my locker?"

"I'm, uh, still looking for it."

He looked crestfallen. "Do you think you'll find it? It's sort of important."

"I'll do my best," I promised.

He clutched at my arms, his sad brown eyes pleading with me. "Please," he whispered, "I gotta get my stuff back, dude."

"If I can't find it, I'm sure I can replace ..."

"No," he said, stifling a sob. "No, you can't."

I went over to talk to Kevin as soon as I could get him away from his crowd of admirers. "How's Boyd doing here?" I asked.

"Don't worry, I'll keep him around. He's a lousy cook. He does take good care of the pool, only he needs help opening the jars of chemicals. He'll be a decent masseur if he ever learns to use his thumbs. He has uses. You wouldn't believe how long the guy can hold his breath."

"I'm not even ... Look, what I mean is, is he happy here?"

"Seems to be. The one thing he keeps asking for is his old wetsuit, which he seems to think you have. I bought him a new top-of-the-line wetsuit right after I bought him those Speedos, but he won't wear it."

"Does he go to the beach a lot, then?"

"Sure, I've let him spend a few weekends in Santa Cruz, even paid for his cab and hotel. So, how've you been? It's great to see you. Too bad Gary couldn't make it."

"Well, it's a really long drive."

"Actually, he was going to come, but then one of his kids got sick."

"I'll have to call him and tell him about all the great food he's missing," I said, taking out my cell phone.

"And the great babes," Kevin added.

"Huh?" I said.

"I made sure to invite enough to share with you guys," he said half-jokingly.

Now that he mentioned it, I noticed there were a lot of scantily clad women around the pool. Many were trying to get Boyd's attention without being obvious about it, but he seemed completely oblivious to them.

I called Gary, politely asked how his kid was feeling and sympathized with his disappointment at missing the party. When he asked about Boyd, I told him about my conversations, leaving out the disturbing hints about his houseboy duties. "I'm pretty sure I cleaned out my dorm room when I moved, so his stuff should have made it to our house. Any chance it got mixed in with yours when you moved out?"

"You know, that's entirely possible. It could be in the basement. But there's tons of Susan's stuff down there, too, and of course there are all the wedding gifts we can't find a use for. Not the one from my best man, of course! The tea kettle was very thoughtful. We use it every day."

"So, do you think you can find the time to sort through it soon? I know it's a hassle, but it seems to be really important to him."

"Tell you what: you're always promising to come see our new house. Come here, and we'll look together."

"Sounds great! I'm not doing anything the next three weekends."

"The weekend after next would be perfect," Gary said happily.

"That'll give you time to find the tea kettle," I said, and we laughed together.

# # # # #

There were a lot of boxes to sort through. "Most of it's Susan's."

"I gathered, from the tons of women's clothes."

"Yeah. Try not to get sweat on them."

"Can I sweat on your clothes?"

"Sure, buddy."

"Look, another box of shoes. And I guess she and her sister will be bringing even more stuff home from their shopping trip."

"You got it. They need this season's fashions. Don't try to make sense of it." He threw his arm around my shoulders. "By the way, her sister's hot! And single."

"Are you trying to fix me up? Again?"

"Absolutely!" If you marry Susan's sister or one of her close friends, the four of us can go places together."

"Wouldn't that be great?"

"We had some great times when you were single, didn't we?"

"I do miss that part of my life sometimes."

We worked in silence for awhile. Suddenly Gary said, "Hey, look what I found,"

I looked up from the box of toasters I was sorting through. "Did you find it?"

"No, but look." He held up a brightly colored shirt that said Santa Cruz. "There are two of them, both the same size. Do you still take a Medium?"

"Last I checked. I can't remember the last time I bought a T-shirt."

"Well, some of us have stayed in shape. I'm sure mine still fits me." He unbuttoned his shirt. He did seem to be in great shape.

"Hey," I protested. "I haven't gained much weight."

"Bet it won't fit." He shrugged out of his shirt. "All those beers over the years had to go someplace."

"We'll see about that." I took off my own shirt and knelt beside him to look in the box.

"I don't know," he said doubtfully, poking me in the belly to confirm that it hadn't gone soft.

"Hey!" I laughed, grabbing his forearm. "You know I'm ticklish."

"I sure do!"

We grappled for awhile, just like old times. The floor of the basement was hard and cold against my bare back, so I struggled to roll on top and let him get a taste of it instead. The feel of his skin against mine, and his familiar scent, brought back memories of more carefree times, even more than the sight of the T-shirts. We wrestled until he managed to get my head pinned against his chest.

"Oh, man, I have missed you so much," he murmured, loosening his grip slightly. "Why don't we ever get together anymore?"

"Well, you know ... you have your own life now."

"Yeah, I guess there's no going back. We can't relive our youth." He released me and we sat up on the floor, side by side, reminiscing about old times. Then, caught up in the mood, I said, "Listen, buddy. This may sound crazy, but is there any way we could coordinate our vacation time and go to the beach together sometime?"

I expected him to say "It wouldn't be the same." Or at best, "Sure! It'll be fun for the kids" – which amounts to the same thing. But what he said was, "That's a great idea! Susan can take the kids to spend the summer at her parents' ranch."

"Are you sure, man? Separate vacations? Won't that feel a little weird?"

"What's weird about it? What could be more natural than kids visiting their grandparents? Or a daughter visiting her parents?"

Grinning, I tried on my old T-shirt. It still fit. Now if only it could magically morph me back into a carefree college student.

# # # # #

I spent half a day in Santa Cruz looking for Boyd. He had checked into a motel but wasn't in his room. Finally, I had an early dinner at a seafood restaurant on the wharf. After that, I wandered over to the opposite railing to look out. There were seals barking out there somewhere. I glanced down and saw that a bunch of them had commandeered a wooden platform that was probably a disused boat landing. It was cute how the animals came out of the ocean and started using human-built things for their own purpose. There were about a dozen, sunning themselves in a huge puppy pile, cuddled up in groups of two or three with a nose resting on a different neighbor's flank or a tail thrown across another buddy. They were doing it deliberately; there was enough space for them each to have some elbow room. Not that they had elbows.

Then, over the constant barking, I thought I heard Boyd's voice quietly saying, "OK, then, catch you later, dude." I looked around and didn't see him in the sparse crowd on the wharf. It had sounded like it came from below. I leaned way over and saw a blond head. I walked down the wooden stairs and found him sitting on the back edge of the platform, almost under the rafters. He was dressed in shorts and a T-shirt, surrounded by seals that were quietly sunning themselves. The animals shied away from me as I approached, of course, and some of them started to slip into the water, but then the rest of them suddenly seemed to decide I was cool and flopped back down.

"Dude!" he said. "What are you doing here?"

I noticed that two seals were leaning against Boyd. He had his arm casually draped around one.

"Kevin said you were in Santa Cruz. I've been looking for you all day. Want some company?"

"The more the merrier," he said with a half-hearted smile. It looked like he'd been crying.

One seal near Boyd suddenly shied away from me and retreated into the rafters, and I sat down in the vacated spot. The other seals seemed to accept my presence now that they saw I was with Boyd. One of them prodded my backpack with its snout and snorted excitedly.

Boyd's eyes suddenly lit with excitement. "Dude! Please tell me you found what I was asking for."

I grinned and swung the backpack off, and took out the folded wetsuit. I'd never looked at it closely, but it felt much softer and more supple than I'd imagined wetsuits feeling, never having touched one before.

Joy filled his tear-streaked face. "Dude!" he whispered, sounding choked up. He grabbed me and planted a kiss right on my lips. I tried to pull away, but he was too strong. The seals started growling and sneezing at this affront to nature.

Finally, he released me and eagerly pulled his T-shirt off. "Dude, thank you so much!" he said hoarsely.

"You're going to change right now?" I just hoped he wasn't preparing for anything weirder than that.

"Yes, I'm going to change. Right now." He pulled down his pants and slipped out of his sandals. "I have nothing to hide from you, man." He hooked his thumbs into the waistband of his boxers.

"Whoa!" I said, averting my eyes to give him some privacy, and looking up to see if anyone could see us over the railing.

"I owe you one, dude."

"Are you decent yet?" I asked, making sure no one was coming down the stairs. But there was no answer, just a commotion from the seals. I turned around, and Boyd was nowhere to be seen. He must have slipped into the water.

I stood up to see if I could see any sign of him. The seals were slipping off the edge, where they were rolling around with each other excitedly and biting each other. I saw neither hide nor hair of Boyd, and started getting alarmed and shouting his name.

The minutes dragged on. No man can hold his breath for that long. Could he have drowned? An ex-lifeguard? I knew his life hadn't been going so well, but I hadn't realized he'd been suicidal. Numbly, I picked up his discarded shirt, pants, boxers, and sandals.

He couldn't have gotten up the steps, or even climbed onto the rafters under the wharf, without my seeing. The only place he could have gone behind my back was into the water, and I'd have noticed if he'd resurfaced. If he was still down there, he was dead. I had to accept that. I trudged back to my car. Eventually, I thought to call Gary. I wasn't ready to break it to Kevin, and Gary and I sort of had practice at this.

"Oh my God," Gary said. "Are you all right, man? I know you loved the guy."

"Loved?"

"You know what I mean."

"I don't know if I'm all right. I just feel numb. He was so happy just a few minutes before. Was it a mistake to give him the wetsuit back?"

"It wasn't your fault. Look, I'll be with you in three weeks, as planned. Will you be all right until then? If I can get away sooner ..."

"I'll be okay."

"If you need to talk, call me. Day or night."

"Thanks, buddy."

# # # # #

I stayed in Santa Cruz. The worst that could happen is I'd drown myself. Better that, than lose it on Highway 17 and take some innocent bystanders with me.

Exercise helped me feel better, so after a couple of days of moping in my hotel room, I started going on long swims. On my second day out, a seal came right up to me and poked me in the chest almost playfully with its snout. That had never happened to me before. I wondered sadly if it was one of the tame ones Boyd had been sitting among.

It dove right between my legs and prodded me gently in the back, then circled around and nuzzled my armpit.

Then it bit my shoulder, though not hard enough to break the skin. Did seals ever eat swimmers who stray too far from the shore, I wondered? Nervously, I started swimming back toward safety.

I almost ran into someone. I stopped and raised my head above the water.

"Dude! It's me!" Boyd said. He was still wearing his wetsuit, unzipped as usual to reveal his muscular chest.

"Boyd! I thought you'd drowned!" Impulsively, I grabbed him in a tight embrace. He managed to tread water for both of us.

"Why'd you think that, you bozo?" he laughed, squeezing me.

"You disappeared!"

"What, didn't you see me changing?"

"No, I didn't watch you change! Not past the boxers, anyway."

"Oh. Sorry if I got you worried."

"I'm just glad you're all right. I'll have to call Gary and tell him."

"How's Gary doing, anyway?"

"He and his wife are fine, thanks."

"Oh, right. I keep forgetting. Mated for life, right?"

"Why are you so cynical about marriage?"

"Just as long as it doesn't mean a guy's wife has to be his life partner."

"Of course she does! I mean, I know the divorce rate is high these days, but traditionally ... My grandparents on both sides stayed together their whole lives."

"And did they do everything together, 24/7, year-round? Or did your grandfathers do a lot of socializing with their buddies?"

"Well ... one of them loved to fish. I don't know if my grandmother went along."

"Dude!" he laughed. "Wake up!" He splashed me playfully. "Promise me you'll at least spend time with Gary and see if anything happens."

"As a matter of fact, we've got plans to spend the summer together."

"That's great, dude! Where?"

"Here."

193

"Awesome! So I'll get to see a lot of you guys."

"Then you've moved back to Santa Cruz? Where are you staying?"

"Dude!" he said, exasperated. "Well, I guess it's no surprise you can't see the truth about what I am. You don't even know what you are! Catch you later, dude. I'm going to go lie in the sun with my buddies."

He zipped up his wetsuit and dove. A sleek shape shot past me underwater, and he was gone.

A VIRGIN IN KEY WEST: A JOE MARTINEZ STORY
By Jesse Monteagudo

Back in the early seventies, before cruise ships and AIDS, the island of Key West was a sexual paradise for a horny young guy. I first visited the Conch Republic in the summer of 1972, when I was just eighteen and practically a virgin. Not owning a car at the time, I boarded a Greyhound bus in downtown Miami on a Saturday morning and headed south. I remember that first trip as if it was yesterday. We traveled through still-undeveloped parts of Miami-Dade and Monroe Counties; island-hopped on the Overseas Highway; and stopped in Homestead, Key Largo and Marathon for piss breaks and a snack. I even saw a miniature key deer cross the road as our bus rode through Big Pine Key; a rare sight then and now.

It was late afternoon when our bus finally arrived at the Greyhound Station on Roosevelt Boulevard in New Town. Not wanting to spend my hard-earned money on a taxi ride or even on local bus fare, I put on my backpack and began to walk in the direction of Old Town. I walked down Roosevelt Boulevard til it became Truman Avenue and Truman Avenue till it crossed Duval Street. My plans were to walk down Duval Street to Mallory Square, watch the Sunset, take in some of the sights, grab a bite, and hopefully make some new friends before taking the first bus back to Miami the next morning. Finding a place to sleep was the furthest thing from my mind. I was, after all, just eighteen years old.

As I walked down Duval Street, I took in the sights and sounds of Old Key West. There were very few cars: most people walked, skated or rode bicycles. Most of the native Conchs were dressed light, for it was a hot summer. I myself wore a white tank top T-shirt, blue short-shorts, black hiking shoes and white socks, and a black cap that barely protected my head from the sun and other elements. I dressed for success as well as for the tropics, for I was proud of my body. After all, I worked out several days a week and wanted to show off what I got. My choice of clothes seemed to have its desired effect: A few pedestrians stopped to compliment my tight round buns and one even had the nerve to grab them right on Duval, just to make sure they were real.

"You shouldn't waste an ass like that out here on the street," said my new admirer, after I politely moved his hand away from my butt. "You should go over to Joe's Blow, where the action is this time of day."

"What's Joe's Blow?"

"Just the hottest gay bar in Old Key West. Just turn into that alley and walk halfway down the block." Though it was getting late, I decided that a visit to Joe's Blow was worth missing the Sunset at Mallory Square. I thanked the man and walked over to Joe's Blow. What a dump! Though I wouldn't have given Joe's Blow the time of day back in Miami, I was in Key West where, after all, anything goes.

"Hey Joe, look who just walked in," yelled one of the customers, as I entered the Blow. "It's fresh chicken, right off the bus!" Coming in from the late afternoon sun, I could barely see my way inside the dark bar. Soon, however, my eyesight adjusted itself to its surroundings, and I was able to take a good look around. As I expected, Joe's Blow was a dingy dive that made Smokey Joe look like the Ritz. A group of men sat along a bar talking to a bearded bear who I presumed was Joe himself. A young bartender kept busy filling the men's mugs with beer while a second bartender worked the pool table and the back room. The back room itself was empty except for three tourists who sat around a table, drinking rum.

"Welcome to Joe's Blow," said the owner, as he stared down at me from across the bar. "What would you have?" Lucky for me, these were the early seventies, when the drinking age in Florida was just eighteen. I showed Joe my ID and ordered a beer.

"It's quite a place," I gulped, as I drank my beer. "How did you get your name?"

"We opened a couple of years ago, right before a hurricane hit Key West. That didn't bother us, for we just turned Opening Night into a hurricane party. But the wind almost blew the place down, and since then Conchs and tourists alike call this place Joe's Blow. It's still the hottest gay bar in town," he smiled.

"I guess it is," I said, as we shook hands. "I'm only down here for the night. I came on the bus and plan to take the bus back home tomorrow morning."

"It's a shame. We lost our go-go boy last week, and you look like you could do the job. Have you ever danced naked, on top of a bar?"

"I don't think I could do it," I replied. In fact, dancing naked in front of some lecherous drunks in a bar was the furthest thing from my mind. Just then my Duval Street admirer entered Joe's Blow, ordered a beer, and sat down next to me. I immediately got up. Not having anywhere else to go, I found my way to the back room, where the three tourists were still sitting around their table, drinking rum. All three men were in their thirties; trim, muscular men with sharp blue eyes and long blond hair. They, too, were dressed in tropical attire. "This is my first time in Key West," I said, to no one in particular. This had its desired effect, for the men smiled and invited me to join them.

"Come over here and join us," one of the men said in what I sensed was a European accent. "This is our first time in Key West, too," he added, as I sat down next to him. As we shook hands he ordered another round of rum, this time for the four of us. We smiled. As it turned out, my three new friends were German tourists who had arrived in Key West just a hours before I did.

"We are three boyhood friends from Munich. My name is Gustav and my pals here are Rudolf and Fernand," he added, as I shook hands with the two of them. "Once we realized that all three of us are gay, we decided to travel the world, to see places and meet cute boys. Key West is our first stop here in America," he added.

Rudolf piped in: "What's your name and where are you from?"

"My name is Joe Martinez and I live in Miami."

Fernand smiled: "Were you born in Miami? You seem to have an accent of your own."

"I was born in Havana, but I lived most of my life in America."

"We heard Miami was full of hot Cuban boys," Gustav noted. "We were going to visit Havana to meet some Cuban twinks but figured Florida was safer. Our plans are to stay in Key West for a couple of days and then go up to Miami. We could give you a ride back if you need one."

"That would be great, thanks." If nothing else, a ride home would save me some bus money. And they seemed like nice guys, I thought, as I drank my rum. It wasn't long before I got mellow, and threw all caution to the wind. Gustav smiled at me and ordered another round. Soon it was getting dark, and the four of us didn't have a care in the world.

"This place is getting on my nerves," Rudolf said, as more people filled Joe's Blow. "Let us go over to the guest house and hang out for a while." Gustav and Fernand agreed. "Do you want to come with us?"

"I guess so. Where are you staying?"

"We are staying at the Casa Cayo on Fleming Street," Gustav said. "You'll love it over there. It's men only and clothing optional." Casa Cayo was the most notorious gay guest house on the Key. It was very popular with European tourists, though its rates were above my pay scale. Here was my one chance to visit this infamous, Key West resort, I thought to myself.

"I guess I could join you," I replied. "I haven't had dinner, though."

"Don't worry about it," Fernand replied, as the four of us stood up. "We'll hang out by the pool for a while and then order a pizza."

"The Casa Cayo is only a few blocks away," Rudolf added. "We'll walk over there." It was already dark when the four of us left Joe's Blow, heading towards the Casa Cayo. We strolled down Duval Street and then up Fleming, alongside a block of gay guest houses that lined the street. At the end of the block was the notorious Casa Cayo. "There are not too many people at the Casa this time of night," said Gustav, as he used his room key to let us in. "Except in the gym or at the front desk, most guests are having dinner or watching the Sunset. It's much better for us."

"Hello, Gustav," an effeminate bottle blond at the front desk looked up as we came in. He frowned. "What did I tell you about bringing hustlers to the Casa Cayo?"

"This is no hustler, Vito. This is Joe, who just arrived from Miami. He's going to spend some time with us." Vito gave me a dirty look but did not try to stop me from coming in. "Just make sure that he behaves himself," he told Gustav. "If he steals anything, I'll add it your bill." At that moment, two whores walked in, looked around, and headed towards the rooms in the back. Vito stopped them in their tracks.

"I told you before that this is a men's only guest house," he screamed. "You can't come in here. Get out and don't ever come back!" The whores were obviously hoping to turn tricks, not realizing that the Casa Cayo was a gay establishment. As Vito escorted the hookers off the premises, Gustav, Rudolf and Fernand led me down the hall to their room.

"The pool is fabulous in the early evening," Fernand gushed as I dropped my back pack in a corner of their room. "The water is cool and there's no one around."

"But I forgot my swim shorts."

"Don't worry about it," Gustav laughed. "This place is clothing-optional, remember? Besides, a cute muscle boy like you shouldn't be wearing clothes."

"Thanks for the compliment but I've never done this before," I said, perfectly honest.

"You'll get used to it," Rudolf added, as he shucked his clothes. "Back home in Munich, we go swimming naked all the time. As long as there are no women around. Besides, the pool should be empty this time of night."

"What's there to lose? I'm game," I said, as I threw off my clothes. Now Gustav, Rudolf and Fernand stood naked before me: a trio of trim, muscular men with thick, uncut cocks and low-hanging balls. Like other Europeans, my three German friends shaved off all their body hair below their necks, even their pubic hairs.

"Over in Germany, we like to keep our bodies nice and clean," said Fernand, as he fingered my nature trail. "But a little hair looks good on you," he added. "At least your parents didn't clip your dick, the way too many of them do over here." With towels in hand, the four of us walked naked to the pool which, as Rudolf said, was empty this time of night. While Fernand showed me around the pool and the nearby tropical garden, Gustav and Rudolf fetched some rum, ice and mixes from the front desk.

"It's quite a place, Joe, don't you think?," Rudolf said, as he handed me a cocktail.

"It sure is," I replied, as I drank the tropical mix. By this time, I'd already consumed several drinks, and didn't have a care in the world. I was an eighteen-year old, hot Cuban-American boy, practically a virgin but willing to try anything. As I lay down on a pool side lounge, I gave myself willingly to these three German hunks.

"Have you ever tried poppers, Joe?" Fernand asked, as he placed an open vial of amyl nitrite under my nose. All of a sudden, my heart started beating faster and my body became more sensitive to its surroundings. To my friends' delight, my eight-inch cock began to harden, and my cock-head thrust forth out of its protective foreskin.

"I think Joe is getting hot, boys," said Rudolf, as he grabbed my stiff prick. "You have a nice *pinga*," he added, breaking into fluent, if accented, Spanish. "Nice *huevos*, too," he said, as he took my low-hanging balls. Before I knew it, Rudolf was on his knees, sucking my balls. I never felt such an experience before, and I enjoyed every minute of it. "There is nothing as beautiful as a young man's balls," Rudolf said, as he briefly looked up. "Don't you agree, boys?"

"I don't know, Rudy," Fernand replied, as he took hold of my hard prick. "I prefer hot *pinga* myself," he added, as he fell on his knees to work on my thick prick. Fernand knew his way around a young man's dick. I sighed with pleasure as he began to work on my hard cock, pushing the foreskin back to reveal the tender head within. An experienced cocksucker, Fernand took my eight inches deep inside his mouth and throat, while at the same time licking the hard shaft with his eager tongue. As Rudolf and Fernand continued to work on my balls and cock, Gustav held the bottle of poppers under my nose, keeping my body at a fever pitch. But Gustav had other plans.

"Give me your sweet *culo*, Joe," Gustav whispered, as he dropped to his knees below me, spreading my muscular thighs apart to allow access to my young and willing ass. Spreading my buns to expose my bunghole, Gustav took some grease, anointed my virgin hole with it, and used it to shove two fingers inside my rectum. I groaned and moaned as Gustav massaged my tender prostate, filling my body with erotic energy. Gustav then took his fingers out of my asshole, replacing them with his hungry tongue. This was a rim job that I would not soon forget.

"Your ass is a mouthful, Joe," Gustav muttered, as he continued to eat my ass. "Who needs pizza when one can have a hot Cuban boy's ass, cock and balls for dinner." His friends agreed. Soon the world seemed to disappear. All that mattered was my cock, my balls and my ass, and the three men who pleasured them with their mouths and with their hands. An eternity passed as my three lovers continued to lick my balls, suck my cock, and rim my ass. I was the passive object of desire for three men who took their pleasure from the taste of an eighteen-year old Cuban muscle boy's naked body. Vials of poppers continued to pass beneath my nose, keeping me in a state of super-charged erotic ecstasy. It wasn't long before I reached the point of no return.

"I'm coming!" I screamed, as I shot my accumulated orgasm down Fernand's hungry mouth and throat. Fernand swallowed my man-milk, not spilling a drop, and then kept my cock inside his mouth for a while, not wanting to let go. He then stood up and stroked his own cock to orgasm, coming all over me. Gustav and Rudolf followed suit, stroking their own restless cocks and spilling their seed all over my tight young body. When we were through, we lay on top of each other, completely exhausted.

Gustav was the first to recover from our accumulated passion: "You have a great body, Joe," he said. "Now let us jump in the pool and get cleaned up." The next thing we knew, the four of us were in the pool, splashing water at one another, laughing, and cleaning ourselves up.

This was just the start of my first Key West weekend. I spent the rest of my time with Gustav, Rudolf, and Fernand, taking in the sights during the day and giving myself willingly to them at night. I even got to see the Sunset on Mallory Square. When it was over, my three

Mickey Erlach

German friends drove me back to Miami, leaving me at my front door after inviting me to visit them in Munich. One of these days, I might just do that.

FINLAND FLAUNT
By Jay Starre

Chad knew exactly when his love of voyeurism and exhibitionism began. But he got more than that from his summer in Finland. Much more.

After his sophomore year in college he journeyed to Scandinavia where he worked on a tree farm as part of a work exchange program for students. East of Helsinki along the coast of the Gulf of Finland, he found himself ensconced in a small cabin with a lone roommate. Kristian was actually a Finn, hailing from a small town in the north. His English was excellent, which put Chad to shame since he spoke barely a few words of Finnish.

Kristian was a quiet dude, with a rare smile and timid manner. Chad was more the gregarious sort, but quickly realized his cabin mate preferred silence to the constant chatter the American was used to.

It was only their third morning together when he woke to find the young Finn sprawled across his nearby bed with covers tossed aside.

His naked, creamy-pale butt was on full display!

Eyes locked on the exciting sight and unable to look away, Chad could barely breathe. Afraid if he made a sound Kristian might wake and cover himself, he moved his hand down to his stiffening cock as quietly as possible.

Lean thighs curled sideways, rounded ass high and in full view, smooth cheeks divided by a deep crack, a pair of hairless nads squeezed between the legs and just visible – Chad drank in every inch of Kristian's naked form with greedy lust.

The young American flushed with a mixture of desire and embarrassment, not only afraid the slumbering Finn would suddenly awake and turn to catch him peeping, but slightly ashamed at his own pleasure in the moment. Not only was he enjoying the forbidden eyeful, he was enjoying the fact Kristian didn't know he was being watched!

It was the first time he'd ever played the Peeping Tom. He had to admit the fun in it outweighed the guilt. He couldn't pull his eyes away, and he couldn't stop himself from jerking off.

In that latitude, the sun rose early in the summer. It was barely four in the morning, and they wouldn't have to get up for another two hours. Chad pumped his cock as quietly as possible as his heart raced and he labored not to gasp.

That early morning sunlight washed over the sleeping Finn through half-open curtains, bathing him in a subdued golden light. He didn't move at first, merely lying still, his bare back rising and falling in a slow rhythm. Eventually, though, he emitted a deep sigh and rolled over completely onto his belly.

Chad froze, afraid to continue staring and risk being caught in the act, yet too mesmerized to look away. Kristian was on his stomach now, covers shoved aside, his legs spread wide, the pale cheeks of his smooth butt rising in two delicious mounds from a narrow waist and muscular thighs. Tearing his eyes from that naked butt, Chad dared a look at the Finn's face.

His eyes were closed! Thank God, he thought. Silky black hair fell over his broad forehead, narrow nose dividing the rather flat face, a bowed mouth open, pink lips wet with drool.

Chad pumped his throbbing cock a little faster, fascinated by that open mouth, imagining all kinds of scenarios involving those lips and his hard-on. Kristian moved again. The watching American froze with fear, unable to look away.

He rolled over onto his back this time, and Chad gawked open-mouthed as a full hard-on reared into view. That was a real surprise, and he barely bit back a thrilled gasp as he took in the sight of that lengthy Finnish pole throbbing along Kristian's flat belly.

Morning wood on a young dude was normal, and he realized it might not mean anything. But still, the stiff cock was just that. Hard. Sexy. Exciting.

More was to come. Kristian proceeded to roll and sigh and display his lean body in all kinds of sensual positions. At one point, on his side with one knee up against his chest, his pale butt-crack gaped apart and Chad was treated to the sight of his puckered, pink asshole.

Hard-on and hole, it was finally enough for the American to achieve an explosive climax, cock in hand, cum spurting out in a juicy geyser as he nearly passed out in an attempt to stifle his gasps.

Exhausted, he fell asleep a few minutes later, regardless of the titillating sight of the naked Finn exposing himself across the room.

That day he couldn't get the memory of what he'd seen out of his mind. Not just the image of the naked Finn, but also the churning emotions raised by that early morning show. On an intellectual level he knew what both a voyeur and an exhibitionist were. But facing the reality was something else.

"I will go to the ruins of Baltasar's Castle after work this day," Kristian announced at lunch in his precise manner. Beneath the shade of a copse of silver birch, the pair shared their usually quiet meal of cheese, rye bread and fruit. The Finn's announcement was unexpected as he turned his bright blue eyes on Chad and offered his shy smile.

"I will return late, so you may eat supper without me if you choose."

Chad nodded, unable to muster the courage to ask if he could join him, especially since Kristian didn't extend that offer.

But when the day was over, and after they'd returned their chainsaws to the tool shed, Kristian glanced over at Chad and their eyes met briefly. A small nod was all the Finn gave, but that direct look was unusual, and to Chad, suggestive.

He hesitated long enough for the Finn to get a few minutes ahead before he followed. Heart beating in his chest, he was careful to pace himself along the wooded trail so that his longer legs wouldn't carry him too quickly ahead and he'd catch up to his cabin mate.

Meticulously tended spruce and fir marched in all directions, Finland's "green gold." The trail was easy to follow for some time before it veered off in a downward meander toward the shore. Baltasar's Castle was a remnant of the Swede's defenses from the time when they ruled Finland and warred with Russia for dominance of the region. He'd been to it once already to check it out, so knew where he was going.

The smell of the sea rose up to collide with the sharp scent of forest just before he reached the ruins. Perched on a rise overlooking the Gulf and facing east toward Russia and St. Petersburg, the tumbled-down walls were overgrown with vines and surrounded by gangly birches that waved and rustled in a gentle ocean breeze.

Moving slowly now, he held his breath as he picked his way quietly off the trail and toward a gap in the stone wall that offered a view of the castle's interior. What did he expect to find?

More of the same from that morning. He wanted to see his new buddy naked!

Something about the look Kristian had given him, along with the flagrant display of that morning gave him hope he'd get to see the Finn showing off his lean body again. Was he going to sunbathe in private in the ruins? From what he'd been told, the Scandinavians were not uptight about nudity, and very often shed their clothes, all of them, to soak up the warm summer sun in secluded spots.

He peered through a narrow opening that might have once been a slot for archers, but was now merely a hole in the stone wall. The roofless ruin was exposed to the late afternoon sun with interior walls even worse off than the more solid outer ones.

There he was! Shirt already discarded, he had one foot up on the low remains of a stone wall and was busy unlacing his boot. Lush summer grass underfoot sparkled in the slanting light. A lone spruce shone with blue-green iridescence to his left as he methodically removed first boots, then heavy work jeans, and then to Chad's delight, his tight white underwear.

He was naked.

Now this was the time for Chad to discretely remove himself and allow his new cabin mate some privacy. That would be the right thing, or at least the polite thing to do. But the American was hooked on the all-too-new sensation of watching. He couldn't shake it. He told himself Kristian just might want him to be watching as well. That direct look earlier, the naked rolling around in bed that morning, he hoped they were signals he read correctly.

And on the other side of the wall, Kristian wasn't making it any easier for Chad to resist hanging around for the view!

The lean Finn stretched languidly at first, planting his bare feet wide apart, face upturned to the glowing sunlight, smooth torso rippling and muscular arms tightening as he clasped his hands behind his neck and actually smiled up at the warm sun and closed his eyes to soak in the golden rays.

Chad drank in the sight with lustful green eyes. Sweat actually beaded on his forehead under the thick mop of his sandy-brown bangs and ran down his armpits under his T-shirt. His cock reared up under his jeans and jerked in his underwear when he noticed Kristian's doing the same.

With eyes closed and face upturned, hands behind his neck, the Finn's lengthy cock began to swell where it dangled between his smooth thighs. Arcing outwards, growing pinker and fuller, it bounced upwards in a sudden spurt, fully stiff as it finally slapped against his hairless belly.

That in itself would have been enough to thrill the spying American – the dark-haired Finn, naked, feet spread and cock stiff, sunlight illuminating him in perfect clarity. His hand in his jeans, pumping his own boner, Chad would have been content to drink in that sight and pump himself to his second orgasm of the day.

But Kristian had more in mind than nude sunbathing. A hand languidly dropped to his crotch, and before Chad's startled eyes, gripped the stiff base of his rearing hard-on and slowly began to slide up and down it.

He was jerking off!

And, not only was his slim hand riding up and down the length of his twitching cock, but his other hand dropped down behind his back and slid over one cheek of his very naked butt.

The half-closed blue eyes swiveled just enough to glance at the overgrown entrance before returning to gaze up at the sun, closed again.

All at once, he felt absolutely certain the Finn knew he was watching!

The entire scenario reached another level of intensity with that realization. He was getting off watching the naked stud jerk-off, while the Finn was getting off by showing off to his American cabin mate.

Kristian proceeded to slowly flail his raging boner while beginning to writhe his slim hips back and forth and work his other hand around over the bare cheeks of his ass. His pink mouth opened and his tongue came out to lick at the bowed lips. His cock-head flushed bright red, while precum began to ooze out the flared piss slit.

Watching another dude jerk-off was a thrill on its own, but hiding out and watching, while the one getting watched grew more and more excited, more and more flamboyant, was totally novel and totally unreal.

Kristian reached up and spit on his palm, moaning loudly as he did, then dropped the goo-coated hand back down to rub it up and down his long, pink poker. His round nuts bounced as he thrust his hips forward and humped the air.

The hand behind his back burrowed into his deep crack, and the Finn turned sideways, with ass now facing the entrance, and coincidentally, Chad's hide-out. Fingers probed around in the hairless valley, then spread open the cheeks and revealed the quivering hole.

It had been violated. Stretched, pulsing and pouting, Kristian had obviously been fingering it! The Finn actually tickled the entrance with his fingertips, grunting loudly and wriggling his cute white ass.

It was all so unbelievable. Chad could only gawk open-mouthed and await the inevitable. It didn't come for at least fifteen minutes as the Finn pumped, humped, stroked and fingered.

He eventually got down on all fours and spread his knees wide apart, pumping his dangling cock between his thighs and fingering his pink asshole right there before Chad's eyes.

Finally, head down in the grass, a pair of fingers crammed deep in his tight young hole, palm flailing his cock, he let out a near-shout as he blew a big wad all over the grass beneath him.

What a show.

Although he hadn't blown his own load, he felt totally satisfied watching the hot Finn do the deed. Flushed and sweaty, he clambered down from his perch and slipped away to return to their cabin and await Kristian. When he finally arrived, he was as shy as ever, but every once in a while Chad caught him glancing in his direction with those intense blue eyes.

After the mind-blowing experience at the castle, it took Chad a week to muster up the courage to take the next step in the game of peek and show he imagined he and the dark-haired Finn played.

The mornings were usually a sensual contest of quiet rolling and tossing in their separate beds, both young men naked and seemingly intent upon showing off what they had to offer. Chad refrained from jerking off like he had the first morning, for two reasons. He didn't want to ruin the languid excitement of the moment, slipping in and out of sleep while his gorgeous cabin mate tossed his covers aside and lay naked across the room, so close yet so far away. And he'd come to believe Kristian knew they were teasing each other with their display and merely pretending to be asleep most of the time. He didn't want to get caught jerking off and thus end their game of pretense, not yet at least.

Cocks stiff half the time, their young asses rising and falling or spreading and wriggling, all amidst sighs and little moans as they half-dreamed and half fantasized separately, but together in a dance of increasingly bold displays; Chad loved it, but it was also driving him crazy.

Kristian's quiet personality didn't make it any easier to take the next step, or even talk about what was going on. The dude hardly said a word unless he was actually asked a question that required a response.

They had no television, or even a radio or cell phones or computers. The cabin did have electricity but was otherwise Spartan. Kristian read a lot, and Chad did the same although his natural inclination was to have some conversation. His cabin mate's perennial silence was at first a little daunting but gradually transformed into something else.

He would look up from his reading to see those quiet blue eyes gazing in his direction, followed by a small nod and a ghost of a smile, and he would suddenly feel reassured. He slowly grew relaxed with that quiet presence.

It was Kristian who suggested they play chess. "Do you like the chess?"

"Uh, sure," Chad lied.

Computer games and sports were more his style, but he did know how to play the game, so it was at least something to do. He imagined they might chat a bit while playing, or get into the spirit of competition and even tease or dare each other, but that was simply not the Finn's way.

He was intent on his moves, contemplating every nuance of strategy with more of the same silence. He smiled when he won and smiled when Chad won. He even laughed a little when the American let out a satisfied whoop or two when he was the rare victor, but otherwise he merely nodded or shook his head or offered brief replies to any ventured questions Chad put out.

"Do you have any brothers or sisters?"

"I have a sister."

"That's cool. I have two older brothers. They're kind of a pain in the ass, always telling me what to do and crap like that. Most of the time I just wish they'd leave me alone."

Silence.

"What about your sister? Do you get along?"

"She talks too much."

Kristian offered a wisp of a smile and Chad couldn't help chuckling. He took the hint though and stopped pestering him with personal questions.

Chad found himself often staring at Kristian's hands as they played, or his bare forearms, or his neck, or the line of his cheek or tilt of his head. He noted the slight wave in his dark hair, how extraordinary were his light blue eyes and the soft lashes that fluttered above them.

Staring at those fine hands, or the handsome face while in the midst of one of their silent games, the American suddenly realized he was enjoying that placid camaraderie almost as much he was enjoying their morning games of ass and cock flaunting. That was a real surprise. It seemed there might be more to his feelings for Kristian than just steamy desire for his naked body and more of that sensual and novel morning voyeurism.

Of course, he relived every moment of the exciting display Kristian had offered at Baltasar's Castle the week before. Images of the young Finn showing off his naked body, pumping his stiff cock and playing with his own firm round ass while Chad watched breathlessly from his hiding place came back again and again to haunt him.

He finally screwed up the courage to make his move.

In the flush of a victory at the chess board, he chortled out a daring suggestion to his placidly smiling cabin mate.

"I think I'll go to Baltasar's Castle tomorrow after work."

Kristian nodded, his blue eyes meeting Chad's briefly. It was enough. Chad's heart pounded in his chest as he got ready for bed. What would tomorrow bring? He could hardly wait to find out.

The following day he worked side-by-side as usual with his blue-eyed cabin mate as they picked their way through the dense woods thinning out young pine and fir with their chainsaws in order to create the neatly spaced forest Finland was renowned for.

The work itself required a great degree of cooperation between the pair. Even though the trees they cut down were mostly small, under five yards or so in height, you wouldn't want to have one of them land on you unexpectedly. They wore earplugs to protect against the high

211

whine of their chainsaws so were unable to communicate verbally. Instead, they used hand signals and nods of their heads to indicate their movements. In that silent manner, they forged their way through the forest in a steady dance of cut and slash and watch and wait.

Awash in his feelings of steamy desire for the Finn and their game of watch and show every morning, Chad discovered that even this grueling labor had become somehow sensual. That arduous work with heavy chain-saw in hand was made easier, also, by his near-giddy anticipation for the upcoming afternoon.

He intended on trying out a little of what Kristian had been doing. He was going to flaunt himself.

When their work was done, he offered the Finn a bright smile as he again announced his plan to head off for the ruined castle. Kristian was still dawdling around the work site as Chad marched off. He was certain the Finn would follow him – just like he'd followed Kristian the previous day.

His cock was stiff in his jeans all the way to the castle. The day was hotter than usual and the light breeze off the Gulf welcome as he descended along the path through the fir forest. Sweat dribbled down his armpits and in the crack of his rounded ass. He was very conscious of his body, wondering if he could possibly be as audacious as the Finn once he got to the ruins.

It wasn't long before he was in the exact spot Kristian had inhabited a week earlier. With trembling hands, he quickly began to strip, excited yes, but also afraid that if he didn't act right away he'd chicken out. Before he knew it, he was in his underwear, the afternoon sun bathing him in bright warmth, the cooler sea breeze stroking his bare flesh.

Fingers hooked in the waistband of his undershorts, he took a deep breath and dared a glance up at the window opening in the wall where he'd perched the previous day.

Amidst the tangled sway of birch branches, he spotted a dark head of hair and a pair of bright blue eyes.

Fuck! Quickly looking away, Chad let out his breath in a shaking sigh and half-closed his eyes as he made the final move and shoved down his underwear. Stepping out of them, his fat cock bounced in the air in front of him, rampant and proud. All too aware of those blue eyes gazing at him from above, his heart pounded and his breath came in rapid pants.

He was embarrassed, and excited, and all at once totally liberated. Naked, bare feet planted in soft grass, he thrust his hips forward, fucking the sunshine with his bobbing cock as his hand seized the base and began to pump.

He was jerking off just like Kristian had! A surge of intense sexual greed nearly overwhelmed him. He almost shot his load right then and there.

Instead, he let go of his grip on his cock and placed both hands on his bare ass, squeezing the smooth mounds as he pulled them apart. With his fat cock jerking between his thighs, he bent over half-way to thrust out his butt as he spread the cheeks.

Almost delirious with the nasty emotion of the moment, he began to writhe and hump his naked ass, feeling the air on his tight hole, and most of all, enjoying the greedy gaze of his Finnish friend from above.

He bent further over, pouting out his pink pucker, lost in the desire to show off, to reveal his innermost desires and most secret spots. With his big cock pulsing and jerking in front of him, he writhed his plump can in circles, kneading the smooth cheeks as he showed off his hungry asshole.

He dared to stroke it with a fingertip, gasping as he imagined his watching cabin mate coming down and touching it himself. His thoughts ran out of control as his body did the same. He plunged that finger deep inside, pushing back against the probing invasion, reaching around with his other hand to grip his cock and begin pumping it wildly.

Chad changed positions, turning in circles, lifting one foot up on the low stone wall behind him, arching his back and showing off his plump ass, then facing the other way and showing off his huge hard-on and the palm that pumped up and down it.

He worked cock and hole with his hands, mouth open, eyes half-closed as he dared a random glance up at the watching Finn to check if his show was being appreciated.

The eyes were there, barely visible amongst the greenery.

He jammed a finger deep into his tight asshole and reared up with his hips, fat cock bright purple as he stroked it to the inevitable eruption.

A geyser sprayed out into the golden light. Heart pounding, gasping for breath, he shot his load for the watching Finn, proud of his copious spew.

That was that. As he came down, his body going limp, his breathing returning to normal, he looked up again. Kristian was gone.

Nothing was said about it that evening, much as Chad expected. Even though he'd been courageous enough to show off at the castle for Kristian, he was still afraid to talk about it or make any further moves. And he was pretty sure the Finn wasn't about to speak out.

But he got a surprise.

"Tomorrow night I will take the sauna. Would you like to have this with me?"

"Sure. That'll be cool."

He hadn't enjoyed the famous Finnish sauna yet. He wasn't sure if they did it in the nude or with towels or what. He hoped it was a naked affair, addicted now to the thought of showing off his body to his buddy, and of course wanting to see Kristian naked, too.

It was all he'd wished for, and in the end more than he dared hope for. The small wooden shed nestled in the spruce behind their cabin was already prepared for use as they entered it. Kristian had turned on the heat under the bed of rocks and they glowed red as heat enveloped them.

"Leave your clothes there please."

The words were music to the sandy-haired American's ears as he shed his clothing just inside the door and placed them in a wooden basket. Kristian was quicker, used to the protocol, and his bare ass was on display in moments. As the Finn moved over to the heated stones, that sweet butt pumped delightfully, encouraging a rising boner from Chad as he stripped down to the buff.

Steam rose in billowing clouds from the heated rocks as Kristian splashed water over them from a bucket.

He turned away from the thick mist to face Chad. Even with the dense fog, his own rearing boner was impossible to miss.

That bold display rocked Chad. With blue eyes wide open and gazing directly into Chad's own, there was no longer any pretense. It was the first time neither was faking sleep, or pretending they were alone at the castle and the other wasn't watching their every move.

Of course neither actually said anything. That was Kristian's nature while Chad himself was too excited and too afraid to ruin the moment by saying the wrong thing.

The next half hour was a game of cock and ass flaunting as the pair lounged on the wooden benches and soaked up the heated steam. Every now and then Kristian rose to splash more water on the rocks, enveloping the small chamber with copious clouds of dripping mist.

Hard-ons never flagging, the two students grew steadily bolder, without saying a word, lying back, cocks pink and twitching between their thighs, cracks opening up as they raised their legs up on the bench and faced each other. Pink holes beaded with condensed moisture, purple cocks slick with it, they drank in the raunchy show with steadily growing excitement and boldness.

Surprisingly it was the Finn who finally pushed them both over the edge. Still facing Chad, feet up and ass-crack wide open, cock stiff between his lean thighs, his blue eyes dared to meet the American's. They didn't slip away, but remained direct and bold.

A hand on his knee slid down toward his crotch. He kept his eyes on Chad's as that hand moved between his spread thighs. With provocative brazenness, he wrapped that hand around his hard-on and began to slowly slide it up and down.

Chad gasped. Trembling, he followed Kristian's lead. His hand gripped his own cock and began to pump up and down the slippery column.

At first they merely pumped their cocks and stared at each other. Then, Kristian put his other hand down between his legs and began to stroke his asshole. Chad did the same, shaking all over and dripping steam and sweat from head to toe.

With the steam billowing around them, they jerked off and fingered their assholes. It was the sexiest thing Chad had ever done, and he actually believed he might have been more than satisfied if that was all they did that night. Of course he was fooling himself. The more he got from Kristian, the more he seemed to want.

The Finn was quiet, but also intuitive. His silent nature allowed him to listen. And Chad had been speaking loud and clear, in actions if not words. After rising to add more water to the rocks, on his return instead of sprawling back on the bench like Chad and pumping his boner and fingering his ass, he boldly approached the American.

"Time to do the fucking."

That was it. Kristian dropped his sweet mouth down between Chad's spread thighs and swallowed his thick meat. Chad grunted, thrusting up into the wet warmth as his hands grabbed the smooth mounds of the Finn's slippery ass and went to work on it. As Kristian sucked, the green-eyed American kneaded and squeezed Finnish butt-cheeks and finally crammed his fingers in the available crack. Finding the slippery hole pouting and ready, he buried a pair of fingers in the quivering maw.

The next half hour was a raunchy wrestle of slippery young flesh. Their lust released, they explored every inch of each other. Cock found hole, mouth met mouth, mouth met hole, and cock found mouth.

It was Chad who scaled the final barrier. He crawled atop the sprawled Finn, looked deep into his eyes and slowly fed him cock. The sensation of that puckered hole opening to his throbbing cock-head, followed by the steamy heat inside and the pulsing wrap of anal lips and twitching sphincter around his burrowing shaft, were deliriously pleasurable.

"It is good. Is it very good," Kristian managed to mutter as he pulled Chad down for a deep kiss. The Finn wrapped his arms around Chad and held him tightly as they fucked their way toward the orgasm they'd been working toward since that first morning when Kristian bared himself for his new American cabin mate.

Their shared release was near ecstatic. Their young bodies thrashed, come spewing. Hearts still pounding and laughing breathlessly, they stumbled outside to the cool night air where they engaged in the sauna's final act. Shrieking and hopping around, still naked, they took turns spraying each other with a hose. The cold water was an exhilarating shock to their steamed-up bodies. It was the Finn who pulled Kristian into his arms and held him tight as they kissed once more, shivering and shaking there under the moonlight.

It turned out to be a spectacular summer and one Chad would never forget. Afterwards, he retained that first time fascination with the game of voyeurism and exhibitionism he'd discovered with his Finnish friend.

Fortunately for the sandy-haired American, his memories of Kristian, the Finland woods, Finnish castles, and the steamy Finnish saunas were not all he gained from that amazing summer.

Back in the States, a huge mirror covered one of his bedroom walls. In it, he could watch himself, and his lover, as they flaunted their bare cocks and asses to their heart's content.

And often when he came home after work, he'd be treated to the sight of a bare ass on display, perched daringly over the arm of the living room sofa. Or come into the kitchen to find that same lithe body sprawled back on the counter, legs in the air and stiff cock jerking between raised thighs. Or he'd notice the bedroom door ajar with a soft light indicating someone there. Beyond that doorway he'd find his lover face down, slowly humping the mattress as he pretended to be asleep but knowing full well his American boyfriend would discover him and pause to watch, thrilled as he made a show of himself.

And who better to find in those exciting positions than the dark-haired Finn himself?

Kristian had come back to America with Chad.

And stayed.

LIFEGUARD DREAM DUO
By Jay Starre

Matthew couldn't have asked for a more perfect day. Strolling along a fantastic beach on the Gold Coast in Queensland as the sun rose out of the sea and a pleasant breeze stroked his near-naked body, it was a dream come true. He'd planned this trip to Australia since he was a freshman in college, and now as a graduation present to himself, here he was.

It was exhilarating that everything seemed different here. They drove on the other side of the street. It was December, and summer was just beginning. Temperature was measured in Celsius, and miles had become kilometers. They even seemed to be speaking in a foreign language, with a tendency toward broad vowels that come out sounding totally different than what he was used to, and missing Rs in the most common words like "here" which sounded like "heah." He had to pay close attention to actually understand what they were saying, especially since they used so many slang terms, some of which he wasn't always quite sure how to interpret.

It had been a hot night. The temperature in the hostel where he was staying climbed to 43 Celsius just before sunset, and even though he wasn't exactly sure what that translated into in good old American temperature, he knew it was damn hot. No air conditioning in the dirt cheap rooms meant a sweaty sleep.

So he'd risen just before dawn and headed down to the beach, which was only a hundred yards away.

Carrying his hiking sandals and T-shirt, he headed south along the endless beach. Apparently it ran uninterrupted for fifty miles. The dark-haired college graduate ran in and out of the waves now and then but otherwise was content just to walk, and walk. Hiking was definitely his favorite sport and this was a spectacular location for that.

It was relatively quiet on the beach that time of morning, and since it was so extensive, he found himself virtually alone most of the time – until he heard the sound of a vehicle coming from behind. Curious, he turned to see an open-topped SUV approaching, tires spitting up sand and salt spray. A bright red sign on the grill spelled out "Lifeguards."

The vehicle slowed then pulled up beside him. A pair of shirtless young studs were the only occupants. "Good morning, mate! We're the slip, slap, slop patrol. Are you wearing your sun screen? If not, we're the blokes for you. We've got plenty of spray."

"Slip, slap, slop" was the phrase repeated on billboards and advertisements for sun screen products nearly everywhere. Australians loved their beaches and their sun, but had one of the highest rates of skin cancer in the world. They promoted slopping on the sun screen with a vengeance.

"You're definitely the blokes for me. You can spray me all you like," Matthew blurted out.

He blushed as he realized how that sounded. Especially since he'd meant it in just that way. If there was such a thing as a typical Australian, these two each filled the bill in their own way. One blond and one red-head, they were tanned, tall and toned. They looked about his age or a little younger.

"Excellent! Arms up then, and close your eyes."

The red-head had already leapt from the left side of the vehicle, which in Australia was the passenger side. Matthew was face-to-face with the freckled complexion of a beaming lifeguard with brilliant green eyes, the cutest pug nose and the fullest pink lips.

Laughing, he did as he was asked. The gentle mist of a sun screen blew over him, starting at his face and moving downward. Due to a mixed parentage, his mother was a black dancer from New Orleans and his father a white construction worker from Connecticut, his skin was already a rich chocolate. But a little sun-screen wasn't going to hurt him. Kept the skin moisturized, he figured.

Then, with his eyes closed and picturing that sexy red-head spraying away, he began to spring a huge boner. It immediately tented the front of his baggy surf shorts, and he could do nothing about it.

To make matters worse, a pair of hands began to slide over his shoulders and then down his back. "Best to rub it in a little, mate. And get some of it on the area here just above your bum."

The hands dipped under the waist band of his shorts and vigorously rubbed in the slippery spray, sending an electric rush downward into his suddenly quivering asshole, then round to the base of his stiffening cock to make it leap outward and totally betray his lusty thoughts.

It was obvious that while the red-head sprayed, the blond was busy employing roaming hands to brazenly grope him! He dared to open his eyes and found himself staring into those bright green orbs. The lifeguard's broad smirk meant one thing, he hoped.

"Should we take this somewhere less public?"

Matthew held his breath as his proposition hung in the air. The fingers sliding around on the upper area of his bare ass suddenly dipped and probed. A pair of hands was right down in his ass-crack!

"Ace notion, mate. Hop in and let's go."

The hands pulled out of his ass-crack, but not before fingers found and briefly tickled his twitching butt-hole. He let out a little gasp, then a nervous giggle as he glanced around to see if anyone was close enough to catch that bold grope. But there was no one within a half mile, thankfully!

Of course the lifeguards weren't fools, even if they were obviously a bit on the nasty side. Now, it only remained to be seen how nasty they actually were! He joined them in the front seat of the SUV where he found himself crushed between the Aussies warm bodies, their bare thighs pressing against his from either side and the red-head's strong arm across his shoulder.

His boner still tented the front of his brightly-colored shorts, an unmistakable bit of evidence that he was up for anything the pair had in mind. The blond driver introduced himself as Sean with a bright grin, then cranked the steering wheel to the right and up off the beach into the woods, while at the same time managing to reach down with his free left hand and seize Matthew's hard-on through the flimsy material of his shorts.

"Brilliant! The randy bastard's got one real nice dick on him, Will. And his ass felt ace, too."

"Let's not waste any more time, then. In the back, mate!"

Sean was a wild driver and the vehicle had stopped in another spray of sandy dirt within the shade of scrub eucalyptus and gum. They had topped a low rise and were now just off the beach and hidden in a small gully. Obviously the pair knew the area.

The two lifeguards wore only skimpy swimsuits that did little to hide their round asses and bulging crotches. Those bulging crotches were revealed within moments as the laughing Aussies scrambled over the front seat and into the rear deck while peeling those suits down and kicking them off. They were buck naked by the time Matthew crawled over the back of the seat and reached them.

Will, the red-head immediately challenged Matthew as he waved a fat pink hard-on and laughed. "On your knees, mate. Let's see how good you are at cock-sucking."

The American was already in a crouch as he came over the back of the front seats and it was simple enough to drop to his knees in front of Will's out-thrust crotch. Drooling and gasping, he lunged for that waving shaft.

He caught the crown with his lips and sucked it in. Tongue twirling, he swabbed the bulbous head lustily while slurping with his plump lips and snorting for air.

"Right nice! He's no bludger in the sucking department!"

Sean crowded in as his mate began to pump into the kneeling American's mouth, straddling him from behind and placing both hands on his head. He pulled back and to the side, Will's cock popping out, and his own lengthy shank sliding in.

"Here's a bit of brekkie for you, some more juicy Aussie dick!"

The pair then battled for Matthew's mouth with Sean's hands on the crown of his head and Will's down on his shoulders. His own cock thrust outward to create a huge tent in his shorts while his lips smacked. Glistening drool coated both dicks and his own dimpled chin and big lips. His hands roamed over each of their taut swimmer bodies, smooth thighs, impossibly flat bellies and firm asses. He was in cock-sucking heaven!

They managed to stick both cocks in him at one point as he opened wide and gurgled loudly. They laughed and joked, calling him "our randy bastard."

It was Will who bent down to grasp the waist of his shorts and yank them to his knees. Out popped his big dark cock, the helmet shiny with precum and the shaft swollen and twitching. His bare ass was exposed, too. A paler creamy chocolate, the smooth mounds jutted out from his darker and trimmer waist. He'd always had a big butt, even though he was slim otherwise. A result of all that hiking, along with generous genetics.

"You're an ace bastard, and this mouth of yours is beaut! That ass looks real nice, too," Sean commented.

By now Matthew had figured out that "bastard" was a loosely employed term of endearment. He gobbled down Sean's ten-incher with a loud mewl and wriggled his butt for the pair, just to emphasize his willingness to give it up for their use, along with his already well-used mouth.

"Let's get the bloke on his back and out of his bathers. Time to get his legs in the air," the red-head said as both his hands found Matthew's melon-cheeks and squeezed.

"Ace idea, mate!"

The lifeguard dream duo worked together with ease as they tore off their American prey's surf shorts, flopped him onto his back, then spun him around so that his head dangled over the back of the tail-gate they quickly dropped down. With his butt facing the front seats, Will seized the backs of his knees and raised them then shoved them forward to his chest. Sean jumped down to the sand and straddled Matthew's face.

Expecting more cock, he was taken off-guard when the red-head buried his face in his up-ended crack and began to lick his ass! Just as he emitted a startled gasp, Sean's firm ass-cheeks settled over his dangling face.

By this time, he realized there was no predicting what these pair of randy Aussies had in store for him.

As tongue found his hole and stabbed into it, hole found his mouth and pouted over it. He stuck out his own tongue and lapped at the twitching slot, his hands grasping the solid lifeguard ass surrounding his face. That ass was coated in a down of blond while the crack itself was virtually hairless. The hole was surprisingly compliant, gaping open for his ticking tongue and actually sucking at it with little greedy convulsions.

That nasty response only made his own hole more willing as Will poked and probed with his tongue. When the lusty lifeguard clamped his lips over the American's hole and began to suck, he responded by squirming around on the truck deck and shoving upwards with his hips, while mimicking that gut-churning action with his own mouth and sucking voraciously on Sean's pouting hole.

Leaning forward, with his muscular thighs clamping Matthew's face, Sean reached down and seized the American's taut nipples. He began to tug and pinch, which had Matthew thrashing even more wildly and moaning incoherently between those firm lifeguard ass-cheeks.

"Time to get the bastard oiled up for a bit of a root!"

Will pulled out of Matthew's ass with a slurp and cute little giggle. "Right, mate. Let's oil him up."

With his face still clamped between the blond lifeguard's powerful thighs, he couldn't see what was going on, but he could feel the sudden spray of suntan oil as it landed on his torso, up-ended ass and spread thighs. The mist felt deliciously cool, especially since a light ocean breeze just managed to reach them at that moment.

Two pairs of hands slid over him in a sensual glide. More oil was sprayed, followed by those hands massaging it in. As he continued to eat out Sean's ass, those hands grew bolder. They seized his thick cock and pumped it. They found his hole and a pair of slippery fingers teased it. More oil was sprayed, his cock was worked faster, and two fingers pushed past his well-oiled ass-lips and slithered deep.

He groaned around the hole pressing against his mouth and wriggled around the fingers digging into his tender asshole. Those fingers began to slide in and out while more oil was sprayed over his crack and torso. Hands played over his body, pumping cock, probing hole and teasing nipples. He drove his tongue as far up Sean's hole as he could while he flopped and thrashed over the deck of the truck and wondered what was next for him.

He found out. Fingers slid from his asshole and cock began to rub up and down his crack. He could feel Will's fat tube pulsing against his flesh as it slid around in the oiled valley and against his slippery ass-lips. He reared up toward it, which had the pair of lifeguards hooting with laughter.

Flared cock-head settled on his hole and pushed. At the same time, Sean stepped back slightly and shoved downward with his own cock. The bullet-shaped tip drove deep between his gasping lips. The cock pressing against his pouting ass-lips stretched and parted them, then slid inside.

"The bloke's getting rooted from both ends," Sean said as he pushed deeper with his cock.

Matthew's head dangled backward as the blond lifeguard continued feeding him the slender length of his very long cock. It easily slithered past his tonsils and into his throat, sending waves of heated pleasure up and down his spine. The cock in his ass, much fatter, took its time sliding deeper inch by thick inch.

A hand pumped his cock, too, slippery with suntan oil. His knees pressed against his chest, and he snorted for air as the cock in his throat retreated, then pressed forward. The cock up his ass steadily burrowed its way home.

Dizzy with lust and lack of air, he found himself relaxing totally. Right to the balls, both cocks impaled him fully. He had never felt so stuffed.

The pair synchronized their assault, at first sliding in and out at the same time, then alternating with the cock up his ass pushing home while the cock in his throat withdrew to rest on his gaping lips. Then that cock slithered back inside his wet mouth and beyond his tonsils while the one up his butt slowly retreated until the flared helmet teased the rim of his hole from the inside and held there.

"Bloody hell, this is some ace ass, mate! Take a crack at it next?"

"I'd love a fair go at that bum. Let's switch it up."

Matthew was quickly manhandled into a new position, on his hands and knees with Sean behind him now on the deck and Will standing in the sand. The red-head winked and snickered as he took hold of the American's face and played the plump knob of his pink cock over his full lips. Behind, Sean wasted no time, driving in deep with his more slender cock.

The two Aussies drilled the kneeling American, slapping his round butt playfully while yanking on his swollen nipples, tugging his dangling balls and pumping his stiff dick. He was thoroughly used and loving it!

He lost track of time as cock plugged him from either end and the two lifeguards hooted and jeered. His dark body writhed helplessly between the two tanned Aussies, on fire from head to toe. Eventually, orgasm loomed, and he thought he was done for, but the pair must have sensed it and cut off that release precipitously.

"He's got a beaut of a cock, mate. I think I'll go for a ride on it before he blows a ripper!"

Sean's roaming hands took hold of Matthew's hips and twisted. Will pulled his cock out of the American's mouth and helped his buddy spin Matthew onto his back again. The pair rearranged themselves once again, this time with the blond facing the front seats and his ass settling down over the American's crotch. Will knelt in front of his lifeguard buddy and began to kiss him as he reached around and grabbed hold of Matthew's cock to aim it at Sean's pouting asshole.

The American let out a huge groan. "Oh my god, what a gorgeous ass!"

"All yours, mate. Root away!"

The well-oiled head of Matthew's dark cock pushed past the gaping pink rim of the Aussie's hole and drove deeper as he squatted down over the American's lap. Matthew reached out and took hold of those firm Aussie melons, squeezing the pale flesh as his cock slowly disappeared up the yielding hole.

It was a tight fit, but with all that oil and steady determination on Sean's part, the hole gulped up all of the dark cock being offered. That firm Aussie ass settled down over Matthew's lap, swallowing the entire fat cock.

Then he rode it. Matthew sprawled on the truck deck and groaned non-stop as his cock got fucked just as thoroughly as his mouth and ass had. He watched mesmerized as that awesome lifeguard body rose and fell over his lap. The blond was broad-shouldered but narrow-waisted, and his solid butt was pale in comparison to the warm tan of the rest of his body. Matthew couldn't tear his eyes off that rising and falling ass, so white, and the sight of his own dark cock appearing and disappearing as the lifeguard rode it.

This time his orgasm couldn't be staved off. The intense pleasure of his oiled cock sliding in and out of that snug asshole drove him over the edge.

"Fuck! I'm gonna shoot!"

Sean rose off just in time to receive a gusher of cum rising up to splatter his spread ass-cheeks and dangling balls. The pair of lifeguards broke their kiss and scrambled around to straddle the sprawled American. While he continued to spurt, the two quickly pumped their cocks over his face and managed to tear off simultaneous loads of their own.

Their nut-cream flew in juicy gobs to land on each other's cocks and dribble down over Matthew's big gaping lips. He laughed and snorted as he licked up the Aussie juice with unashamed alacrity.

"Good onya, mate. A ripper of a root."

Will chimed his agreement then bent down to kiss Matthew, getting a good taste of the splattered cum while he was at it.

"I reckon we better not play the bludgers any more and get back to work," Sean reminded his fellow lifeguard with a tap on the shoulder.

Will rose from his kiss and laughed. "I reckon you're right, mate. But first, we better get cleaned up."

With a smirk and a wink, Will crammed his cum-dripping cock down into Matthew's mouth. As he gulped and licked, Sean joined in by shoving his own cock in. The American opened wide and took them both as the two lifeguards kissed each other.

Licked clean, they pulled back out and bent down to kiss Matthew. Two mouths and two tongues swabbed his plump lips.

Then it was all business at the pair rose and retrieved their abandoned swimsuits while Matthew did the same. He climbed out of the back and slammed the tail gate shut for them as they climbed in the front and started up the engine.

With a jaunty wave and a blown kiss, Will shouted back to Matthew as they roared up the gully slope and away. "My mate and me, we're back on patrol at dawn tomorrow. Shall we get in the nudely again for another beaut of a root?"

Matthew waved and nodded enthusiastically. He guessed Will meant get naked and fuck, and hoped he was right.

He was. The following morning, bright and early, the pair came roaring up the beach to greet him again. Another wild fuck ensued, this time in a lifeguard shack hidden in the gum woods up from the beach.

Two weeks of the same followed. The pair were creative in their choices of location and in their varied performances. One time they even picked up another morning hiker and had him join in on the fun and games.

It certainly turned out to be a summer to be remembered, even though it was in December!

THE SHOWER POLICE
A Novella
By R. W. Clinger

PART 1 – PALM-LUST

1.

Camp Minnowtah. 672 acres. Nine cabins. Eight counselors. Thirty boys under the age of sixteen. It's mid-summer in Samoy, New York, chilly and just right. July-something. I'm out for my morning exercise, run my ass off, and try to stay fit. Everything about the run is peaceful and enjoyable, quiet and serene. After running for a half mile on Chipmunk Trail, I slow my pace down to a considerable jog, work my way around Lake Samoy, and start to head back to camp for breakfast with the six boys I'm in charge of.

The jog becomes pleasant and just right. Eventually, I take it down to a walk and suck in the fresh air, breathe daylight and woodsy life into my lungs. I'm cautious and alert, trained well to be in the wilderness. Everything seems to be perfect and serene on my walk. Just right. Now, as I pass a tiny rest area with a natural spring, which is approximately .4 miles from Camp Minnowtah, I hear a strong and strange grunting sound echoes and lifts in the distance. It's not from a bear or deer. The sound is not from an upset raccoon or squirrel. The grunting is more potent, more alive, less aggressive. I really don't know where it comes from at first, but I become curious, alert, and follow the sound, searching it out. I head south, walk slowly and carefully, peep my head through the thick oak and pine trees of western New York, and soon enough ... I see where the grunts derive from.

2.

The boy is well-built, stands in the distance, and drips wet with morning sweat. He is four feet from the natural spring, positioned among ferns, which lay around his feet. Tree canopies and greens of various colors shadow his naked body. The blond jock-type has his shorts pushed down to his ankles and his shirt rolled up into a ball on the ground next to his feet. Two hard-working fists rock up and down on his ten inches of veined and pulsating cock. He grunts madly with his vibrant movement, works his private part to an exhilarating pulse, groans and moans like a woodsy creature, and pleases the both of us.

Instantly, a brief arrangement of shock settles into me. "Holy shit," I whisper, recognize the young man's tight looking legs and sweaty-glazed chest. I've gawked at his massive biceps and rock-hard thighs before. Relentlessly, I've studied his blond hair, thin and semi-parted lips, muscular biceps, and curly hair that gleams on his climbable, mountain-like torso. I've craved the guy's solid abs, the thick cords that line his neck, his fresh nipples, and bumblebee-size ears. The dude's no stranger at all to me, in fact ... he's just right, and I know his name – almost everything about him.

3.

Ian Pierce. Twenty-three years old. A blond cutie with fall-into blue eyes. A Camp Minnowtah Officer's Assistant for the past five summers. Someone to look up to and learn from. A resident of Canton, Ohio. Graduate of Templeton College with a degree in sociology. The only child of Herbert and Barbra Pierce of 56912 Walnut Drive. Hobbies include: rowing, fishing, climbing, and poker. Always wears tight shorts. Enjoys paperback mysteries by James Patterson, Sue Grafton, Janet Evanovich, and Robert B. Parker. Eats healthy foods. Doesn't smoke. Keeps a journal next to his cot filled with his daily events, thoughts, and endearments. Ian's the kind of guy you want to have as a boyfriend and dance under the stars with. The kind of guy you want to be out in the woods with, because he'll protect you. By no means shy. Not flamboyant. Never is fowl-tempered or out of line. A gentleman at all times. Someone who will ask you for a walk in the woods – just the two of you – and he ends up kissing you on the neck, cheek, and lips. One of those kisses that melts you, makes your knees wobble, and causes you to helplessly fall under his spell. Hot to look at, to study, and drool over – if you're into that sort of thing, of course.

4.

Ian Pierce carries out some morning naughty/exercise on himself. Pierce is my supervisor, a step above me in the chain of command, and can eat me whole if he desires. I'm just an eighteen-year-old baby-sitter with twelve weeks at Camp Minnowtah and a six-boy squad. Pierce is hot and steamy, dreamy and refined, an experienced Minnowtah counselor for as long as I can remember. He's well-built and sweet looking, has these adorable lips you can just cuddle up against by the burning, evening fire. A not-so-pleasant boy with his strictness, his procedures and directions, but very attractive in all other aspects.

Something stirs within me. It feels the same way as when I wake up at night from one of my bathroom dreams. Three naked guys surround my naked body, offer me soap and shampoo, kisses and hugs, and other hard objects. The cock in my shorts grows with life, becomes instantly hard, and has a mind of its own. A tiny spot of liquid flows out of its head, and causes me to feel warm and tingly all over, perhaps even dizzy and delusional.

5.

One is supposed to mind his own business and allow privacy for others. It's not written down in my Camp Minnowtah Handbook; therefore, I stand behind one of the hulking trees and watch Pierce carry out some erotically intense movements. He humps and thrusts his fists, pokes and pulls at his hard-on with force. Pierce seems to be a master at his vibrations and motion. The cords along his neck tighten up as he grunts with built-up pressure. He swings his hips to and fro, sweats fiercely ... and now, with a constant trembling, he shoots a white stream of assistant-goo out of his shaft, bucks forward with the heat and rays of sun, with moans and grunts. The white stream arcs out of his massive cock and flies to the ground. What is leftover simply hangs from his ten-incher. Pierce knows what he's doing, has read his helpful masturbation handbook a hundred or more times, I guess. He simply rolls a hand down to the base of his cock, meets fingers with blond pubes, and gives his long beast a hard shake. The clinging jizz flies off and swirls into the woods.

I'm taken aback by his actions. He's delicious looking and totally perfect. I've been questioning myself these days about who I am, what kind of man I will eventually turn into. I enjoy looking at guys instead of girls, and this slightly throws me. But as I stand here behind the tall pine with my eyes glued on Pierce's masculine actions, an understanding forms within the ripples of my confused mind and I clarify: I really like dudes.

Pierce catches me half-hidden behind my pine. Our eyes lock instantly! Utter fear collapses my chest and my pulse races. He discovers my intrusion and calls out rather suddenly, "Hide, I can see you ... Step out from behind your tree."

I listen to him because I have to, because he can have my ass in a ringer if I don't. It's not boot camp or anything like that, but the supervisors and higher counselors take their jobs seriously, especially him. A steaming and firm rod is at full attention in my running shorts, which causes me to feel embarrassed and half-dizzy, but I listen to Pierce and step out from behind the tree.

"Come over here, Brett." He uses my first name, which means that he isn't as pissed as I think he should be.

Slowly, I move forward and comprehend that he's more beautiful and dashing up close. Sloped chest and all. Pecs like bubbles. Hard pointy nipples. The blond V-area between his chiseled legs is silky-nice, and smooth looking. I can reach out and touch any part of him, but don't, and won't, if I know what's best for me. Immediately, I respond, "I'm sorry ... I was just ... I was just ..."

6.

Camp Minnowtah and its counselors are not new to me. For the past thirty-nine days I have devoured Pierce with my eyes, longing to connect with him. Brett Hide – me! – wants nothing more than to brush his shoulder against my shoulder, drag his lips over my smooth and hairless chest, pinch my erect nipples with his fingertips or teeth, and dine on my cock with a hunger that is ...

Pierce is not going to fall for me, let alone carry out these naughties with me. I'm only eighteen years old, fresh out of high school, sexually inexperienced, and wet behind the ears. I still have a boy's face that consists of dark eyes and cocoa-colored hair, rosy cheeks, a dimple in the middle of my chin, narrow shoulders, and a tiny birthmark at the back of my neck that is shaped like the letter S. The only thing I really have going for me is my height. I stand over six feet tall, can play a killer game of basketball, and swim in Lake Samoy like a fish. In truth, I know very little about coming onto a guy, bluffing my way through dates, a city boy from Pittsburgh who sometimes tells people he's still a virgin. If Pierce finds this out about me, I'm screwed. Better to keep away from him, avoid him, and ...

7.

He pulls up his khaki shorts and closes the twenty-four inch gap between us, wraps one hand around my shoulder and places the other hand across my mouth, holds me still, keeps me as a prisoner, and threatens me with his bad boy blue eyes. Our hips touch by accident. Pierce's chest is up against my chest; I can feel our two hearts beat as one. It's like we can kiss or something, but his palm is snuggled against my mouth, totally in the way, and attempts to suffocate me and keep me quiet. Softly, he whispers with wide, aqua-blue eyes, "Just tell me what you saw, Brett. That's all I want to know."

I wriggle free from his weight and force. He's going to beat the shit out of me if I stick around. I escape the palm over my mouth, sharply inhale and exhale, but can't quite pull away from him; a place I find comfortable while in his hulking arm, pressed ever so closely to his naked and firm chest. I say, "I didn't see anything."

He smells like sweet boy-ooze and perspiration. His cheeks glow with new sweat. Pierce questions, "Nothing? ... You had to see something, Hide."

I shake my head and begin to tremble. Everything about me is too heated. Totally on fire. Scared and horny at the same time. Completely unsure of what's about to happen next between us. "I didn't see anything."

"You should be a man and tell me the truth, Hide. Tell me what you saw."

"Really ... Nothing."

"What's that then?" he points down at my private parts and shares a broad smile with me across his handsome face.

I have a steaming hard-on in my shorts. The tip of my cock's head pops out, saying hello. "Nothing ... Nothing at all." Before I can say anything more, or embarrass myself to the fullest limit or degree, I break free from him and run away ... for safety and privacy, pushing my rod down and keeping it hidden.

8.

The counselors' cabins are named after horses: Mustang, Palomino, Stallion, and Appaloosa. I know Pierce is in the Stallion cabin, next to the lake. I bunk with Marco Tuvetti in the Mustang cabin, next to the woods and a trail marked Saxifrage Path. There are two counselors per cabin; a requirement in the Camp Minnowtah Handbook. Our six Minnowtah boys bunk in the cabin next to ours called Clydesdale. When I return from my run/walk and hardening experience with Ian Pierce, I escape into Mustang and find Marco fresh out of the showers, drying off with a Martha Stewart towel that he brought from home.

Like his name, Marco's all Italian, right down to his oak-dark eyes and thick head of black hair. The guy is twenty years old, severely straight, and has the thickest cock I've ever seen. As he dries off, I stare at his two-inch wide uncut hose, his clean-shaven balls, and muscular thighs.

He asks, "Where have you been?"

I can be a sarcastic little shit at times, like now, and respond, "I went to the mall."

Marco has a pretty great sense of humor, is turning out to be a trustworthy friend of mine, and replies, "I hope you got me the new Muse CD I've been dying for." His session of drying doesn't last long. He finds a pair of white boxer-briefs and slides into them. The Unico cotton perfectly outlines his six inches of soft cock, his nicely developed thighs, and his ball sack.

I climb on my bunk, turn on my side, and continue to watch my roomie's dressing period. "Shame on me, Marco ... I forgot to pick that up for you. I'll get it the next time I'm there."

He slips into a pair of blue Nike shorts, a green-and-white Camp Minnowtah T-shirt that clings to his abs and pecs like plastic, and a pair of Reeboks. In the process, he rattles off our afternoon agenda with our six boys, which consists of craft time, an archery lesson, a nature walk, and play time in the lake, swimming.

I daydream of starting a bitch fight with his girlfriend – Renee Wilde – back in Erie, winning Marco over. My mind envisions the redhead attempting to slap my cheeks, pull my hair, and stomp on my feet.

Marco pulls me out of my daydream by accident. The guy reaches between his legs with his right palm, re-adjusts his goods, lets out a little grunt, and informs me, "Come on, Brett ... We've got a lot of work with the boys today. Get off your lazy ass and let's get a move on it."

9.

The six boys we're responsible for are Matty Padilla, Brick Martin, Bobby Rake, Harold Schmidt, Coyne Masterson, and Chris Needles. Marco and I take the boys swimming in the summer sun down at Lake Samoy.

I can't keep away from Pierce. My concentration strays from the boys swimming to Ian Pierce sunbathing on an azure-colored towel. The hot guy looks edible, a model out of the pages of *Instinct*. Pierce has on a bright yellow bikini, a pair of cheap sunglasses, and nothing else. I study the mound of yellow-covered crotch between his impeccably-built legs. I consume the fine blond hair that decorates his firm chest, thick thighs, and pointed nipples. Pierce lies still in the sun, glowing and gleaming, waiting for me.

Marco's thirty feet from me on the sandy beach, watching our six-pack. I walk up to him and ask, "Hey, I'll be back in a second. Can you cover for me?"

He says he will, tells me to take my time, that he has the six-pack under control.

Pierce doesn't see my approach. I stand over his still body, stare at him for over a minute, and eventually say, "Nice abs ... How many times a week do you work out?"

The young assistant pulls off his shades, squints up at me, checks me out from head to toe, and shares a smile. Pierce adds, "Who's watching your boys?"

"Marco. He's fine."

Pierce looks from his left to his right, back up at me, and inquires, "You want to touch my cock, don't you?"

Actually, it's not a bad idea at all. There's the thirty boys swimming in the lake and eight counselors that intrude though, preventing a finger-fest. I nod my head and reply, "You must be reading my mind."

The blond guy shares a hearty laugh with me, puts his sunglasses back on, and adds, "You're too desperate, Brett. I don't like that in the guys I fuck."

Pierce is right ... I am too desperate. I back away slowly, think about his comment, decide not to be so forward, and find my six-pack again, next to Marco. Here, I ponder Pierce's comment, watch the boys swim, and ask Marco, "Have you ever been desperate to get laid?"

Marco looks adorable in his red Rufskin suit. He beams a smile at me and supplies, "Every day. That's my life."

"Welcome to my world," I share.

He asks who I'm interested in.

I lie and respond, "No one in particular. I just want to blow a load," and leave it at this, still horny, needy of Pierce's skin, understanding him better.

10.

There's one problem bunking with Marco Tuvetti that distracts me from sleep. Marco's obsessed with his cock and constantly plays with himself. This action takes place after we go to bed and he thinks I'm asleep.

I hear his heavy breathing and his mattress squeak on the other side of the cabin. He lets out a few grunts and moans while he toys with himself. He whispers things I can't understand, murmurs of sexual delight, vulgarities defining sex.

I lie in bed watching him; a silhouette in the summer moonlight. The jock strokes his pole with fury, up and down, continuously. His breathing intensifies and his chest rises and falls. I study the outline of his muscled hips thrust into his palms. The shaft between his legs rolls between his fingertips like he's churning butter. He jerks his beef for a good ten to fifteen minutes, inhales and exhales, and eventually shoots his sticky load over his bare chest, splashing the juice against his hairless abs and taut navel, becoming spent.

Afterward, Marco fingers the dots and dribbles of sap off his abs, and swirls his appendages through the pools of sticky (bittersweet?) cream. He gathers up the goo from his skin and feeds himself a midnight snack, which leaves me to listen to his lips form a suction around his fingers, one by one, as the sexy sidekick consumes all of the spew, leftovers of his fun time without me, ready for sleep.

PART 2 – SWOLLEN INCHES

11.

It's the next night, and I'm the Shower Police; a title that each counselor carries out at least once a week at Camp Minnowtah. I have my clipboard in one hand and my Bic pen in the other hand. My job entails checking the showers to see if they've been cleaned by one of my boy-squad, and make sure no one's fucking around inside.

It's eleven o'clock at night and the boys are at an evening powwow by the lake where they sing campfire songs and share hair-raising ghost stories.

I walk inside the antiseptic smelling bathroom/shower area, make a direct left and see three empty and clean urinals. Beyond the urinals are two toilets, both are fresh and tidy. Someone's showering by the sounds of the rushing spray in the far-left corner. I wonder if it's Pierce. I can only hope it is Pierce, needing a good eye-dose of his body again

– this time soaped up and ready for some action with his hands, or even with me.

It's not Pierce in the showers. Some naughty/rule breaking Minnowtah boy has left one of the showers on. To my disappointment, I find myself inside the stall, turn off the shower, and exit the facilities with a smile on my face, carrying out a job well done.

12.

Every boy has his toys; Marco Tuvetti is no exception. He enjoys his tube of lube, a gold cock ring, a cock pump, and ...

Accidentally, after playing Shower Police, I'm back at Mustang, walk in the cabin, turn on the light, and see my roommate handling a lubed dildo. The plastic cock is eight inches long, considerably veined, and is almost two inches thick. Marco's on his back, and in his bed. The dude has his legs wide open and the dildo shoved up his ass about four inches. Upon my entrance, he lets out a quivering grown, sits up with the dildo still inside him, turns an auburn red with embarrassment, and asks, "What are you doing here, Hide? You're supposed to be with the boys at the campfire."

No, he's wrong. Marco is scheduled to be watching the six-pack, not me. "I'm the Shower Police tonight. It's on the schedule."

I scan the dildo inside his ass, his taut nipples, sweaty thighs, and the few dribbles of spew that line his succulent chest; a half-burst from his rod that I apparently walk in on and interrupt.

From his bed, Marco claims, "Pierce is going to fucking kill me for this," and removes the lubed toy from his ass, placing it on the towel beside him.

"Don't worry about it. I'll handle Pierce. Trust me, you're not going to be fired or sent home over this."

"How are you going to do that?" Marco asks, closing his legs, covering himself with a second towel.

"I have my ways, Marco. I told you not to worry about it." I wink at him to add some comfort and take in his cut chest with its dribbles of liquidy ooze.

"Why do you want to help me?"

"Because I'm your friend."

"What's in it for you?"

I answer in a playful manner, "Your ass. Let me be the dildo next time." I spin around, exit Mustang, and head down to the campfire where I know Pierce is dying to share an ass-beating with me.

13.

The campfire reaches into the treetops, crackles with fury, and licks the sky. Red-orange-yellow flames devour the oak logs as the thirty boys sing The Doors' "People Are Strange," instead of the common "Michael, Row Your Boat Ashore."

Following the song, one of my six-pack, the writer in the group, Coyne Masterson, begins a campfire creep story about a displeased ghost in the Samoy Woods. As Masterson startles his pals with a nicely crafted tale, Pierce makes eye contact with me across the fire pit; it says: I'll deal with you and Marco in the morning, Hide.

I try to smile at him, continue to play my game of 'I'm Into You,' but it doesn't seem to work at all.

Pierce is too pissed to even look at my boyish looks. Instead, he directs his attention to Masterson's ghost tale, and ignores me, breaking my heart.

14.

Back in Mustang, following the campfire bash and settling in my six-pack, I find Marco in his bed, asleep. Half of me wants to wake him up and tell him that shit's going to hit the fan in the morning with Ian Pierce. The other half wants to leave him sleep. While I make up my mind whether to wake him up or not, I hear three taps on Mustang's door.

I open the door and expect Pierce to be standing there with an awkward grin of disgust smeared over his face. It's not Pierce, though – fortunately. One of my six-pack stands at the door shivering, and explains, "I can't sleep and have a stomach ache."

239

It's a classic case of homesickness for the red-headed Rake boy. I tell him to come into the cabin and have a seat in the rickety chair by the window. Bobby Rake looks like the world is about to crumble around him. I find my cell phone, believing it the perfect anecdote for his homesickness. Within seconds, I settle down beside him and ask what his home phone number is and dial the number.

Rake talks to his mom and dad for the next ten minutes. Following their conversation, he has a wide grin of happiness on his face. I pat his head like a puppy, and ask, "How do you feel now?"

"Better. Can we do this again sometime?"

"Absolutely. Any time. This is why I'm a counselor."

After Rake leaves, heading back to his cabin, Marco confesses, "That was really sweet of you, Hide. Way to go. Nice work."

"I thought you were sleeping?" I spin around in the semi-darkness and check out his still body in the full-size bed.

"I woke up when the kid was knocking on the door."

I watch Marco turn on his side and show off his sculpted torso in the dim light. The guy should be a fashion model; he's this cute. I study his nicely developed abs, the trail of treasure hair beneath his navel, and his firm pecs. Marco's nipples are rock hard solid and his ...

"You're a pretty cool guy, Brett. Do you know that?" he inquires.

"No. You've got the wrong guy." I do think I'm pretty cool. But who cares about me? I'm too interested in him. What a nice face he has. No scars. No acne. Perfectly coiffed hair and pouty lips. Entrapping brown eyes that I find mysterious. Just handsome and sexy with enough muscle to hang onto.

"How'd things go down by the campfire, anyway?"

I bring him up to the minute concerning Ian Pierce's quiet rage, his eye contact made with me, and interpret what I think he was trying to share with me, which was pissy anger.

"The fucker has a stick up his ass, Hide. He probably just needs to get laid. I'm not going to worry about it. How about you?"

I shake my head and reply, "What's the worst he can do? He'd be a fool to out us from Camp Minnowtah, then he'd have to hire on new counselors, which he doesn't have time for."

With this said, I strip out of my clothes, flick off the cabin's interior light, climb into my sheets, put bygones behind me, and fall asleep, dreaming.

15.

Ian Pierce punishes both Marco and me. Marco gets punished because he wasn't with the six-pack at the campfire when he was scheduled to be. I get punished because I attempted to cover Marco's shift. So we're on bathroom clean-up duty, scrubbing the tile flooring with our Crest toothbrushes, just like guys in the Army.

In truth, it's not so bad to be on my knees with Marco Tuvetti. He's in front of me and wearing a pair of ass-clenching shorts. The shorts are so tight I can see the outline of his goods, which makes me steel-hard.

Together, it takes us approximately three hours to clean the tile floor. Pierce checks our work after we finish and approves our labor, sends Marco back to Mustang to look after our six-pack, but instructs me to stick around because he wants to have a private conversation with me.

Of course, I'm still on my knees when Marco leaves. Pierce wears his summer navy shorts, a white T-shirt, Nikes with half-socks, and a silver whistle around his neck. He walks up to me, practically brushes his V-spot of cock and balls against my chin, and asks, "So tell me, Hide, why did you want to save Marco's ass from getting in trouble?"

"We're a team. He's my friend. I think he would do the same thing for me."

"That's real noble, Hide. I'm afraid Marco only cares about his cock, though."

Pierce has a valid point. Marco is one horny dog who has nothing on his mind except sex. I certainly would not be surprised to find out that he's a maniac in bed, knows exactly what he's doing between a girl's legs, under the sheets, against a tree, anywhere. In truth, Marco seems the type that can never get enough sex, especially solo-acts in Mustang.

Pierce places a palm on my shoulder, gives it a little squeeze, and rattles off, "Listen to me, Brett. You're a nice guy. Super kind. Always looking out for your six-pack. Just a well-rounded counselor. Marco's got to look out for himself. I don't want you putting your neck on the line for him in the future. You hear me?"

I nod my head as Pierce removes his palm from my shoulder.

"Good. Now, get back to your cabin and help your six-pack out. We're going canoeing this afternoon, and by the looks of their skills, they're going to need all the help and support you can supply."

I understand, agree with Pierce, nod my head again, and escape the bathroom, running back to Mustang, Marco, and the six-pack.

16.

I'm on duty again, doing my rounds as the shower police. It's after eleven o'clock at night. There's only one light on in the boy's restroom. I hear a shower running, see steam billowing inside the room, hear grunting, moaning, and a male voice say, "Keep it down ... Someone's going to catch us." Cautiously I move forward, on the prowl, and stay alert. I hear kissing, more moaning, and the same male voice whisper, "Right there ... You've hit the jackpot." When I turn the bend, head into the shower area, I see ...

Ohmygod! Holy hot! Underneath the shower's translucent spray, a naked Marco's in the stall with another guy, a stranger that I don't recognize. The stranger has red hair, a thin build, is about nineteen years old, stands at five-ten, has some very white skin, a bulbous ass, droopy balls, an uncut shaft about eight inches long, big feet, a bigger shoulder span, emerald-colored eyes, pierced nipples and earlobes, and clean-shaven underarms. The red-haired stranger is bent over, toying with his own cock, and has his legs spread open. Marco stands behind the boy, holds onto his narrow hips, bangs the dude hard and harder, pushes himself to and fro in a speedy manner, pulverizing the stranger's rump again and again, deeper than each time before. Marco wears a red condom on his cock, digs his fingertips into his gentleman friend's skin, thrusts continuously, bucks his weight into the redhead, huffs and puffs, ready to let the stranger blow his load – soon.

They don't see me. I'm inside the mist and watch their heated guy-on/guy-in action within the shadows, half-hidden by one of the surrounding walls. I can cause mega trouble for them if I want to be a prick, but decide it's more fun to watch the duo in motion as they continue to ride each other, connecting sexually.

The redhead whispers, "Shove it in harder, dude," and Marco does. The stranger instructs, "Good job ... do it again," and Marco listens, bolting his weight into the naked boy. "Keep up the good work ... Ride that fucking ass, dude."

Marco's beautiful in motion as he slips his cock into the horny redhead, and pulls it out. He's an animal with the stranger's ass, pounding it profusely, banging it with speed and prosaic movements. Marco's chest is rippled with the shower's spray, and his shoulders are dappled with droplets of sweat. He resembles a professional porn star in the shower, pivots his weight forward, backward, forward again, rides the redhead's ass with enjoyment, and has a smile laced over his pretty boy face.

Neither can take their ass-to-cock connection any longer, I surmise. Gingerhead exclaims, "I can't hold it in, dude," and stands up with Marco's cock still inside his body. The redhead doesn't even have to touch his cock – he's this turned on by the action with his Camp Minnowtah friend – and shoots white spray out of his joint, becoming spent.

Marco isn't far behind, of course. He shoves his pole into the upright stranger twice, eventually pulls free from the tight boy-cavity, rips off the red condom, and tosses it to the shower's floor. He begins to stroke his beef a few times with his right hand, balances his weight with his left hand, and fires off a load onto the redhead's back and ass, and murmurs the guy's name again and again, "Patrick ... Patrick ... Patrick."

Following their bliss, I leave them alone and let them wash up. I find my way back to Mustang, undress, climb into bed, feel the erection between my legs, and tug on it a few times. I imagine my rod in Marco's ass like his rod was in the redhead's ass. I finger my goods with speed, carry out some heavy breathing, and shoot a sticky load onto my stomach, rub the ooze into my skin, close my eyes, drift off to sleep, and dream again of being with Ian Pierce.

17.

The next morning, I sport a thick chunk of wood between my legs. Sunbeams flood in Mustang's window, illuminating the shaft and its head. The summer sheet is down by my ankles and my cock slips through the opening in my boxers. When I open my eyes and turn my head to the right, Marco stands in the middle of the room and studies my mast, shares a broad smile with me; perhaps the shittiest grin I've ever seen on a guy. He says something crazy like: "That's bigger than I thought it was going to be." I tug up the sheet, clamp a hand over my goods, tame it down, and venomously share, "What the fuck do you care?"

Marco doesn't answer me. He's too busy rolling fingers up and down on the briefs-covered V-area between his legs, bringing about some hard life to his plaything.

We stare at each other for a few seconds. It's the kind of stare that might just lead into a kiss – who knows? Now, he checks out my pumped chest, sun-dappled nipples, and my boy-cute face. I observe his ten fingers roll over his cotton briefs and make himself hard. Eventually, I snap out of the boy-voodoo and say something crazy like: "Marco, what about your girlfriend?

"What girlfriend?"

"Renee ... Renee Wilde. The girl who you say sends you pictures and letters from home. The girl who you say you sometimes talk to on your cell phone. Isn't she your girlfriend?"

He snaps out of his hand-game, drops his palms and fingers to his sides, spins around, checks his pretty boy looks in a mirror, and rattles off, "Yeah ... Renee. Of course she's my girlfriend."

It sounds odd slipping out of his mouth, unconvincing, if you want to know the truth. Marco Tuvetti sounds like he's lying to me, keeping a secret from me, playing make believe or something juvenile like that. Renee, I assume, is just a figment of Marco's imagination. Or, maybe Renee is just a friend and not a girlfriend. Whoever Renee Wilde is, I decide to go along with my roommate's game, and say, "I'm glad you have Renee, Marco. Everyone needs someone important in their lives. Having a girlfriend must be nice."

He ignores me while he dresses. The guy doesn't utter a single word to me.

Whatever. I roll over on my side, face the wall, close my eyes, and drift back to sleep for another twenty minutes, knowing he's going to walk out of Mustang and lead the six-pack on a nature hike without me.

18.

Later this morning, I am face to face with Ian Pierce. He calls me into his cabin, tells me to sit down on the edge of his bed, paces from left to right in front of me without a shirt on. Pierce says some crazy stuff about committing myself as a Minnowtah Camp Counselor more, and putting my ass into my job. I wonder if he's purposely using this ambiguous statement with me or not. Half of me hears what he says and the other half doesn't. Again, I consume his muscled chest, the perspiration under his clean-shaven arms, his taut-looking navel, and the way his navy-blue and marigold-colored running shorts cling snugly to his hips and outline his dick and its lust-sack beneath.

"Do you understand what I'm trying to get across to you, Hide?" Pierce eventually asks me as he stands directly in front of me. He shows off his engorged package, plump abs, inflated pecs, and the succulent cords that line his neck and semi-sweaty arms.

It's like boot camp, but it isn't. I nod my head in a politically correct manner, and add, "Yes, sir!" for effect.

"Are you being a smart ass with me, Hide?"

"No, sir!" I shake my head.

"Because if you are, I'm going to fuck it out of you right here and now."

What did he just say? Fuck it out of me? I share a questioning look with him by squinting my eyes, and pursing my lips together.

He is certainly not amused with me, though, nor my look of puzzled astonishment. He closes the gap between us, moves up to my face with his crotch, presses the back of my head forward, and rubs it against the cotton fabric of his shorts. He now adds, "You heard what I said. If you don't stop being a smart ass, I'm going to fuck it out of you right here and now. Understand, buddy?"

The tube of his cock lays against my opened lips. If I want to, I can easily slip my hand into the rim of his shorts, yank the cotton down, and start giving him head right here in his cabin. Brett Hide is a good boy, though, and knows his manners. I merely breathe the jock into my lungs, feel high by his sweaty and powerful aroma, and take an early lunch by extending the tip of my tongue against his cotton Nikes, obtain a short and speedy lick, and enjoy my time against his goods.

Pierce is naughty to the third degree. He dry humps my face, pushes my teeth against his cotton, buries my nose to his goods, and implores, "Sometimes I can't keep myself away from you, Hide. It's hard to do for me. You see something you want and you know you can't have it because it's unprofessional, because it's the wrong thing to do. But then you think ... What the hell, right? Go get it. Suck it up. Take whatever you want of it ... What do you think, Hide? What's your opinion on this matter?"

My opinion is buried against his hard cock and balls. I suffocate in Pierce's shorts, unable to breathe, and lose air by the seconds. I try to pull away from him, but he only pushes the back of my head harder to his crotch and leaves me put up a bit of a struggle.

He finally catches onto the severity of my face buried in his cotton and pulls my head away from his goods. He sort of chuckles above me and says, "You were turning blue, pal ... Sorry about that."

I gasp for air, choke on oxygen, feel light-headed and dizzy ... happy to my queer core.

He pats me on my back, adjusts his merchandise, and shares before leaving his cabin to join his own six-pack, "The next time you're in my zone, I'm going to let you blow me. Until then ... you can think about having my cock in the back of your throat. That will certainly give you a good reason to lose your breath."

19.

Late afternoon turns into a disaster. The temperature rockets to ninety-nine degrees, and we have one boy who suffers from heat stroke and a second one with a pretty bad sunburn. Fortunately, neither of the boys are in my six-pack, but still.

Because of the scorching heat, everyone's instructed to take a siesta in their cabins for a few hours, until the day begins to cool off, just before dinnertime. Of course, camp counselors are not above this instruction and also end up locked in their cabins.

Marco lies on his bunk in his birthday suit, which is no surprise. I try not stare over at his chiseled body, but can't help myself. I think about moving onto his bed and messing around with him. There, I want to cordially slip his tube of beef into one of my holes, play with his scrotum sack, lap the sweat off his chest or ass, and attempt sexual naughtiness between horny guys who just happen to shack up together in the same cabin. I stay put though and casually drift off to sleep in the extensive heat.

I really don't know how long I'm asleep. An hour? Eighty minutes? Maybe even longer. I dream of getting it on with Pierce in the showers. Pierce is busy with a bar of green soap. Meticulously he rolls it up and down the plane of my chest, shoves his tongue down the back of my throat, and brings my cock to life with a mixture of suds and water. I'm blown away by the action, ready to hump him like a wild dog, and will the action of his cock to firmly press into my taut hole.

It's not the heat wave that brings me out of sleep. It's not the thick humidity, nor the lack of water. It's Marco's tongue and mouth that pulls me from the Pierce-dream, which sucks/licks/kisses my swollen inches between my legs. He becomes happy as a cannibal at my middle. The dude toys with my balls, laps at their extra skin, and murmurs with pleasure.

"Marco," I whisper, and drag my fingers through his black sweaty hair, "... what about your girlfriend? What about Renee?"

There is no Renee Wilde; I know this. There has never been a girlfriend from Erie. Marco Tuvetti isn't straight and ...

I pull out of him in a speedy manner, stroke myself off, and fire cream against his left cheek like a good boy under his lust-spell. Sticky white shoot slaps his cheek and begins to roll down and along his neck. I share a grunt, groan, and grind my teeth together in pure satisfaction.

He wears my load like a pro, which I lick up, drop by drop. I work on his face for the next minute, unable to prevent my hunger from the snack.

"That fucking rocked," he whispers, wildly breathing.

"Just the way you wanted it done."

"Fuck yeah," he admits, crazy for our united sex.

At his side, spooning him, I feel my lids close and my mind drift off to a fun-filled bar of naked jocks. I feel lost and bemused under his romantic spell, nostalgic and bliss-filled. And here, under the heat of the day, I selflessly give into sleep and dreams – wholly.

20.

I never confront Marco about his suck-job. Instead, I mind my own business, chalk it up as a wet dream, and move on.

Marco doesn't bring it up, either. What's done is done, unsaid/unshared words about an event that ... never took place. A misdemeanor between roomies. A misunderstanding of the flesh that is never discussed, mutually, of course.

It's not all about boy-connected-to-boy sex at Camp Minnowtah. Honestly, we are busy counselors who take care of our six-packs like doting mothers. We hike, bike ride, raft, canoe, and practice archery, which Ian Pierce helps me with, showing me how to stand, how to pull the bow string back, and release the arrow into midair at a distant bull's eye. On Wednesdays, we share an afternoon of crafts. The boys learn how to whittle and make wooden utensils. We create in-ground toilets, dreamcatchers, and wind chimes. We write letters to their aunts/grandmothers/mothers/fathers and tell them about our adventures at summer camp. Although the adult counselors are quite promiscuous, severely guilty about hopping in the sack and sharing some protected sex, we teach our six-packs values, ethics, and high morals, to the best of our abilities. We help the boys with questions about sex, Mother

Nature, school, and their families. We bond with the six-packs, become positive role models, and lead them in the right directions, out of turmoil/danger. We realize we've all been boys once, just like them, with the same inquires and activities, the same camps and boyhood friends. They are us, of course, except they are younger, inexperienced, and innocent.

PART 3 – BOY-HUMP

21.

Two days after his suck-job, Marco leaves a photo album on his bed, purposely. Our six-pack is watching a Walt Disney movie in their cabin, which gives Marco and me almost two hours off; Pierce will check on the kids in the meantime. My roomie exits Mustang and heads into the rain, claiming he's going to take a walk on Rostraver Trail, which leads away from Lake Samoy, a three-mile trek. I sit on my bed and read a David Leavitt novel, but I can't concentrate on the words/sentences/paragraphs. Instead, I keep looking over at the photo album, listen to thunder roll overhead, the rain fall, and stare at the album's faux leather binding and wonder what's inside it.

Curiosity nips me in the ass. I can't take another page of Leavitt with the photo album just sitting there and waiting to be thumbed through and invaded by my eyes and fingers. So I put the novel down, cross Mustang, find myself on Marco's bed, place the album on my lap and open it to the first page.

There are over forty Kodak prints inside the album of the redhead I saw in the shower with Marco. I learn that the guy's name is Patrick Mulldon. A green-eyed boy with an adorable smile and freckles that cover his face. A nineteen-year-old guy who is obviously Marco's obsession. A boyfriend, significant other, or companion. Someone Marco cares for, dearly.

A story unfolds in the photographs: Marco and Patrick are teammates on the Erie Eels swim team and pose on their blocks with their maroon and gold Speedos tight around their private parts; Patrick lounges in his dorm room at West End College; Marco and Patrick are on a vacation in Atlantic City; Patrick showers, looking pissed off at his boyfriend for snapping a shot of him while he's naked because he wants some privacy. It's a romantic story, needed on my part, and explains a lot about my roommate's behavior and likeness for Patrick, which causes me to smile.

An hour later, Marco enters Mustang. He's a drowned rat, dripping everywhere. I find him a towel and toss it his way. As the Italian jock strips out of his clothes, he looks at his bed and sees that the photo album isn't where he left it. "Where's my album? What happened to it?"

I calm him down and say, "I put it under your pillow. No one needs to see it except for you and Patrick."

"About you and me ..." he begins with a serene and confused look on his face.

I cut his words off, though, and confess, "I'm glad you have someone like Patrick. I'm your friend, Marco, not your boyfriend. I know that. And, I promise I won't tell Patrick or anybody else about our fling in the heat the other day. How's that sound?"

He lights up with a glowing smile, trusting me. "You're a good man, guy," he chides.

I give him a hug because he needs one, and maybe I need one. "You're not so bad yourself, Lucy. Now, what do you say we check on our boys and see what kind of trouble they're getting into?"

He agrees, places a delicate kiss on my right cheek, and whispers, "Thanks, Brett ... Thanks for everything."

22.

Chipmunk Trail. Pierce runs in front of me and bolts through the woods. The dude is shirtless and sweaty from head to toe as he exercises in the morning. I pick up my pace and follow him, but keep enough distance between us, so he doesn't see me. He slows his run down to a jog and checks his pulse. The trail zigzags through Samoy Woods, left and right, back to the left again. I don't know how it happens, but I lose Pierce in the dense woods, slow my jog down to a walk, and decide to head back to Camp Minnowtah and see what Marco's up to with the six-pack.

I'm alone in the woods, huff and puff, begin to leisurely walk and catch my breath from running. Eventually, I stop and listen to the summertime sounds: blue birds chirp, a deer grunts, maple/birch/oak leaves rustle in the wind. Everything around me is a brilliant green and brown; a woodsy landscape waiting to be articulately painted by an artist's steady hand. I take a rest and stand still for more than a minute.

Out of nowhere, Pierce surprises me. His hands wrap around my chest and drop to private parts. Lips connect to my earlobe, and I hear my abductor whisper, "I know you were following me, Hide. Can't get enough of me, can you?"

"Pierce, I thought you were in front of me." I feel his chest against my back and his biceps touch my skin. The cock between his legs nudges up against my bottom. He breathes heavily, intoxicated with his run/me. He rolls his right palm up and down my chest, teases my nipples, and turns me on.

"I worked my way into the woods and circled back around. Now, I have you right where I want you."

I spin around in his grip, tease his chest with my own hands, slip a palm and fingers deep into his Nike shorts, find his cock and balls, play with his goods, and ask, "You want me?"

He becomes hard under my touch. Alone in the woods, just the two of us, I realize he can have his way with me on Chipmunk Trail if he wants. He hungrily nods his head, leans into me, takes a whiff of one my sweaty pits, shares a blistering smile, and says, "I want you here and now."

"You'll have to catch me first," I share, pull myself away from his tantalizing grip, and run away from him with speed. I zigzag crazily through the woods, hope he catches me, want him to entrap me in his massive arms, tackle me to the ground, and have his way with me. I'm a fast runner, though, and he doesn't catch up. I outrun him, purposely playing hard to get. Before I know it, I'm back at Mustang and Pierce isn't anywhere in site. Our sticky and sweaty moment ends as quickly as it started, without our bodies entwined in a boy inside/over/behind boy action. And here, my chest heaves up and down, I cunningly smile, and whisper out loud, "I'm such a tease ... He'll have his way with me later, I'm sure."

23.

Marco says:

When Patrick Mulldon isn't around, I'm his fill-in boyfriend or fuckboy for the summer. It's not that he's unfaithful to his boyfriend, a liar and cheat. Rather, he's over-sexual, and desires boy-intimacy on a regular basis. I'm his toy, a substitute for his red-headed boyfriend's body. He really doesn't like me, not in the way he likes Patrick. I'm just a temporary sexual fix for him, a guy with a nice cock and set of balls, chiseled body, and exactly what he needs until Patrick returns to his life again. He uses me for sex. There's no connection between us. Our moments together are about sweat and getting off. He hopes I understand. He doesn't want me to have any hard feelings. Can he make it up to me with a kiss/blowjob/a hump to my ass – something?

Marco says:

"Climb on top of it, slowly ease your ass down on my chunky piece of rod, play with my nipples, take inch after inch of my pick up your chute, start to ride it like I'm a cowboy, take it like a man, take it real hard, take it all, choke on it, deeper and deeper, that's the way you like it, bucking your bottom like a man, rough sex that you enjoy, pull on my nipples, work them with your fingertips, hard and harder, let me buck your tight ass, I'll drive you crazy with my cock, I'll send you to a different place, I'm going to call you Patrick as I come ... Patrick ... Patrick ... Patrick."

Marco says:

He wants to keep me for as long as he can while he rolls fingertips through my hair. He likes the way our bodies press together, so sticky and sweet smelling, like candy. It's impossible not to think of Patrick while he fucks me. He doesn't want to hurt me, and won't, but our relationship will be over at the end of summer, when he returns to Patrick and Erie, beginning/attending his junior year at West End College. He likes the arch in my cock, its perfect mushroom cap, the way I grit my teeth when I explode ooze over his chest. He's my friend and he will always have a bond to me, being united to my skin, no matter what.

24.

Again, I become the Shower Police, fulfill my duty, and search out the boys' shower. He's there, just as I suspect, since his cabin is empty. It's definitely him on the far side of the bathroom, perpendicular to the three American Standard sinks is an American Standard Pierce, showering, just as I predict. I stand far enough away with my clipboard and keep a steady gaze on him. He lathers his steel-like body with soap, swirling it over his chiseled chest, beefy thighs, and deflated crank. The guy is strong and hard looking, muscled from head to toe, and drop dead gorgeous; a summer boy in a man's body. The orange bar of soap continues to roll up and down his massive chest, strays easily between his spread legs again and again. His piece of meat is soft looking, long and veined, wet and slippery, perfectly munchable to me. He yanks on his balls, heavily breathes, and has his cock hard as steel in a matter of seconds; its mass points north toward the ceiling. I watch him move his right hand up and down on his thick oar, hear him huff and puff, and train his beast to shoot an evening load of sticky cream.

I lose control of myself. The stem in my shorts begins to bulge and I start to sweat. As I watch Pierce quickly give his Minnowtah-flesh a few yanks, I begin to lose the clipboard and pen in my hand, dropping both to the floor:

Smaaaaack!

Click!

"Who's there?" He sounds surprised, knows someone is in the shower with him.

I can't answer. I shouldn't be spying on him. I've totally crossed some kind of unspoken and moral line. Slowly, I hunker down and attempt to pick up my clipboard and pen. My intentions are to bolt away, out of the showers. Pierce catches me, though. He steps out of his hot shower and jerk-off session with a hard-on between his lumber-like thighs, which satisfies me.

"Hide, I should have known it was you."

I become helpless and nervous for some strange reason, yet my attraction for the boy is intense and on fire. I stand, salute his chiseled body, and gawk at his firm cock. "Yes, sir ... I was policing."

"I'm glad to know you were doing your job. Find anything interesting in here?" He toys with his beef with one palm. Excess skin rides up and down on his shaft and a gasp of excitement escapes his mouth.

For a brief second in time, I am swept away into the oak forest again where I spied on him: He simply rolls a hand down to the base of his cock, meets fingers with blond pubes, and gives his long beast a hard shake. And now ... now he's caught you again, Brett. But you wanted him to, didn't you?

"Are you going to answer me, Hide?"

I decide rather clearly that the guy is more than hot. He causes prickles to form on my spine and forces my legs to wobble. Half-frightened, I fear that he'll beat the nonsense out of me. He is gallant and charming, though, and he catches me from my fall, places his lips directly in front of mine, and suggests, "I have something else to show you ... Are you up for it?" He snuggles his slippery and firm cock against my khakis, causes them to grow damp, smiles hard at me, dazzles me, kisses me with an opened mouth, with his long tongue that digs at the back of my throat, and makes me think: Yes, I'm up for it ... I'm up for him ... All of his commanding boy-toy.

25.

"You're totally into me, aren't you?" Pierce asks.

I nod my head, perhaps blush, and feel as if I have to run away again.

He smiles, runs a hand along my pretty boy-cheek, and shares, "I won't hurt you, Hide ... Now, let's teach you a few things."

He orders me out of my counseling clothes, assists me with buttons and shoelaces and zippers. Pierce moves steady hands against my muscled skin and finds my solid nipples, pinching them. He says something wild like, "I've had my eye on you for a long time. I'm glad we could come to some agreement out here in the middle of nowhere."

I'm nervous as hell, wobbly, and half-disoriented. I feel his tongue along the slip of my chest, over abs, and against my navel. He cups fingers around my fuzzy balls, squeezes them generously, and whispers, "Nice set, guy ... You should have these out to play a little more here at camp."

My eyes roll into the back of my head as his kissable lips clamp over my seven-inch rod. I'm oar-hard, numbed with interest, and pulsate above him as his mouth crams over my sweaty goods. He rocks his head to and fro, carries out an action that I've always wanted to conduct with him, flogs my boy-like spike with his long tongue, and excites me more. He groans beneath me, begins to play with himself, rolls a hand up and down on his own shower meat, and toys with his stiff lumber.

I'm quite prepared to come in his mouth if I have to, but something lavishly sweet convinces me to hold out longer, to enjoy this moment until I utterly ... burst! I grab onto the back of his head, push and pull on his skull, and mix fingers with his blond hair. He eventually comes off for air, breathes hard and harder, smiles up at me, connects infatuating eyes with me, and whispers, "What a chunk of pure beef, dude ... Just my style." He rises from his knees, shoves his tongue into my mouth, kisses me, and presses his naked and steamy body against my own.

The urge to come right now, blow my load, and fill the shower area with a spray of Brett Hide, is overwhelming. But I'm so taken and moved as boy clings to boy, as a voluntary function between guys carries out with rock-hard ease, that I steady myself, breathe slowly in, and then out, pull off and away from his lips, and dominantly whisper, "It's my turn. Get ready."

26.

I'm a quick study, use my extension of tongue along his veined neck, over a hard pec, and now a pointed nipple. I hold tight to his hips, balancing him so he doesn't fall. My tongue drives over solid abs and the blond splay of hair on his lower torso. The aroma that wafts about us is stinging-hot, masculine as the tip of my tongue polices the top-slit of his spike.

Pierce moans above me as my movements take over his shaft, lather it with sucks and constant licks. He places his palms over my shoulders, pushes into my mouth, pulls out, groans, "Are you sure you've never done this before?"

I back away from him, jack him off, and prepare him to spray his torso with his thick juice. Now, I respond, "No ... I haven't." It's a lie, but who the fuck really cares?

Pierce smiles down at me and suggests methodically, "Well, you could've fooled me."

He dives his cock into my mouth again, places his hands behind my head, starts to buck his erect cock inside my mouth, and pushes it deeper and deeper into the valley of my throat. I feel dizzy beneath him, trapped in his hearty boy-hold, heated by our combined desire and connection.

"Thatta boy, Hide ... Show me what you have ... Use your tongue," he coaches from above me like the assistant that he is.

Every shove stings my mouth, but I find it utterly delicious. Inch after inch plasters me, bucking me with a fierce and ecstatic motion until Pierce begins to breathe heavily, and chants, "It's too soon to shoot a load ... I've got other things to show you first."

27.

With a condom affixed to his ten inches of throbbing dong, Pierce informs, "It's going to hurt, Hide ... Keep your hands flush against the shower wall."

I feel his fingers lube my hole, separate my jittery legs, and pivot three fingers inside my boy-tomb; a place where I want/desire/need his cock. Now, he preps me like a good Minnowtah Commander's Assistant for his swollen pole, twists his three fingers inside my narrow chute, laughs in a masculine voice behind me, and asks, "Did you read this in your handbook, dude?"

"Never ... Ouch! ... No, sir."

He begins to push knuckles up and inside me, and causes me to feel faint in a nice way, purely magnificent ... as if I float with him in the hot shower's spray, locked against his ready-to-fuck-me body.

"I think you're prepped, guy?"

For what? Policing? A game of his own? A boy powwow?

"Bring it on. Fuck me ... and fuck me hard."

28.

He grabs my hips and pulls me onto him. Four inches of his shaft enters me, prompts me to cling to pipes and tile, squint my eyes, and grit my teeth. It feels wonderful and painful all at the same time, diligent and resourceful. The faux virgin squad leader gets plowed by Ian Pierce. Brett Hide finally obtains a shower-fix from one of the hottest dudes in New York.

Hot spray lashes my skin as he goes to town on my ass, does a little investigative work, probes, and leads on his own. He pushes three more inches into me, explains, "It's supposed to hurt ... Just hang on." His vibrations are rich and rhythmic, steady and fine. They continue for what feels like forever: boy rubs inside boy; long shaft invades young Hide; interests between the two are hot and heavy; breathing ensues in the far reaches of the wild. He pumps and grinds my hole with perfection, a style that is gold winning. Up and down. Emphatically. He causes my eyelids to bat open and closed, and nibbles on one of my shoulders as I wilt within his strong arms.

"I ... I ..."

He slaps my ass with one palm. "Spit it out, dude."

"I'm going to blow ... I can't help it ... It's happening by itself."

He pushes into me hard and fast. The boy is on a mission and carries out some conductive friction with me. He thrushes all of his wood into me, plows me with the speed of a buzz saw, and groans and moans behind me. Hot jizm flies out of my rod by itself, explodes into the shower stall, and splashes against the green tile and orange bar of soap between our cocked feet. Ian Pierce fixes blast after blast into my boy-tunnel, works my cock with his right hand, drains it, and plows every part of my body. With ease and simplicity, with busy hands and rod, he creates a connection between us that I find exalting.

Before he blows his load, he pulls out of me, tosses the condom to the tile floor, spins me around by my hips, and says directly to me, "Make me come, dude."

I'm apt, reach forward with my right hand and strap it against his pulsing and veined Pierce-monster. As this hand busies itself, my left hand pivots against the massive structure of his chest and begins to pinch his right nipple. I hear him moan to the movements of both hands, watch him buck his hips upward, into my grasp, stare at me wildly, and breathe heavily, charmed by an innocent and young Brett Hide.

"It's time to show you what I'm made of, Spying Hide" Pierce pants strongly, bucks into my hand, groans and grunts. The cords along his neck tighten up and his hips move upward with a rhythmic speed. He chants with a thick grin, "Ready or not, here I come," and pumps my fist with two more blows. The guy then showers my torso with white goo, glazing my nipples, abs, and even my chin.

Hot and fiery jizm blows against my skin, washing me down. Boy-stuff drips from my nipples in thick globs. I listen to Pierce say, "Time for a campfire snack, my friend." He slips three fingers to my pec, gathers up his ooze, and slides the sap into his mouth. My sidekick takes in his sticky burst, seems to enjoy it by the enlightened smile on his face, and finds it appealingly sweet and salty, thick and creamy, a scrummy guy-treat for the shower stall boy.

When he pulls sticky fingers away from his mouth, he smiles and asks, "Was the fuck everything you thought it would be?"

"Yes, Sir," I nod my head, "better, in fact."

"Would you like some more, Hide?"

I nod my head again, anticipating another fuck with him. "Yes, Sir."

He laughs, kisses me in a complex manner between guy and guy locked together, pulls off, and adds, "I thought you would say that."

29.

I believe he'll ask me to leave, so he can finish his shower. Instead, we shower together and draw the orange bar of soap over each other's hard bodies. Pierce leans into me, causes my boy-finder to grow stiff between us again, strums the boner like a guitar, and says, "Did you ever use your cock on a guy before?"

I'm nervous and comfortable at the same time, enjoying a summer of heat, fun, and a naked Ian Pierce. I trust him, find him to be a flesh-guide for my Samoy needs this late summer. "No ... I haven't," I lie for the hell of it, because it's hot to see the expression on his face to learn that I'm a so-called virgin, even if I'm really not.

"I think it's about time you learn, Hide. Right here and right now." He bends down in the spray again, decides to take charge of the moment, teaches me how to plug his mouth with a chunk of boy joy, and smiles up at me with his charming and dashing aqua-blue eyes. Water sprays over our bodies with ease. He starts something between us that leaves me intoxicated and merciless, hungry and steamy – the way I've always wanted to feel with him. He becomes an impulsive, licking, and craving leader with ease. As he envelopes my tube of fat cock into his mouth, I think: I'm up for him again ... and all summer long, if he's up for me.

30.

Night after summer night, I stay with Pierce on his cot, snuggle up against his sweaty biceps and firm chest. I breathe him into my world, cuddle his body next to mine, and play with the blond hairs on his chest. We become romantic boyfriends through the rest of summer, learning each other. He falls for me hard, obeys his thirst for me, and adores me for months to come.

One night in July when it is steamy hot, he spoons me from behind and asks about Marco. "Is he still using your skin as Patrick?"

"Yes, but not as much."

"Is Patrick coming to visit Camp Minnowtah?"

"Yes. He'll be spending nights with Marco while I'm here with you. No one's supposed to know. It's a secret."

"You know that's against camp policy and ..."

I block Marco's words off with a kiss, drag fingers down and over the plane of his solid chest, and whisper in his ear, "What you don't know won't hurt you."

"Of course," he replies, begins to place kisses against my ear, neck, and then my chest, and initiates something untamed and sticky between us, again.

The Writers

A.J. DAMIAN is based in England and is a part-time writer and part-time worrier. Her articles have appeared in *Love Romance Passion*, and her short story has been published in *Quail Bell Magazine*.

DAVID CONNOR lives in rural New York, with his dog, Max, where he just finished his first novel. He's been writing professionally since 1982, everything from soap opera to satire and is finally putting his nighttime dreams and daytime experiences to good use in the gay erotica genre.

DERRICK DELLA GIORGIA was born in Italy and currently lives between Manhattan and Rome. His work has been published in several anthologies and literary magazines. Visit him at www.derrickdellagiorgia.com.

HL CHAMPA is an extensively published writer of erotic fiction. Find out more at http://heidichampa.blogspot.com.

Residing on English Bay in Vancouver, Canada, **JAY STARRE** has pumped out steamy gay fiction for dozens of anthologies and has written two gay erotic novels. Contact: Jay Starre on Facebook.

JESSE MONTEAGUDO is a freelance writer who lives in South Florida with his partner. His column, "Jesse's Journal," appears in *South Florida Gay News* and Bilerico.com.

JOSHUA SKYE is the author of the fantasy adventure *Xerxes Canyon*. He lives in rural Pennsylvania with his partner Ray of 15 years and their son Syrian. Contact: joshua_skye@hotmail.com.

LANDON DIXON's writing credits include magazines such as *Men*, *Freshmen*, and *[2]*, and anthologies such as *Teammates*, *Boys Getting Ahead*, and *Best Gay Erotica 2009*.

LOGAN ZACHARY (loganzachary2002@yahoo.com) is an author of mysteries, short stories, and over forty erotica stories, living in Minneapolis with his partner, Paul, and their dog, Ripley, who runs the house. www.loganzacharydicklit.com.

MARK APOAPSIS'S recently published works include erotic science fiction, two erotic period pieces in *Mob Men on the Make*, gay horror flash fiction in *Henderson's Chilling Tales*, and an erotic epic poem about a fraternity initiation.

MILTON STERN is an author living in a Mobile Home Community in Maryland with Esmeralda, his rescue beagle. Check out his blog: http://gayjewmobilehome.blogspot.com/ and his website: www.miltonstern.com.

R. TALENT is a freelance writer who is putting the final touches on his debut novel along with the series he hopes to come from it.

R. W. CLINGER has written six novels, four of which are for a gay audience. His short erotic fiction has appeared in many compilations. He is currently at work on a new gay novel. R. W. can be reached at kenitorico@verizon.net.

ROB ROSEN, author of the novels *Sparkle: The Queerest Book You'll Ever Love*, *Divas Las Vegas*, winner of the 2010 TLA Gaybies for Best Gay Fiction, *Hot Lava*, and *Southern Fried*, has been published in well-over 150 anthologies, with more than a dozen from STARbooks Press. Please visit him at his website, www.therobrosen.com.

The Editor

This is Mickey Erlach's eighth anthology for STARbooks Press. When he was a boy of summer, OP shorts and tube socks were in style.

any underwear. "Excuse me," I said, having a hard time looking
by that bulge in his crotch, "but don't I know you?" "Maybe," h

before I knew it, I had his rod in my hand, and mine was in his. "
o?" he asked, his tone challenging. I knew exactly, and sank to n

www.ingramcontent.com/pod-product-compliance
Lightning Source LLC
Chambersburg PA
CBHW031116030726
47496CB00002BA/573